ODIN'S WORD

ODIN'S

WORD

D. A. SPRUZEN

Table of Contents

Chapter 1 1
Chapter 2 10
Chapter 3 20
Chapter 4 24
Chapter 5 34
Chapter 6 39
Chapter 7 42
Chapter 8 45
Chapter 9 50
Chapter 10 74
Chapter 11 83
Chapter 12 96
Chapter 13 113
Chapter 14 122
Chapter 15 137
Chapter 16 147
Chapter 17 167
Chapter 18 187
Chapter 19 201
Chapter 20 208
Chapter 21 213
Chapter 22 220
Chapter 23 230
Chapter 24 235

Chapter 25 249
Chapter 26 253
Chapter 27 258
Chapter 28 272
Chapter 29 276
Chapter 30 279
Chapter 31 282

Book Club Questions 293
Author Bio 295

1

Yggdrasil now soared well beyond the clouds. This time last year, the Norse tree of life had been no more than a large twig that Lin snapped off after Ragnarok, the final battle. She'd planted it everywhere she lived, but it had neither thrived nor died. When Loki had finally been destroyed the previous summer, it started to leaf out and grow so fast that Hunter knew if it were to be replanted, it had better be soon. He chose a spot between the woods and the house at his and Lin's new estate on the Chesapeake Bay. Even on a clear day, we could barely see the glorious canopy we'd admired so much only a couple of months before.

Hunter (formerly known as Hoenir, brother of Odin) felt beyond a doubt that its branches, still blanketed in summery green at Christmastime, had reached his heaven. One night, as we cuddled in bed, he dropped a bomb.

"Mary, I am quite sure that Yggdrasil has reached whatever is left of Asgard."

"It certainly looks as if it could touch the sun."

"Well, I hope not that far. You know, I must climb it. I must know if anything of Asgard remains. It was our world, and we ruled it."

I clutched him tightly. "Will it be dangerous?"

"Yes, I am afraid it will. There will be furious winds, all kinds of precipitation, and arctic cold. And it will take a very long time without rest, sleep, or food."

"Oh, Hunter, why don't you just leave it alone? You are happy here in your wonderful home with your family. Why risk everything now?"

"Because I must."

That sonorous tone meant the discussion was closed. It would be an exhausting, perilous journey—and even with his godly powers, he might not survive. While Hunter and his wife Lin (former handmaiden to Odin's wife, Frigg) were theoretically immortal, that trait had weakened after Ragnarok to the extent that they must now undergo rebirth at regular intervals. Who knew the true limits of their strength?

I didn't sleep much that night. In the days that followed, I tried not to think about the climb, as it jangled my nerves to the point of rendering me inept. I couldn't imagine living without my love. While Hunter was Lin's husband, he was also my lover and my daughter Rose's father. No one in the family minded. We all loved each other.

Our traditional Christmas celebration left me flat, although I put a good face on it for Rose and the rest of the family. Lin seemed a little sad, too. Her Syrian protégé, Reem, delighted her a few months ago by announcing her plans to join a practice in the Washington area. Those plans changed when she decided to join Doctors Without Borders, sought after because she was now bilingual in English and Arabic. Lin doted on Reem as she'd had a daughter with the same name in Egypt many years before. Always outliving her children weighed heavily on Lin.

Apart from Reem, the usual crowd had joined our celebration: Dr. Ayre (formerly Eir, Norse physician to the gods), friends Joe, Helen, and Lettie (who still managed Lin's private investigation agency). Lin and Hunter's children, Sven and Margareta, were home from college. Rose and I were considered family, together with my Auntie Peggy. I still marvel that I, a very ordinary young woman called Mary Lambert from a small town in Pennsylvania, had stumbled into this extraordinary situation. While I'd been hired to ghostwrite Lin's memoirs, that had become sidetracked by more compelling events.

At Christmas dinner, five-year-old Rose sat next to her Papa, with her beloved Uncle Joe on her other side. Joe Paglietti was a detective with whom Lin, a private investigator, had collaborated from time to time. He had recently married Helen, a lawyer. I, my Auntie Peggy, and Rose lived in a house on the Chesapeake Bay not far away, but we all spent a great deal of time at "the castle," as we called the huge house Hunter had rebuilt, also on the Chesapeake Bay. Lettie, partner and manager of Lin's detective agency, was still unattached. She thought she'd met Mr. Right, but he turned out to be a racist, so she broke it off. I looked around at them all, so merry. Our last Christmas all together? Lin watched me with her annoyingly enigmatic smile. She knew what I was thinking.

The maid Dora clattered around in the kitchen, getting ready for her second grand entrance, the first being the presentation of a perfectly golden turkey. Formerly a Greek wood nymph, she was married to Stan, who managed the grounds, did odd jobs, and took care of the cars. Stan was surprisingly normal for a man with a leprechaun for a mother. To say we were a motley crew is an understatement that would put any British stiff upper lip to shame.

After clearing away the turkey and side dishes, Dora marched the flaming Christmas pudding around the table, as she always did, and set it before Lin, who dished it out. We all nibbled at our helpings slowly, lest we test our capacity to breaking point. Silence reigned as we soldiered through, while Christmas tree lights winked their jolly patterns, reflecting off shiny ornaments and bathing the faces of those nearest in their flashy hues. Lin finished her pudding before everyone else and pushed back her chair.

"Hunter and I have something to tell you."

We all froze at this ominous announcement, several with mouths open and loaded forks poised. She paused as if making sure she had our attention. Lin was never averse to creating a little drama. I knew what was coming, of course, but an official announcement would make it—official.

"Yggdrasil seems to have stopped growing. That means, we hope, that it has reached our former heaven, Asgard. Hunter will climb it on New Year's Day to see where it leads."

"No, Papa, you mustn't, it's too far, too dangerous," Margareta said, her voice unusually panicky for someone usually so stoic.

"I must find out if Asgard is still there. I must see what remains. It was our home, our kingdom. From there, we ruled the world." Hunter crossed his arms.

"Papa, this is not wise. Please think it through again." Sven sounded breathless.

"Papa, please don't go away. I want you right here." Margareta's alarm had shaken Rose. Hunter drew her onto his lap.

"I must do this thing. I must find out. I will never rest until I do. But I am strong. I am a god. I will survive. And that is the end of it." His voice left no room for argument.

"When will you start?" asked Joe.

"10 a.m. on New Year's Day. I have purchased all the necessary gear."

"May we come to cheer you on?" asked Lettie.

"Of course, I would welcome it.

"I will also come. I will bring you a useful salve," Dr. Ayre said. Her salves and potions were legendary. I went through childbirth happily high and feeling no pain; wounds and burns healed in minutes; Auntie Peggy's arthritis barely bothered her anymore, and she'd made remarkable progress after her stroke, probably due to an ointment she rubbed into her forehead each evening; and Loki died for good after being shot while occupying the body of a fox, when the good doctor seized the moment to administer an injection that turned his immortal soul and mortal flesh to dust.

As the big day approached, I felt as if Hunter had been diagnosed with a fatal illness. The love of my life was about to risk all, for the sake of what? The possibility that his heaven would still be waiting? All the gods had perished in the final battle. Maybe he'd find that the ice giants—Jotuns— had taken possession. They would kill him for sure. Maybe Loki's son, the voracious wolf Fenrir, had survived and would wreak revenge for his father's death. The massive creature had swallowed the sun and the moon, after all. Who knows what else he had managed to consume? After the battle, all the worlds had supposedly sunk into the void, and only Midgard had reemerged as far as Lin and Hunter knew, but what if others had popped up? I tortured myself with these "what ifs" as I lay in bed at night, often alone. When Hunter joined me, I clung to him like a limpet. I couldn't lose him. Nor could little Rose.

Finally, the waiting was over. We all stood around the tree, wrapped in our warm jackets and scarves against the cold wind sweeping off the Chesapeake Bay. Auntie Peggy, still using a wheelchair outdoors since her stroke the previous summer, insisted on being present. The mood was subdued enough that even Rose knew this was a serious moment. Hunter kissed us all, even Joe and Stan, men not used to male-on-male displays of affection. Dr. Ayre rubbed one of her wondrous ointments on Hunter's face and hands. She also handed him a little plastic bag of pills, "For when you feel weak or overtired."

When he came to Lin, they stood with their eyes closed, foreheads touching, and seemed to stop breathing. I felt at once touched and jealous. I'd long accepted that Lin was Hunter's wife and had been for millennia. He loved her and their bond was unbreakable. He loved me, too. I would get old and die, as would all his children—but he and Lin would not. It was a tragedy that stalked them through the ages. And now it haunted me.

We stood around awkwardly while the two communed, not liking to stare or disturb them with chatter. After a good ten minutes, they separated. Hunter wore some sort of dark green padded jumpsuit. Given his enormous size, he must have had it custom-made. A thick rope encircled his waist and a long knife lay sheathed at his hip. His beautiful thatch of blond hair was tucked into a cap that fastened under his chin, covering his ears. He pulled on gloves that had some sort of rough surface on the palms.

He approached the tree, climbed several branches, then turned and waved. We waved back. No one said a word. The keen wind cut into my cheeks while Hunter's receding figure cut into my heart. He climbed so fast that, after ten minutes, he looked the size of a cat. Another five and he disappeared from view. Maybe forever. The enormity of losing Hunter, the love of my life and Rose's hero, almost paralyzed me. Would we lose Lin, too? What would happen to us?

"Bye-bye, Papa, I love you!" called Rose. "He waved to me," she told us.

We all looked at her curiously.

"He's gone above the clouds. How could you possibly see him?" asked Sven, his voice angry and resentful.

"I can see above the clouds," Rose answered, glaring at her half-brother, her eyes wide and reproachful.

"Let's go in now," I said.

"No, I want to stay until I can't see Papa anymore," she replied in the rebellious tone I knew so well. Rose was not a normal child. Wonderful, but not quite normal. How would I cope with her on my own without driving her away?

"Why don't you all go in and have some hot chocolate," Lin said. "Rose can stay out here with me."

"I want to stay," said Margareta. "I can see him, too."

The rest of us trudged into the castle, Dora pushing Auntie's chair. After Dora heated the milk and made our cocoa, we all sat around the kitchen table, staring glumly into our steaming cups. Sven sulked over his. I guess he was beginning to realize that his sisters had inherited a few powers that had bypassed him. They were modest as far as godly powers went, but I'm sure he resented it, even though he was a brilliant mathematician—unlike Margareta. Maybe he inherited that gift from his father, who played the stock market to great advantage.

After draining my cup, I went to my room, climbed into bed, and wept. I'd slept poorly for so long that I fell asleep and didn't awaken until Auntie wheeled herself into our suite to knock on my door and announce dinner.

"I'll be there in a while. I have to freshen up," I called back. I knew my eyes must be puffy. I'd rather have remained alone but must think of Rose.

A few minutes later, Lin knocked and entered without waiting for a reply. I was sitting on the edge of my bed, trying to muster the energy to get ready.

"I know you're upset," she said. "So am I. But it's something that he has to do. He's the brother of Odin, a god of the Aesir. He must find answers. It's his destiny."

She flopped into my armchair. "I have mixed feelings about the gods rising once more. Suppose Frigg wants me to resume my former life as her handmaiden? I like being married and having children. I like food, drink, and sex. I like dressing up and having fun. I can't go back. It's been too long and I've changed. I'm not that innocent handmaiden anymore."

Lin clutched the edge of the chair and bent her head, her pale golden hair curtaining her face. She was dressed entirely in black. She almost never wore black. Did the gods wear black to mourn?

"Why are you dressed in black?" I asked. "Do you think he's going to die?" My voice quavered.

She laughed and looked up. "Of course not. A sales lady told me last week that I should wear black because it would look stunning against my fair skin and hair. She was right, don't you think? I wanted to surprise Hunter. But he didn't notice." She dropped her head again.

"I guess he had other things on his mind." *So vain.*

"In case you're wondering what we were doing, head to head like that, we were forming a special connection."

"What do you mean? You already have the deepest connection imaginable."

"I can now enter his mind to see and hear whatever he does. I will record everything on my phone if you are not around to help. I haven't started yet as the worst part of his climb is yet to come. I will sleep tonight and enter his mind in the morning. I will probably not sleep after that until his return."

"What a relief that we'll know what's happening to him."

"Just us, Mary. If things go bad, we must sugarcoat it for the others."

"All right. Do you want to do it here or at my place?"

"Here. We need to keep Rose away from it. By the way, she said she was going to tell all her friends at school that her Papa climbed up to heaven. I told her in no uncertain terms that she was to say nothing of the sort."

I couldn't help seeing the funny side of it. "I can imagine how that would sound. I'd start receiving condolences!" Funny in the moment, the idea upset me once more.

"Why don't we meet in my room after breakfast?"

I got up and went to the bathroom to wash my face and brush my hair. How soon would it be before I saw streaks of gray appear? At the first sight of one, I'd head off to the beauty salon. And plastic surgery was always a consideration. I sighed. Who was I kidding? You can only put off the inevitable for a few years. There would come a time when Hunter was still young and handsome and I was old and gray. To be accurate, Hunter would be reborn a rambunctious baby when I'd be in a casket, ready to be lowered into the soil. Lin would come back as a sixteen-year-old maiden who'd hire a nanny to take care of Hunter until he reached the necessary stage of maturity to take his place in her bed once more. The rebirths occurred every 130 years or so for Hunter and 150 years for Lin. Their powers had weakened considerably in the millennia after the fall of their world. Their immortality, while still in place, necessitated these inconvenient hiccups.

I managed a scrambled egg for breakfast. I loathed it when Hunter ate his very rare steaks so early and avoided looking his way, especially when he fed bits of it to Rose. In fact, I'd gone off beef completely, thanks to him. Today, though, I missed seeing those bloody smears.

Rose said, "Dora, can I have steak for breakfast, like Papa?"

"No, precious, I don't have any, since Papa will be away for a while." Dora gave her a hug. "How about some oatmeal, or an egg, like your mother?"

Rose crossed her arms and scowled.

I heard a tapping sound behind me. "I know you miss him, Rose. We all do. We just have to make the best of it and carry on," Auntie Peggy said.

"Auntie, you're only using a cane. Well done!" I said.

"I've been practicing in my room. I feel like an old crock being taken everywhere in a wheelchair or rolling a walker along. I'm getting stronger, and I mean to keep it that way."

"I'm so proud of you," I said. "But I do think the wheelchair is safer in places like the grocery store or the mall."

Auntie looked sulky. "I suppose so. But I don't like it."

CHAPTER 2

"I know you don't, Auntie, but we just have to make the best of it and carry on," Rose chimed in.

After an incredulous pause, we all roared with laughter.

"Cheeky little miss," Auntie spluttered.

"Lin and I have some things to attend to," I told Rose. "Can you occupy yourself?"

"Would you like to do some reading?" Auntie asked her. "We can take it in turns."

"I got a new puzzle for Christmas. We could do that," Rose suggested.

The two of them went off to our wing of the house, while Lin and I went upstairs to her room. I hadn't been to their bedroom in this house before. The spacious room had been painted a delicate shade of blue, and the solid wood furniture was the golden blonde of Lin's hair. Several large abstract paintings looked as if they portrayed the deepest reaches of the ocean or the outer edges of our galaxy. The combined effect was once of utter serenity.

She lay down on the silky cream bedspread, while I sank into one of two armchairs that felt as if it enveloped me. Thankfully, I carried the old-fashioned tape recorder with me whenever I stayed at the castle because I never knew when Lin would want to record a story for her memoirs. Because of her godly powers, she drained the battery of any electronic device she came close to. We'd discovered—actually, I discovered—that this energy came from her feet. A mixture of a mineral called shungite and silicone glue spread over the soles of her shoes solved the issue, as long as the soles connected fully with the ground.

Her feet were up, so I set the old machine on a small table between the chairs, plugged it in, and inserted a new tape.

"Be ready to switch it on as soon as I start talking. I have to connect."

"Okay."

She closed her eyes and chanted in a whisper. I didn't know their old language, but picked out Hunter's old name, "Hoenir." I sat with my finger poised above the switch until my arm started to ache. Finally.

Tape 1,
Volume 4

"The wind screams around me. It is all I can do to hold on. Nature sometimes tries to outdo gods. I tied myself to a branch for a few hours, but the wind does not drop. I think maybe it is always thus in this layer of the sky. I must keep on up. Damn. That was close. It feels as if the wind is deliberately trying to throw me out of the tree. I must close my mind and think of nothing but up."

Lin stirred. "He closed himself off. I'll wait awhile. Perhaps his mind will alert me when he has reached a safer place. If not, I will try again in an hour."

It had been unnerving to hear Hunter's deep voice coming out of Lin's mouth. And hearing how even one such as he suffered from the dangerous, perhaps hostile, wind.

"Shall I go down to the kitchen and get some hot chocolate?" I asked.

"We have a kitchenette just along the hall. Come, I'll show you."

Lin got off the bed wearily. Entering the mind of a loved one who faced great danger must have been taxing. We opened a door at the end of the corridor to a narrow room that had a sink, a hotplate, an electric kettle, a microwave, a small fridge, and an array of cabinets. Lin pulled a carton of hot chocolate packets from one of the cabinets, two mugs from another, then filled and plugged in the kettle. While the kettle boiled, she selected a packet of cookies from several sitting on the counter. We soon had our comforting drinks and snacks and ambled back to the bedroom.

Lin sat in the other armchair, where we sipped and munched in silence for a few minutes.

"You know, it occurred to me that Agna would want to know about this," I said.

"I know. She won't be pleased I haven't told her. I don't know what to do about her."

"Why? She's like your sister. What's the time there now?" Agna, a Norse witch, lived in London.

"It's early afternoon over there. Remember, her mistress was Freya, who plotted to bring down my lady Frigg and take her place at Odin's side." Lin slapped her cup down on the table, picked up another cookie, and bit it in half as if to kill it.

"I had forgotten. And you don't know where her loyalty will lie."

"Right. I'm scared, Mary." Her chin trembled. I'd never seen her so vulnerable. It made me feel scared, too.

"You're scared of big changes, dangerous discord."

"Exactly. I don't want to give up the life I have now. Unless I can gain immortality for my children."

"I don't think Agna will want to, either," I said. "Maybe you should give her the benefit of the doubt. She knows about Yggdrasil, after all. She must be wondering."

Lin sat up straight. "But still. It's risky."

"If her loyalty still lies with Freya, you will lose her friendship. If you show your distrust at this stage, you will most likely lose her friendship. Trust her, but with your eyes open."

"You are very wise sometimes, Mary. I'll call her right now."

They spoke in English, so I listened to Lin's side of the conversation, in which she told Agna about Hunter's expedition and how she was trying to follow his progress. Then the plaintive tone, wondering about what changes might come about, and how Agna felt about it. Lin looked happier by the time she hung up.

"You were right. She's worried about changes. She doesn't want to use her powers for evil. She doesn't want to give up her life. She's flying over in a few days."

"Plane or … under her own power?"

"The Atlantic's too wide for her to fly under her own steam these days. Don't forget, we're none of us as strong as before."

I hoped Agna was telling the truth. She'd struck me as a decent sort of person—well, witch—who was unlikely to double-cross her best friend. But who knows?

Lin stiffened. "He's opened up again." She sprinted to the bed, lay down, and closed her eyes.

Tape 1,
Volume 4 (continued)

The wind dropped some, but now the rain has started. Hard rain. Hail, I suppose, biting my face. I must shelter and close my eyes to protect them. I have goggles in my pocket. I am afraid of dropping them. The wind is picking up again. If only I can get well above the clouds, where there can be no rain. But there might be wind, I think. Or maybe not. I will tie myself to the tree again.

Goggles. Must hold them tight. They should be under my cap. But I cannot hold the cap and put on my goggles without dropping one of them. I must not lose them.

That wind roars, maybe it roars my name. Yes, Hoohoo-nir, hoohoo-nir, over and over. It will drive me mad. I put my cap in one pocket. I get my goggles out of the other pocket. My hair is soaked. I am putting goggles on. My cap is back on. It is hard to fasten with gloves. I will put one glove in my pocket. My cap is fastened. Water is dripping from my hair down inside my jacket. My other glove is on. I must continue on up.

The ice comes at me harder, driven by the wind. It gets worse the higher I go. Are the Jotuns still alive, still warring with us gods? Oh, such a gust, I almost lost my footing.

I am not feeling so strong now. But it is too risky to get out a pill. I can hardly breathe, the air is so cold.

No more thinking now. Just up, just up. Up.

Lin sat up. "Closed off again. Poor darling. How he suffers."

This was a horrifying ordeal. Only a god such as Hunter could have survived this long. How long could he tolerate this onslaught of brutal weather?

"I'm really afraid for him," I said.

"Me, too. He has great strength and endurance. But even gods have their limits. Would you mind going to the kitchenette? There's a bottle of white wine in the fridge. You'll find a corkscrew in the drawer next to it, and a couple of glasses in one of the cabinets. We need a glass or two."

I struggled with the corkscrew. To this day, I'm not very good at it. I finally got it open and managed to fish out a crumb or two of cork. I grabbed the bottle by the neck with one hand and the glass stems with the other, and triumphantly bore them along to the bedroom.

Lin was seated in the armchair, drumming the fingers of her right hand on the table. When I poured the wine, she almost snatched it from the table, draining it in one go. I poured another. It didn't take me long to down my first glass and start on a second. We both felt rattled. Not so unusual for me, but unheard of for Lin.

"You should go to Rose, Mary. She's missing her Papa."

"Yes, I should. And maybe you should go to Sven and Margareta. They must be very worried, too."

"I'm just afraid of missing a communication."

"Even if you're with everyone, you'll feel it. You can just excuse yourself. Go to the bathroom, if necessary."

"I suppose you are right. Let's finish the bottle."

Before long, we went downstairs, Lin steadily, me not so much. I went through to my wing and reclined on the sofa in the living room. Rose and Auntie were engrossed in their puzzle on the small dining table.

"How's it going?" Auntie asked.

"Fine, thanks. Lin and I spent some time talking about household matters. And so on."

"That's nice, dear." From the look she cast my way, I could tell she didn't believe a word of it.

Out of the blue, Rose asked, "Mama, why don't I call you Mom like the other kids in my class?"

"I guess everyone referred to me as your mama, so that's what you learned to call me. Don't you like it?"

"Well, I like Mama best, but I'm tired of being different and keeping secrets."

Auntie broke in. "Every family has secrets. When you are older, you will know which things are important to keep to yourself, and which are not. Meanwhile, it's best to be very careful."

"I see. I think I'll stick to Mama. It sounds more cuddly. I don't really care all that much what the others think."

"That's the spirit, Rose," said Auntie.

I smiled and nodded. I didn't have the energy to do much more.

"Will Papa be home for dinner?"

That took me by surprise. "Didn't you understand he was going on a long journey?" I asked. "He won't be home for some time."

"I thought so, but I wasn't sure. No one said, exactly."

She climbed down from her chair and came to me for a cuddle. It felt good. Comforting for both of us. Auntie went on with the puzzle.

I don't remember what we had for dinner, being so torn up with worry and pity for Hunter's situation. Here we were in a nice warm house, eating a hot dinner, and soon to be tucked into a cozy bed. Most of the conversation took place between Sven, Margareta, and Auntie. The kids decided that they should help Auntie practice walking with a cane along the driveway every day, as long as conditions were not slippery.

"But you have to go back to university," Auntie said.

"Until then," Sven said.

"Two days from now," Auntie retorted.

"Well, Mary can help, can't you?"

"Of course," I said. "Happy to."

"Well, then," Margareta said with an air of finality.

I kept glancing at Lin. It may have been my imagination, but I thought she looked as if she were waiting to hear a distant phone ring. But, no interruptions. She wasn't wearing black anymore, but a cashmere sweater in her favorite sapphire blue, and gray wool pants. She looked stunning, as always, with her long, golden-blond hair, perfect face and complexion, and a figure that was flat and curvy in all the right places. Hunter took care to tell me often that I was beautiful, too, but I could never compare.

We all moved into the living room for coffee. Auntie and I didn't drink coffee so late, but all the others did. We had lemon and ginger tea with a spoonful of honey.

"I really must put Rose to bed," I said. "I'm pretty tired, so I think I'll just read in my room."

"Good night, see you at breakfast," said Lin. "We can continue our discussion after that."

I hoped she wouldn't mess up recording on her phone if Hunter connected again. She had to remember to put on shoes and be grounded, too. I remembered coating the soles of her slippers, so maybe it would work out. At least she had a good memory.

Lin didn't come down for breakfast. I could hardly eat, torn up with fear for Hunter. I felt pretty sure Lin's absence didn't bode well. I was glad the kids were still here, as they distracted Rose from asking about her father all the time.

After I'd pushed down the last forkful of scrambled eggs, I went back to my room and paced for a while. Supposing it was bad news? Should I invade Lin's privacy? But I had a right to know. Didn't I? I went upstairs and knocked on the door.

"Come in," a sleepy voice answered.

Lin was still in bed, and I had woken her. She turned over to face me and frowned.

"Lin, I was so worried when you didn't come down. Is everything all right?"

Her face relaxed. "It is. Let me play you something." She sat up, picked her phone off the bedside table, and fiddled with it. That made me nervous. I moved to take it until Hunter's voice stopped me. He sounded hoarse and weak.

"The top. I have reached the top." A thud and a pause. "I fell. The ground is so soft and spongy. It is lovely and warm up here. Bright and dry. I cannot get up right now. Crawling away from the hole where I came in, although I am no longer sure where that was. Perhaps it closed up. Hope I can find it again. So soft and warm. Lots of little clouds coming toward me. They are covering me like blankets. One slipped under my head. I shall sleep now. A good long sleep, I hope."

Lin turned off the recording. "That's it. He's still asleep, or I would have woken up, too. We will just have to wait."

I felt like doing a little dance. "He's safe." I sat down. "I haven't slept much since he started. What a brutal climb."

"It was. But you know how strong he is. Not only in his body but in his mind." Lin lay back on her pillows and closed her eyes.

"I guess he is. I'm confused, though. I expected the climb to take longer. And what about the airlessness of space? And how can there be wind and hail up so high?"

"Once you get to a certain point, the route to Asgard takes a different path. A path that is hidden to all but the gods."

"Oh, I see." I might have known. "Shall I ask Dora to bring up a tray?"

"Yes, why not? I don't feel like getting ready yet. Coffee and pancakes."

Dora received my request with a grunt and a snort.

I found the others in the family room. Sven was helping Rose with another puzzle, 1,000 pieces this time. Margareta had her nose stuck in a book, and Auntie knitted, rather more slowly than she used to. I noticed she sat in an armchair, a cane by her side. She had made excellent progress. Her weakened left hand managed the needle quite well, and her face had regained its normal appearance. She had spoken clearly for a few months now, which I knew gave her tremendous satisfaction. She'd always been articulate and precise in her speech. Dr. Ayre's salve had also made a drooping left eye and jaw straighten up and probably accounted for the speedy return of mental acuity. Walking was taking a little longer, but she had made great strides, to coin a phrase.

I cleared my throat, suddenly feeling emotional. "I just want to let you all know that Hunter has reached the top of Yggdrasil and has emerged into a warm, dry, and soft place where he is enjoying a well-earned sleep."

"Is it Asgard?" Sven asked.

"He didn't say. When he wakes and starts exploring, we'll know more. Your mother is exhausted and having a lie-in. As soon as he wakes, she'll sense it."

"When is my Papa coming home to me?" Rose asked, her chin quivering.

"Just as soon as he can, Rose," Margareta said. "He's our Papa, too, you know. We also miss him."

"Yes, but you and Sven are away all the time. You're used to it. I'm not old enough yet to be away from Papa." She started to sob.

"Come on, Rose. Let's go look for shells," Sven said. "It's really cold, so we'll have to dress warmly."

He led her out. "I think I'll go too," said Margareta. "The sea always makes me feel better." While glad the kids were so good to Rose, I couldn't help feeling like a third wheel. She had so many adults looking out for her. Well, I was her mother when all was said and done, and she knew that.

"She's a lucky little girl," Auntie said. "She's got loving siblings that will always look out for her, no matter what."

"I know," I said. "It's just that sometimes I feel she doesn't need me much anymore."

"Oh, she knows who her mother is. You are still her main rock. And her Papa, of course. You are all traveling a sticky road."

That was the first time Auntie had acknowledged out loud that Rose was Hunter's daughter. It must have been obvious for a long time, but it was one of those things not spoken of.

"Are you very shocked by the situation?" I asked.

"I was at first. But I suspected the Thorens were different, even before we were officially told. It seems completely normal to me now. And you'd be surprised by some of the things I've seen. A Russian spy who was a circus clown midget, for example. He traveled all over Europe with that circus. The ringmaster, his father, was a big burly chap, and his mother was a contortionist. His family had no idea what he was up to. They were devastated when he was found dead in a ditch just outside the last Serbian town they camped in. But at least they didn't have to know his history. He had a lot of blood on his hands. And you never heard this story."

"You mean he was assassinated?"

"I will say no more." Auntie closed her mouth in a tight line that ended the matter.

It was two days before I saw Lin stiffen and her eyes open
so wide I could see the whites all around the irises. We had
just finished breakfast and had been sitting around after all
the others left the table. She got up and almost ran upstairs,
beckoning me to follow. Once we got to her room, I quickly
inserted a new tape into the machine and switched it on.
We sat in the armchairs on either side of the small table.
Nothing happened for a few minutes. Lin sat completely
still, her eyes closed. I could have used my phone, since her
feet were planted firmly on the floor, but force of habit made
me think of the tape recorder first.

She opened her mouth a few times, but nothing came
out. I wondered if I should rewind the tape. I stretched out
to the switch, but then she started to channel Hunter.

Tape 2,
Volume 4

I feel better ... strong now. The sky is bright blue, but everything around me is clouded in a wall of mist. My cloud blankets have tumbled away. I will walk. I have to get used to this spongy ground. I feel as if I will tip over if I am not careful. It is like that time we first set foot on Olympus. I see the blue outline of trees and hills ahead, hardly misty at all. A long way ahead. There are many beautiful flowers growing along the road. They are the color of jewels. I only see them clearly when I draw alongside. They smell sweet, too, sometimes like roses and sometimes like lilies.

I hope I find some other remnants of our heaven. Some little thing.

Is that a house? Just ahead on the right. It keeps disappearing behind the mist. I am drawn to that place. I walk toward it, but it does not become closer. I will run now. I seem to run as fast as I used to, before Ragnarok. It is good to feel so strong.

Finally, I reached the portal of a very big house. The ground shakes with a kind of rumbling noise. There is no door, only an arched entry with a very high threshold. I am going inside.

Damn! Every time I raise my foot, that threshold spikes upward as if to break my leg. Ha! This time I kicked it. The ground shifted fast under me. I almost fell but jumped into the place. It is more than a house. This is a vast hall. Like Valhalla, but misty. There is one long hall with archways leading off from each side. Big thrones line the walls. Some are empty, some have statues sitting on them. How did these come to be?

I stand in front of the first throne and marvel at the immense figure before me. Its one eye stares straight ahead, hands resting on its lap. It looks like pictures of the Pharoah statues Mary brought back from Egypt. I look into a big face without expression. But it begins to seem familiar. And that one eye. Can it be? It has taken on the appearance of my dear brother. It makes me feel so sad. My brother, my father, my lord. Odin, father of the world. Now just a figure of stone.

"Hoenir, is it you?"

He has not moved, yet he has spoken.

"It is I, my dearest brother. It is I."

I kneel and rest my head on his lap. The stone softens and warms my cheek. It smells of wood smoke and herbs. I rise again.

Lights dance around the wall behind my brother. They move around him, now darting over and around his statue. Now they circle his head like a halo, all the colors of the rainbow. The mist in the hall has cleared. Lights dart everywhere now. It has become as bright as day in here.

"You survived, Hoenir. You are whole. And Lin, she is in your mind, too. What are you doing with Frigg's handmaiden?"

"Yes, I only just survived. I was grievously wounded. Lin found me and carried me to Hel. We rested there for a millennium while I recovered, before journeying back up to Midgard—Earth is what humans call it—when it arose from the void and became fertile once more. We have lived there together ever since as man and wife. Midgard is the only one of the nine worlds remaining—unless Asgard comes back to life."

"Have you offspring?"

"Yes, three. A boy and two girls."

"Only three after all this time?"

"Yes. Our powers are not what they were. We have had very many, but our children are not immortal."

"A great sadness for you. How came you here?"

"Yggdrasil. Lin cut a sprig after the battle. She planted it wherever we lived, but it never thrived. Until Loki was finally killed last summer, that is. Then it started to grow and gained many branches and leaves. I had to wait for it to grow all the way up here."

"Loki survived also?"

"Yes. He was as wicked as ever. Freya's witch, Agna, also survived. She hid deep in the mountains. We had many terrible troubles with Loki. Finally, when he took the form of a fox and was injured, the physician Eir—another survivor—injected him with a potion that destroyed him. Before that, he had pursued and bothered us for such a long time. He wanted to kill us."

"So, Yggdrasil led you here?"

"Yes, I climbed the tree for several days. It was an ordeal, but I had to see what, if anything, remained of our world."

"I have been waiting for eons, never knowing if there was anything to wait for. I can rise again if enough people believe and call my name. A few people on earth still believe—I hear their prayers—but I must hear my name called loud and clear by many, feel their love, hear them spread my word. Only then will I be freed from this stone prison."

"Most people on Earth have other gods now. Some become very angry if they think anyone is challenging their beliefs. But I will see what I can do."

"Thank you, brother. I have had so long to think and dream. I do not need worship or sacrifice. I do not need temples or statues raised in my name. I need to spread Odin's Word. I have caught glimpses of life in Midgard, the chaos of want and war. They need to hear me and believe my way is best."

"What is your word? Religion on earth often leads to war, starvation, and other unspeakable atrocities."

"I ask no one to give up their religion. My word is that people shall take the good from their religion and refute the evil. I suspect humans still use religion and warp the message to gain power. I have seen it before, using my name to commit some small or big bad deed. Of course, I was able to correct the situation. Why do these new gods not do likewise?"

"Humans think those who are good will be rewarded in heaven, and the sinful will be punished in hell. It does not work very well. No one ever reports back, you see.

"We need not rob them of that belief. It is very comforting, I am sure. But they need to believe that Odin's Word will help them find their way to heaven."

"That might work. But I am no preacher. My family and I must think hard and plan carefully to find a way to accomplish this. It will not be easy, because it is important that we do not call attention to ourselves. Life is very complicated down there now. The rulers want to know where people come from, and especially where your wealth comes from, for example. They intrude into one's affairs without shame."

"Where does your wealth come from?"

"After Midgard emerged, we found the dwarves' treasure. The dwarves did not reappear to claim it."

"I see. Why don't you visit my dear wife, Frigg? She is nearby. Also Freya, who constantly pours honeyed words into my mind, I am not sure why. I think some of the others are here, but I do not know if they are mindful yet. I have not heard them."

"I will come back to you, my dear brother. Later, I will explore the outside part of this world."

I am walking along the hall toward the next statue. It is a surprisingly long walk, and the scent of lilac grows as I get closer. It looked closer. This one glows white amid a rich blue halo. It is a lady. I stand before her and wait.

"Is that Hoenir?"

"Yes, it is Hoenir."

"You live."

"Yes. Are you my lady Frigg?"

"I am. I wish to be able to move once more, like you. How did you do it?"

"I was badly wounded. Your handmaiden, Lin, carried me to Hel. When Midgard rose again, we left Hel and have lived there ever since."

"Dear Lin. Such a faithful girl."

"She loves you dearly. But she is not a handmaiden any longer. She is my wife and mother of my children."

"I understand. And she is with us now. I feel her presence. I would dearly like to see her, but not to pluck her from her life with you. Just to kiss her sweet cheek."

"And I know she would love to set eyes on you once more and kiss your hand."

"But not like this. Is it hard to come here? Why did you not come before?"

"Lin took a sprig of Yggdrasil and planted it everywhere we lived. Not until we killed Loki did it flourish. It only recently reached all the way up to here. It was an arduous journey. It was almost as if the winds wanted to throw me to my death."

"There is evil here. Freya is nearby, and she is jealous of my husband's love for me. She torments me with hurtful whispers day and night. Not that we know the difference between day and night anymore. She says she will kill anyone who tries to rule here and will take Odin for herself. She is trying to enter me now, but I have closed myself to her."

"We learned this from the witch Agna, my lady. She also survived. Freya trained Agna to be a powerful witch to further her plans. Agna will not be a party to this anymore. She is our friend."

"Be careful not to let Freya take over your mind. Her powers are still strong, more than you can imagine. I can only block her until I grow weary. Then she slithers back in."

"I will find her, my lady. I will be careful. And we will find a way to bring life to Asgard once more."

"Go, my dear brother. And be careful."

Her halo fades. The mist closes in around her.

I am walking farther along the hall.

"Hoenir. Dear Hoenir."

Where did that voice come from?

"Come, Hoenir."

It seems to float in a wave from underneath one of the archways. It is darker through here. I look to either side as I walk. I see nothing, but there is a faint odor like rotting tropical flowers.

"Hoenir." That startled me. A statue sits in a niche I did not notice. I can hardly see through its deep purple shadow.

"Who is this?"

"It is Freya. Surely you remember. I heard you talking to Odin."

"My dear lady Freya. It is wonderful to hear you. It is so dark down here, I did not see you."

"I caught some of your conversation with Odin. We are very close, you know."

"I am happy for that, my lady. It must be a lonely existence."

"Very. Frigg is not so accommodating. She blocks me out."

"Why would she want to do that?"

"She is jealous of me. She thinks I want to take Odin away from her."

"Where did she get that idea?"

"Well, he talks to me often. I know he likes me better than her. And what are you doing here? Have you come to take over Odin's role as supreme leader?"

"Oh, no, my lady. I am no leader. That takes more wisdom than I can claim. I will return to Midgard and try to find believers to bring not only my brother but all of you, back to life."

"See that you do. But I do not know if I believe you. Gods crave power as much as men do."

"Believe me, my lady, I do not wish to give up my good life on Midgard. I have been there ever since it rose from the void. It is my home now."

"I hope so."

"I will take my leave now. I must explore this place and see how much is restored."

I backed out of that dark place into the great hall. But it does not look the same. Maybe that is because of the mist—more like a fog now. I will go back to Odin. He must be told of Freya's plan.

This seems like an even longer walk. I only came down one side corridor and then back again. But am not in the same place. I cannot find Odin and Frigg. There, I see light and a way out. It is not the place where I entered. It is so foggy outside that I cannot see my own feet. At least the threshold did not try to trip me this time.

I cannot see anything. It is like walking through a black cloud. I will keep on walking, though. I hope my way clears. I must get back to Odin. Suddenly, I am very tired. I suppose the climb is still taking its toll. It is warm, so I will just stretch out on this soft, mossy ground I feel beneath me. The air is fresh and warm, despite the fog.

Lin's tears still ran down her cheeks.

"To hear the lovely voice of my dear lady, Frigg. To know she still exists, even trapped in stone. We must set them free."

"Her voice sounded like music," I said. "But not the other one. Freya's voice was low and sultry, but with a harsh edge. What's to be done about her?"

"I don't know. She will have to be destroyed, somehow. Ooh, I can't breathe!"

"What's the matter?" I got up and raced to Lin's side.

"Hunter is suffocating. Hunter! Wake up! He's waking and choking. He's fighting the clouds that have closed him in and pressed down on his face. He's ripping them to shreds." Lin was breathing normally now. "It's Freya's doing, I know it. She thinks he wants to rule Asgard."

"What's Hunter doing now?" I asked.

"Running back the way he came. He knows it's Freya. I hope he doesn't do anything foolish. He has nothing with which to defend himself."

"He needs an axe to destroy that statue."

"Yes. No, wait. How do we know that wouldn't release her?"

"I guess we don't know much of anything. Aren't you connected anymore?"

"No, he's closed me off. I've got to know what he's going to do. I wish Agna were here."

"She'll be here tomorrow."

"That may be too late."

Lin didn't come down for lunch or dinner. She texted me.

[I'll let you know when to come up.]

I slept restlessly that night. Things up in Asgard were not as serene as one would hope, considering it was supposed to be some kind of heaven. I worried about what Hunter might do. Freya seemed to have a lot of tools at her disposal. She was a witch, after all. Agna would be with us later that day. Her insight might prove useful.

Lin didn't come down for breakfast again. I hesitated to go up and perhaps wake her like I did before. She needed her sleep, too. Or did she? She was a goddess and could do perfectly well without food and drink. She even had to learn how to eat and drink when she got to Midgard. Thinking of that incident still made me want to giggle because, after her first meal, she also had to learn about pooping. But she was accustomed to earthly delights, now. If she thought she needed sleep, she did.

I took Rose out to the gates to wait for the school bus, then went back to my sitting room, where Auntie Peggy joined me.

"I should have taken you to wait for the school bus," I said. "We can do that tomorrow, weather permitting. I can wheel you there, as there isn't much time, and then you can walk back. The driveway is nice and level."

"Yes, that might work. You seem very edgy."

"Do I? I've been trying to appear calm, for Rose's sake."

"But I see how your mind drifts off when we're talking, how you jiggle your foot when you cross your legs, how you rip a tissue to bits you seem to have plucked from the box for that very purpose."

"You don't miss much, do you?"

"No, I was trained to be super vigilant. It's not an easy habit to break."

"Hunter has run into a problem."

I told her about Freya and her wicked plans. "According to Lin, she used to be good and sweet until she became ruined by ambition."

"It might be worth asking Lin what she thinks brought about the change."

"Lin didn't know about her plans until Agna told her. Maybe Agna knows."

"A vulnerability can often be used as a weapon."

"I guess you would know."

"Now, now," Auntie said, rapping my hand. Her smirk belied her reprimand.

We stayed in our suite reading. I kept reading the same page, as my mind wandered while my eyes scanned the words. At one o'clock, we went to the dining room for lunch to find Agna already seated. After exclamations, hugs and kisses, we sat down.

"I thought you were coming later," I said. "I'm sorry we weren't here to welcome you."

"Oh, that's all right. After I landed, I took a limo from Dulles. It broke down after half an hour or so, so I decided to fly. I told the driver I had to answer a call of nature and disappeared behind a bush. And really disappeared. I hope he's not still looking for me." She laughed with that strangely musical, tinkly sound.

"Now, Agna, that's very naughty," said Auntie. "He might get into terrible trouble. You'd better call the company and tell them you flagged down another car."

"I hadn't thought of that." Agna pouted. "I think I've still got the company card."

"Right now, Agna."

"All right, Auntie."

My Auntie telling off a witch and giving her orders—typical. I wished she'd tell me all about her career. Obviously a spy, clearly high ranking. What a story that would make.

Agna was soon back at the table. "They said they were glad to hear from me. They would go and post bail for the driver right away. I left my number in case of other inquiries."

Her phone rang about twenty minutes later. I heard her say, "Yes, detective, this is she." She moved into the kitchen to complete the call. "Well, that's the end of that, then. Everything is sorted."

It's funny how British people say, "sorted" instead of, "sorted out." She didn't seem to have much sympathy for the poor driver who'd been suspected of doing her mischief.

"Agna and I have some catching up to do," Lin said. "We'll go upstairs to my quarters. Why don't you join us, Mary?"

Lin reclined on her bed while Agna and I sat in the armchairs. Lin brought Agna up to date with Hunter's ordeals and discoveries, and how we hadn't heard from him for more than a day.

"Freya is dangerous," said Agna. "She will stop at nothing to get what she wants. And she is a powerful witch, although I had become more powerful. Our powers lie in our minds. Did Hunter discover other gods?"

"No," said Lin. "He intended to go back to see Odin and look for others after he'd explored the terrain. But he couldn't find it. She must have been concealing the hall, just like she concealed the way back past Odin and out. He started to run back the way he came."

"I have a question," I said. "The stories show Freya to be such a sweet and beautiful goddess. Was that all lies, or did she change? If she changed, why?"

"She was married to the god, Odr, and they had a beautiful daughter called Hnoss. She took a lover on Midgard, a handsome warrior called Erik. One day, Freya decided to make a surprise visit to Erik and found him making love to Hnoss. She cast a spell on her daughter, ravaging her face with scars and pustules. The girl went to her father, crying. Odin knew everything with his all-seeing eye and told Freya she would no longer be the goddess of love and beauty, only of war. Odr left their palace and built another one of his own, taking one of Freya's handmaidens as his wife." Agna sighed and lay her head back on the chair. "The humiliation embittered Freya. She might claim to want Odin for herself and displace Frigg, but I suspect she will try to kill Odin to avenge her punishment and rule alone. She will have become too powerful to depose by that time."

Lin sat up. "We have to do something."

"But what?" I said. "She has a vulnerability. She is not loved. She is not revered as a goddess that humans worship to ensure fertility. How can that be used against her?"

"I really don't know," Agna replied. "Odin must suspect her plot. That's probably why she wouldn't let Hunter find him again. I think we need to find Odin some believers."

"Mary, the recorder. He's coming. No, he's fading in and out. He's running, he's falling, No!"

I leaped to my feet. "What's happening?"

"He's falling, falling." Lin's voice had become a scream. She clutched her head and let out an almighty roar—Hunter's roar.

Agna stood now, head slung back, her mouth moving without sound, her arms spread wide above her head.

"He's holding on, arms and legs clasped around something." Lin sounded less panicked.

"Round what?" I asked.

"Yggdrasil," Agna replied. "When he was running to find Odin, Freya must have opened the portal in front of him. He will be home soon. She has cast a spell to call the winds to assault him, but I have managed to block it for the time being. I hope it lasts long enough. She will realize it is I who has done this. I don't think she can attack me from so far, but I'm not sure."

We sat around for an hour before Lin connected with Hunter again. He was descending fast, exhausted from the precipitous dive, but at least it had landed him more than halfway down. There was no wind, rain, or hail, and it wasn't even that cold. Lin was to make sure there would be steak for his breakfast.

I went to my room to take a long nap. "He's on his way home," I whispered to Auntie.

Dinner was a cheerful affair. Margareta and Sven would leave for college the next morning, so Lin told them the good news, warning them to save it as a surprise for Rose, as she'd never get to sleep otherwise.

The kids had to leave by ten, so hoped desperately they'd see their father before they went. We all drank too much wine and watched a movie—which one, I have no idea. I thought I'd be unable to sleep, but I guess the wine did its job. I woke at seven and went into the shower at once. I wanted to look good when he arrived. Rose woke soon after and I dressed her in a fluffy pale blue sweater and navy pants. Thank goodness it was a Sunday, so she didn't have to go to school. We got to the breakfast table by eight.

"Papa?" she shrieked, and flung herself into his arms. Fortunately, he managed to put down his steak knife and fork in time.

Lin's smile was radiant as she watched the happy scene. The other two kids rushed in, so I had to wait some time for my hug.

We all sat down. The two older kids clamored to know all about his adventures.

"Ask your mother later," he said. "You must finish your breakfast and get off to the airport."

Auntie arrived a little later. "Good morning, Hunter. You are looking well." She pecked him on the cheek—which she had never done before.

"It is very nice to see you again, Auntie," he said, pleasure lighting his face.

The family continued to eat, Hunter rather awkwardly as Rose would not leave his lap. We all trooped outside where Stan waited in the car and said our goodbyes, Rose tearfully.

"I like having a brother and sister. I will miss you."

They both hugged her and waved to her, hanging out of the car windows until the car was out of the gate and had rounded the bend leading to the road.

"Where's Agna?" I asked Lin.

"I think she is thinking through our options. Perhaps planning some magic. Eir's coming over later."

We all trooped back into the house and sat in the living room. Rose snuggled up between Hunter and Lin. I wished it was between Hunter and me. *Practice gratitude, Mary.*

"You and Odin managed to communicate up there. Can't you try to reach him from here?" I asked.

"I have not thought about that. Odin always initiated our conversation. Perhaps if I sit in the dark and concentrate. I must rest for a while. I will try when I wake up."

CHAPTER 8

"Perhaps Eir can help, too. And Agna." Lin said.

"Well, I must go upstairs now." Hunter got up.

"No, Papa, you mustn't leave me again."

"Be patient, little one. Papa is very tired and must take a nap."

Rose pouted and crossed her arms as Hunter left the room. I moved over and cuddled her. "Papa will be back downstairs later. Why don't you draw him a picture while you wait?"

She rushed out. "Mama, come and help."

7

Eir arrived in the late afternoon. We all sat around sipping tea of one sort or another. No one talked, which I found odd, considering all the decisions we had to make. Agna looked as if she was asleep. I decided to break the ice.

"So, now what?"

Agna opened her eyes. "I have been communicating with Freya. She can communicate with me, but weakly. I believe I am beyond harm. Hunter, have you felt anything from her?"

"No, I have not. I keep getting snatches of talk, but it is like a radio that keeps losing the signal. It is all broken up. It is sometimes a deep voice, and sometimes a high one." He stood up and went over to the sliding glass doors. "Another is coming in now."

Lin went to stand beside him. "Hoenir, do you hear me? It is Odin." It was beyond eerie to hear that mesmerizing voice emanating from Lin's throat. Now we heard Frigg, her voice quavering, rising and fading. "Hoenir, she is trying to kill me, poison my mind, and that is all I have left. Help me. I grow weaker with each passing hour."

CHAPTER 7

Agna joined them and put her arms around both, leaning into them. They all stood in this tableau for about five minutes. Now, the evil voice. "Agna, you are a traitor. I must fulfill my destiny. All those who stand in my way will die. I am your mistress. I am stronger than you ..."

The trio broke apart and sat back down. Rose had sensed the gravity of the moment and had not complained when Hunter left her on the sofa. She sat up straight next to him, crossing her ankles and setting her hands on her knees in a comically sedate manner.

"I managed to fog her brain. She won't be able to intrude into the others for a while. It will give Frigg time to restore herself. In a while, I will give her some tips to keep Freya out."

Lin said, "One thing that troubles me is that we don't know how many up there are sentient. And if there are more, we don't know where their sympathies lie. Freya can be very charming and she will no doubt spin some terrible lies to win people over."

I had been doing a little research. "Would it surprise you to know that there are a few groups, both here in the United States and in Europe, that worship the Norse gods? I have discovered them in California, Pennsylvania, and Florida. And even here in Maryland. I think there are a few more, too. There's a big group in Iceland, and they're building a big new *hof*—that's what they call their house of worship."

"You've done well, Mary," said Dr. Ayre. "Do they only worship Odin?"

"No, they worship all the major gods, including Freya."

"Ah," said Lin. "We have some work to do. We must visit them all. Tell them about the situation and warn them about Freya."

"I think we need a plan," said Agna. "Let's make an agreement with other groups that we will all call upon Odin on a certain day and time. That might do the trick."

"That's a great idea," said Lin. "I'll plan the visits. Hunter and I had better do Iceland. Mary, can you take Maryland, if it's not too far away? Eir, can you take any time off to visit another group? It could easily be done on a weekend because that's when they probably meet. Agna, would you like to do California? Perhaps some of the groups are in contact with each other and can help with the arrangements."

So, we had a plan. Lin and Hunter would leave in a couple of days. Not the best time of the year to visit Iceland, but they wouldn't be affected by cold temperatures. I'd contact the Maryland group. It was only about an hour's drive away. Agna would fly commercial to Sacramento and make her own way farther north. Eir would drive to Pennsylvania within the next couple of weeks. She'd fly to Florida as soon as she could. In fact, she'd find a locum and spend a week in the warmer climate.

I felt a little nervous about my mission. It was so far out of my league. And it wasn't as if I were a god like the others. But maybe that was an advantage.

Dora announced that dinner was ready. Happier faces ringed the table now that we had a way forward. "I'll come to Maryland with you," whispered Auntie Peggy. She walked a lot better now, and I'd be glad of her wisdom. I wasn't sure what kind of people we'd be dealing with. Whacko or ordinary?

I drove for just over an hour the next Sunday morning to get to a small town not far from Annapolis. The directions took me out to a farming area. My written directions matched the GPS instructions so far, which was a comfort as I bumped down a rutted track into what looked like a farmyard. I drew to a stop outside an old house that looked well kept, as did the surrounding outbuildings. There were five or six cars and trucks parked around the yard.

A slight man with sandy, thinning hair appeared in the doorway. I got out of the car and approached him. "Mr. Evards?"

"Yes. And you must be Mary Lambert. Come on in. We are about to sit down for lunch. Most of our group were able to be here, so you'll have a good audience."

His manner was pleasant and his tone welcoming. He didn't come across as odd in any way.

"I'll just help my aunt, Peggy Lambert, out of the car. She wanted to meet you all."

"She is most welcome. My name is Lenart."

He walked back to the car and opened the passenger door, assisting Auntie out as they exchanged greetings. Inside, the door opened into a huge kitchen with a long table running down the middle, where smiling people sat, staring our way. They all looked friendly enough. An angular woman swathed in a huge blue apron stirred a massive pot on the stove. A witch's cauldron? She turned and held out her hand. "You are most welcome, Miss Lambert."

"Thank you. Mary, please. And this is my aunt, Peggy Lambert."

"And I am Anita. Please, sit down while I dish out the food. Nothing fancy, just a big stew, but it's filling."

She began to ladle the stew into a pile of bowls beside her. Her husband carried them to the table, setting one in front of each guest. Another woman got up to help. Platters of rolls and butter lay at regular intervals down the table.

I was directed to sit at the head of the table. Or was it the bottom? Lenart sat at the other end. As soon as everyone had a full bowl before them, the Evards sat down. Everyone held hands to say grace, a simple chorus:

> We thank you, Father Odin, for the rains and the sun that nurture our crops and animals.

The people within earshot spoke of normal, everyday things related to farm life. It seemed that they were all farmers. They were curious about me. I told them a few selected truths. I was from a small town in Pennsylvania and now lived in Calvert County near the Chesapeake Bay. I had met dear friends nearby who introduced me to the Norse gods. But, I said, more about that later. They didn't press me. I noticed that Auntie Peggy was enjoying an animated conversation with everyone around her.

After a few of the women cleared away the bowls, a selection of pies appeared, already sliced, and each guest received a clean plate. Jugs of cream were passed around, as were the pies—apple, or cranberry and pear. I had a slice of each. I hoped my overindulgence wouldn't make me burp or have hiccups. All I really wanted at that point was a nap. But there was work to be done.

When Lenart rose, so did everyone else, as if it signaled the start of business.

"We have our *hof* in one of the barns by the yard," he said. "Please follow me."

We entered the barn, which had been transformed inside. There was a long table at one end, which I assumed was some sort of altar. Various carvings of farm animals and human-like figures—gods?—flanked the altar, before which two rows of chairs had been set out. Small tables around the walls each held a vase of sunflowers. They must have cost a small fortune in the depths of winter.

Lenart went to another table and opened a few bottles of white wine that had been sitting in ice buckets. He poured a glass for each congregant as they filed past.

"We give thanks to the gods by appreciating their bounty," he said. What a sensible outlook.

When the last glass had been dispensed, he turned to the congregation, who now each stood behind a chair. "Thanks be to Odin!" he cried. They all repeated the refrain three times, taking a sip between each "hallelujah." They all sat.

"We will now sing our paean to the gods."

It was a strange song. Not quite a chant, but neither did it have a tune to remember. They turned their faces up to the heavens, cheeks flushed and expressions earnest. And it wasn't sung in English.

That was the end of the service.

"What language was that?" I asked Lenart.

"We sing in Swedish, as most of us hail from Swedish forebears in this area, and it is probably closer to the language of the gods than English."

"Most commendable," I said. "A beautiful tribute."

Lenart placed a chair in front of the group. "Please, give us your news."

I told them that very few gods had escaped Ragnarok, including Loki. I had gotten to know two of them and was now part of their household. I thought it best not to mention Rose. I told them a sanitized version of Loki's death, which caused Yggdrasil to flourish and grow once more. The group gasped when they heard that. Hoenir had climbed to find out if Asgard was coming back to life. I told them how I had been privy to Hoenir's conversations with Odin, Frigg, and Freya, and Freya's disappointing betrayal.

"We must free Father Odin from his stone prison so that he may guide us once more. Freya must not be freed. Hopefully, the lady Frigg will also be able to join her husband in his good works."

One of the men remarked, "There are many different religions. There will be trouble."

"Maybe," I said. I then repeated precisely what I heard was Odin's Word. "So, you see, he is not asking anyone to give up their beliefs. Only those that are harmful or hateful. Of course, there will be those that won't like that."

A murmur of assent rippled across the rows.

But then, "How do we know you are genuine and not some sort of government agent?" asked a dour woman, who I'd noticed spoke to no one at lunch.

"We live with Lin, once the lady Frigg's handmaiden. Not many people have heard of her. In fact, not many have heard of Hoenir. One day, they will visit you." Auntie's voice seemed to calm the ripple of unease the woman's challenge had caused.

"And, who knows, perhaps you will get a glimpse of Odin if we can bring him back to life," I added, emboldened by Auntie's intervention.

"How can we free our Lord?" asked Lenart, obviously eager to turn the conversation to a more positive note.

"He needs to hear our voice believing in him and calling on him. We are contacting other groups and have set a date and time for everyone to call Odin simultaneously. Friends are traveling to other groups in California, Pennsylvania, and Florida. My two friends have just left for Iceland, where there is a large group of believers. We have agreed on the last Sunday in February at 3 p.m., Eastern Standard Time. That allows for convenience in each time zone. Can you do it? Will you do it?"

Indeed, they would. There were lots of questions, as might be expected, not all of which I was willing to answer. Auntie held her own, though, masterfully stepping around awkward topics. I gave Lenart a card with Lin's phone number in case he had any further questions. We shook hands and hugged the same rapturous people many times (except the doubting Thomasina) before getting back into the car. We wouldn't get home until after dark, which fell by around five-thirty at that time of year.

"Well, that went well," Auntie Peggy said, sighing her satisfaction. "You did very well, dear."

"Well, you helped a lot. I was really nervous. Did it show?"

"Not at all. You could have been a teacher. You explained everything so clearly."

9

We restrained ourselves to telling each other—mostly by phone—that our visits had gone well, knowing that when Lin and Hunter returned, we would meet and each tell our stories to everyone. I, of course, would record them, although I didn't say so.

Dr. Eyre needed to get back to her practice, so didn't stop by after her visit to Pennsylvania. She planned to fly to Florida the following Wednesday and visit the hof over the weekend. Agna was still in California, apparently doing some sightseeing after her visit. Lin and Hunter should have been back within a week, but Lin texted me to say that they'd had a successful visit but had been delayed. Knowing her, that wasn't necessarily good news. We only had a couple of weeks before the big day.

Dora was relieved to have the house to herself. She was hearty and strong, but getting bigger and clumsier by the week. She was due in the middle of March. She complained about an aching back and feeling tired, so her nymph qualities (whatever they were) didn't seem to be much help. Auntie worked beside her in the kitchen a lot and didn't spend much time with Rose and me anymore. I didn't mind, as they both enjoyed each other's company. I couldn't help wondering why, given Dora's humdrum existence and Auntie's crackerjack past.

At last, Hunter and Lin returned on a Friday evening after more than ten days away. Dr. Ayre had returned from Florida by that time and would join us the next day, and Agna flew in the same morning. I made up beds and Dora prepared dinner, while Auntie shopped online for the weekend. I decided to go home after picking up Rose from school. The weekend promised to be intense. I worried about how much Rose might overhear, but one of the other mothers from her class called and invited her to spend the day because they were planning a picnic at a farm where the kids could ride ponies.

I dropped Rose off at her friend's house at ten and went on to the castle. Everyone was sitting around the living room sipping tea or coffee.

"There you are. I think we should go around the room and report on our visits."

"Welcome back," I answered, miffed by Lin's abrupt welcome.

"Thank you."

"Where is Rose?" Hunter asked.

"She was invited to play with a school friend for the day. It was good timing because I really didn't want her to hear all of this."

"Okay. You will bring her over tomorrow?"

"Sure. Or you can come to us."

"Why don't you begin, Mary?"

I went to the sideboard and poured myself some coffee before sitting down and telling them how it went, with occasional input from Auntie.

"Interesting," Lin said, looking less irritable.

I got my phone out of my jeans pocket and put it on the side table.

"That's better," I said. "It's so uncomfortable when I sit down." I hoped they hadn't noticed me set it to record.

"Let's hear from you, Eir."

Tape 3,
Volume 4

The Pennsylvania hof was hard to find. It's a good thing I wrote down the directions the priest gave me over the phone because the GPS instructions to that address took me way off course. Soon after I finally got out my notes and followed its instructions, I pulled up outside a plain brick rambler set in a large piece of land covered in close-cropped grass. It must have been an acre or so, its perimeter ringed with old oaks.

The front door opened and three people stepped outside—a middle-aged couple and a teenage girl. I wondered if I was lost again. I got out of the car and called out, "I'm looking for Mr. Collins."

"You must be Dr. Ayre," the man said, walking quickly over to meet me. "Come inside and meet everyone. Please call me Peter. This is my wife, Kathy, and our daughter, Annabelle."

We walked inside and it was not as it appeared. The house had been more or less gutted and we stood in a large room that must have taken up most of the building's footprint. Peter laughed when he noticed my surprise.

"Yes, we took down all the walls and placed columns where there were load-bearing walls. We kept the kitchen, of course, and the bathrooms. There are a couple of rooms in the basement we use for storage and an office."

"The GPS took me out of my way. And I see the house number on the house is different, as is the street name."

"Yes, someone found out about us a few years ago before we bought this place. A lot of very conservative Christians live in this area, and some of them take exception to our beliefs. A couple threatened us with their hunting rifles. Not very Christian. So, our real address is not the address on our website. That one doesn't exist."

"I'm sorry. People can get very emotional about religion." I looked around. "I see you have a nice altar and lots of flowers, even at this time of year."

"Oh, yes, we like to always have flowers for our Blot. And this is a special occasion, I believe?"

"Yes. How would you like to proceed?"

"Why don't we hold our service first, and then you speak to us and tell us why you came?"

The altar was built of pine polished to a high sheen. Ceramic symbols were set on it that I would have to ask about later. One of them looked like a facsimile of Thor's hammer. A tall vase of sunflowers stood at each end. Small tables had been set here and there, each adorned with lilies, and a few rows of chairs faced the altar.

Peter poured me a glass of white wine before introducing me to each of the attendees, about thirty in all. They seemed to come from all walks of life. One young woman and her boyfriend were lawyers, one man was a retired civil engineer, a middle-aged couple owned a convenience store in the nearest town, another was a poet, and two were farmers. I only picked this up from the general conversation, so didn't find out what everyone did for a living. Peter didn't mention his line of work.

After a half hour or so, Peter asked everyone to be seated, ushering me to a place in the front row. The poet passed song sheets around, and a couple of musicians took their seats in one corner—a flutist and a harpist. Peter stood in front of the altar and recited a prayer, thanking Odin for the bounty of last year's harvest, the joy of good friends, and the sun and the rain.

"Thanks be to Odin," they all chorused.

The musicians struck up an introduction. It was a strange tune, written in a minor key, which lent it a discordant and haunted note. They all sang the song heartily, while I mostly mouthed it, as the music was hard to follow. To my surprise, the words were written in Danish, Swedish, or Norwegian. I'm not sure which. I caught the gist of it, though, and the names of Odin, Frigg, Freya, and Thor featured often. I suppose they got a native speaker to write the lyrics, which they thought might be closest to old Norse. I found that rather touching.

"Now, friends, our guest, Dr. Ayre, would like to say a few words."

He pulled a chair to the front and invited me to sit. I explained the situation and what was at stake. They groaned when I told them that Freya should no longer be worshipped. I mentioned the date and what we were proposing to do. I also mentioned some of the other groups we were approaching.

The room fell as silent as an arctic night. I had expected questions, but no one ventured any.

"Thank you for your invitation to assist our Lord Odin, sister Ayre. I'm sure we would be delighted to stand outside and call on him to be freed from his stone prison and reborn. We will now sing our final song of praise. Please substitute Odin for Freya. It won't hurt to mention him twice, under the circumstances."

I turned over my song sheet, and, sure enough, there was another one, this time in English. The music was more in line with the predictable tunes of Christian churches that I've heard at weddings and so on, so I was able to sing along. Substituting Odin for Freya was a little awkward as most of the congregation forgot to also change her to him and she to he. Oh, well. The thought was there.

A few of the ladies brought a simple buffet dinner out of the kitchen, and the men rearranged the chairs around the tables and set a bottle of wine on each. I sat with Peter and a few of the older attendees. My hearing is excellent, although not quite as good as Lin's, so I overheard muted, breathless chatter from all sides about what I'd just told them. A few were skeptical, most excited—they felt validated.

"So, does running this group take up most of your time, Peter?" I asked.

"No, I'm a high school English teacher. Another reason why I have to be discreet. This area is pretty conservative."

"I can imagine. Are you in touch with other groups?"

"Yes, four."

"We have people going to Maryland, Iceland, and California. I'll be going to a group in Florida next week."

"I am in contact with the Maryland group, but not the others. My other contacts are in New York and Massachusetts."

"Can I ask you to contact them and tell them what I told you today? The more people who call on Odin as one united body, the better."

"We will do everything we can."

"Here is a card with Lin Thoren's cell number. She is the main contact for this endeavor. If you have questions, feel free to call her."

We finished our dinner, I said my farewells, clasping the hands of each member in mine, and that was it. They seemed convinced.

A week later, I flew down to Tampa and checked into my hotel. I spent a few glorious days either on the beach or by the hotel pool, drinking cocktails and reading mysteries. On Sunday, I took an Uber to the hof. A black car with two men in it was positioned opposite the hof in Tampa. They tried to be surreptitious, but they took a photo of me going in. FBI, I suppose. They can be so paranoid. I had to ring the bell twice before it was opened a crack by a stooped old man with a white beard that blanketed his thin chest.

"Yes?"

"I am Dr. Ayre. I am expected."

"Ah, yes. Sorry, but we are not very popular around here."

He opened the door wide enough to let me slide in.

"I noticed the car across the road."

"Yes, we seem to be on a list. They probably think we're terrorists. I'm George Cameron, by the way."

About fifteen people, mostly middle-aged, stood awkwardly around in a bare living room, sipping wine. They looked at me as if I were the taxman. An oak table had been set against sliding glass doors that led into the backyard, which seemed to be mostly dormant grass with a few shrubs dotted here and there. The table, clearly the altar, had a large vase of the kind of mixed flowers you find in grocery stores, a couple of brass candlesticks graced by tall white candles, and a few small wooden carvings of wild animals placed here and there. It actually looked quite charming. The room was painted pale blue, had two small tables containing vases of flowers and snacks, and a bucket of ice filled with wine bottles laid on a shelf in front of a hatch that presumably went through to the kitchen.

George handed me a glass of wine and introduced me around. I smiled and chatted until they began to warm up.

"Oh, so you're from up there in Washington?"

"Yes, I'm a doctor, and that's where I have my practice. I'm thinking of moving to Maryland, though, close to where my other Nordic friends live."

(I know that's a surprise, I've been thinking about it for a while. I want family time.)

"What kind of doctor?"

"Obstetrician and gynecologist."

"Oh, yeah, lady stuff." This stringy man sporting a crew cut and checkered shirt reddened and shuffled his feet.

"Quite."

"What about all of you? You all live close by?"

Many of them didn't, to my surprise. One couple had flown up from Miami, another drove down from Alabama, and four more had driven from Orlando.

"I guess there aren't too many of you around here, then. How often do you meet?"

"Only a few times a year," said George, sadly. "The surveillance we've been under lately has frightened off a lot of our congregation. We used to number fifty or sixty. You'd think the feds would know by now that we're harmless, but I think a few evangelicals spread some conspiracy theories. You know how those grow and how gullible people are." He set his glass on one of the small tables. "I think we should begin."

The group unfolded chairs that had been stacked at the back of the room, setting them in three untidy rows. I sat in the front and was handed a sheet of paper with some lyrics typed on an actual typewriter, replete with White-Out and fuzzy letters.

George started with a short sermon on the subject of slowing down and noticing—people and their needs, animals and their welfare, the beauty in small things, and intentionally looking into everything we might be grateful for. He spoke well, sincerely, and persuasively. Then we stood up to sing. I hadn't registered that there was no instrument in the room, and, sure enough, we sang *a cappella*. I just mouthed the words, since I didn't know the tune, and the others didn't seem too sure of it, either. It sounded like a cats' chorus.

At the end, they all threw up their arms and yelled, "Thanks be to Odin!" several times. They were all sincere in their beliefs and seemed inspired by their little service, which warmed my heart. Now it was my turn to talk about why I'd come. I stood in front of them and related the facts, the same as the rest of you did, and suggested the date. They became animated and enthused by the possibility of saving Odin, although saddened by Freya's betrayal. They all agreed to the date and time of the call, and this led to a discussion of how to get the whole congregation to participate.

They agreed to call every congregant—George had a list—and to get together with those fairly nearby if they couldn't get to the hof. I agreed that just a few people in different places would be nearly as good as the whole congregation together. I hope that's right. But they were doing their best. I liked them a lot.

A couple of men set up some folding tables down the center of the room and moved the chairs alongside. Apparently, a couple of the women had been busy in the kitchen before the service, and one of them set two big pots of chili on the table, one at each end and another came with plates and cutlery. Then two oversized bowls of salad arrived, and a few baskets of warm sliced bread with pots of butter. I hadn't expected a feast. Even in Florida, the weather was chilly that day, so the warming food was welcome.

George tried to insist on driving me to the airport. I didn't want him to because it was dark already, and he was old. I handed him the card with Lin's number and called an Uber. The surveillance car was still there, so I waved to the guys. They scowled back.

"Well done, Eir," Lin said, looking more relaxed. "Agna?"

I tell you, California is something else. It's like another country. People are so free and easy. I took a flying visit to several places after my visit to the hof. I didn't go to Los Angeles because of everything I've heard about the traffic, but San Francisco has some funky places, and I went to lots of beaches farther up the coast. Surfing's a big thing. And some of those guys are amazing, keeping their balance like that. It develops their muscles quite nicely, too. And...

"Agna! The hof!"

"Oh, yes, sorry. I believe I got carried away. I really liked it there."

"No kidding."

Lin was certainly on edge.

I flew up to the hof, which probably wasn't such a good idea. When I rang the bell at the wrought iron gate, the young woman who came to let me in asked me where I'd parked the car. I hadn't thought how odd it would look, arriving at this place in the middle of nowhere without a vehicle. I said I'd hitched a lift from a truck driver. She didn't look convinced. I should have rented a car and driven at least part of the way.

"My name is Felicity," she said.

"Mine is Agna."

"That's an unusual name."

"Yes, it's old Norse."

She looked a little awed by that. As well, she might. We walked across a spacious compound planted with slender trees and shrubs full of buds that looked as if they would open soon. None of them were plants I was familiar with.

"Our service will begin in one hour. The ladies are preparing dinner and the men are setting things up."

"How many are in your congregation?"

"Eighty-two. We got three new people just this week. The word is spreading."

She said, "The Word," as if it were some sort of name.

The hall was the size of a gymnasium. An altar placed at the far end was covered by a rich blue velvet cloth, its centerpiece a marble rendering of Yggdrasil. Various statuettes of wild animals carved from the same marble were arranged around the tree. A vase of sunflowers stood at each end. A long table covered with a white cloth stood along one wall, already laid with plates and silverware, vases of flowers, and trivets. On the wall opposite were two tables with more flowers. White wine in ice buckets and stemmed glasses stood on one, and on the other, juices, mineral water, and tumblers. I could smell food, so there must have been a kitchen in one of the rooms off to one side.

Seven or eight men carried chairs in from another room and set them up in rows. The women hadn't appeared. I hoped a few more would show up.

"We will have dinner after the service," Felicity said. "People will start arriving soon. The socializing takes place after the service, so they tend to arrive just before it starts."

"How did you become involved with the group?"

She smiled. "My boyfriend. We're going to get married next year. Right here." Her smile faded. "My parents don't like it. They're Christians, you know. The kind that tries to convert other people all the time. It's awful. I can't wait to get away. I'll be eighteen in a couple of months. Then they can't stop me."

"Ah," was all I could come up with while trying to decide if I should offer a word of caution. But it wasn't the time or place.

"You're supposed to sit in the front," she said. "Then it will be easier to get up and stand in front of us to say whatever you came to say."

"Thank you." I was glad to sit away from those now arriving and avoid premature questions.

People started to arrive soon after I sat down. I listened to the greetings and scraping of feet and chairs. The chatter rose louder every minute. Others came to fill the front row. I smiled and nodded to them as they returned the compliment. Eventually, a young man came to introduce himself.

"Welcome, welcome, Agna. My name is Malcom Stimes. I'm so sorry I was not here to welcome you. A minor crisis arose at the office, something that had to be dealt with."

"That's quite all right," I said. "Felicity has made me very welcome."

"We will have our service first, which will last about half an hour. I usually give a sermon, but I will cede the floor to you instead. People will be wanting their dinner!"

I thanked him and looked over the song sheet he'd handed me. Words and music. I eventually learned to read words in most languages, but I never learned to read music. A group of musicians had assembled on one side of the altar, accompanied by a flute, a violin, a harp, and a keyboard.

Malcom stood in front of the congregation and rang a small silver bell. It had the effect of a remote control mute button.

"We will first recite the prayer of thanks to our Lord Odin. We will then raise our voices in praise of those gods of Asgard who provide this earth's bounteous gifts. There will be no sermon today because we have a special guest who has a very important message for us." He moved to the other side of the altar from the musicians.

A small murmur arose before everyone stood. I noticed out of the corner of my eye that everyone flung their arms heavenward as they began to recite, so I did likewise. I couldn't recite, of course, because I didn't know the prayer. It was actually a long poem that sounded like a translation of some ancient text.

I didn't do much better with the hymns. Both were set in a minor key and sounded plaintive. They went on for some time. Perhaps some composer's idea of what a Norse paean might sound like? After the music finally drew to a close, everyone sat down. Malcom gestured to me. I faced the congregation. Quite a sea of faces and expressions—eager, wary, skeptical, blank. I told them more or less the same things as Mary and Eir. When I'd finished, I saw the same expressions, but on different faces.

"Thank you for your insights, Agna. We are distressed to hear of our Lord Odin's woes. I must ask the congregation to vote on your request."

"How do we know this is true?" called a voice from the audience.

"How do you know Odin is real?" I asked him. "You have faith, as do I. Although I have seen him, as I hope you will soon."

"How could you have seen him?" asked another.

I decided to take a risk. "I am not what I seem." I turned to face the altar. "There are other gods on earth who survived Ragnarok. Yggdrasil had been carried down the ages and now that Loki has finally perished, it has grown to touch Asgard." I gestured to the altarpiece. As I raised my hand, it grew." There was dead silence. I withdrew my hand and turned back to face them.

"Will we join our brethren and call on our Lord Odin so that he might be freed from his prison of stone?" Malcom cried.

"Yes! Yes!"

It was unanimous.

"Time to eat," Malcom announced.

A few women got busy in the kitchen and a parade of them bore dishes to the table. I took a plate to be polite, although I wasn't hungry. The white wine was a loathsome oaky chardonnay. Everyone smiled whenever I looked their way, but they didn't come close. Malcom kept me company. Even Felicity stayed on the edge of the crowd. I soon decided it was time to leave.

"How will you get home?" Malcom asked. "Felicity mentioned you have no car."

"Someone is picking me up, just a short walk away."

"I see." He clearly didn't.

I handed him Lin's card and waved goodbye to the group with both arms. They all waved back, staring at me bug-eyed as I walked backward to the exit. As soon as the door closed behind me, I took off. So, they will do as I asked.

Lin had started pacing as soon as Agna came to the part of the story where she talked about gods and Yggdrasil.

"Agna, how could you? You've exposed us all. People talk, it'll get out."

"No, it won't. They thought I was waving goodbye. I was actually making the whole thing seem like a dream, except for the call out to Odin. Even their altarpiece is back to normal."

"Are you sure? Some of your spells haven't been too reliable in the past, you know."

"That was because my powers had weakened over the millennia. Odin made us all stronger when he spoke. You know that. You're stronger than before. I can tell."

"As long as you're sure."

"I'm sure."

"Well, now I guess it's my turn. We had a successful trip, but ran into a few complications."

I was very excited to see Iceland again after seven centuries. Apparently, it was much as I'd left it until World War II, when the Allies used it as a base. They brought modernization and the money to bring the country in line with modern-day Europe. Now it's become one of the most advanced countries on the continent, despite its small population and harsh climate.

When we landed at Keflavik airport, we walked off the plane through a covered walkway to immigration and customs. Everything was spotlessly clean and orderly. The line at immigration moved quickly, the baggage was already on the carousel when we exited, customs was an unimpeded walkthrough, and we soon emerged into a concourse, where the head of this branch of the Asatru and his wife waited for us.

"Welcome, welcome," he cried, his white collar-length hair flopping around as he nodded and smiled. "We are so much looking forward to your visit. I am Aki, and this is my wife, Dania."

Dania, a slender woman with white hair braided down to her waist, echoed his welcome, taking me by my arm as we strolled.

Aki led us through another covered walkway to the parking garage, where he'd parked his van. He and Hunter loaded our bags while Dania and I got in the back seat behind the driver.

"The van is rather large, I know," Dania said, "But we often drive to places as a group. And our hof is just outside of town, so we usually pick up friends to take them to our Sunday service."

"How many are there in your congregation?" I asked.

"Quite a few hundred now. We grow every month. And you are just in time for our official opening. It has been a long time coming. We started building in 2015, you know."

"By the gods, why so long?" I asked.

"The planning process took a long time. The first space was not approved, so we had to acquire a second one. Then Iceland had its financial difficulties. Then came Covid. And after all that, the production costs rose so much because of engineering problems. The hof is built into a hillside, you see. And we had to wait to raise money because it is against our principles to take a loan."

"That sounds daunting. But congratulations, you made it."

Her face took on a glow of certainty. "We knew we would. And now, we will help our lord Odin as much as we can. He has blessed us with sun and rain for all these years."

"Not to mention ice and snow," I said, laughing. She didn't seem amused. So, one of those earnest types.

The men had been talking outside while Dania and I chatted but now got into the car. I was eager to see how things had changed. I was in a different part of Iceland before, but I had a feeling that it was much the same all over in those days.

"How far are we from Reykjavik?" I asked.

"About 50 kilometers," Dania said.

"Wow, a long way."

It was quite tedious for the first half of the drive. Fields of snow lined the highway, although the road had been well cleared. Winter is not the best time of year to visit Iceland. It can be quite pretty once the snow melts and it starts greening up. I leaned back in my seat, disappointed. But after twenty minutes or so, the view began to get more interesting as we came to a small town. The houses were so colorful, even their roofs, which I glimpsed where the snow had slipped off. We passed walls of yellow, red, blue, green, and everything in between. Ah, I made a poem! Anyhow, there was nothing like that last time I was here. Well, there wasn't an airport, either. I tried to eavesdrop on Hunter's conversation with Aki. Hunter was speaking a sort of broken Norse to Aki's more fluid sounds, that I assumed to be close enough to Icelandic to work.

Eventually, we reached the outskirts of the city when it was almost dark—at three in the afternoon. "You will be staying at the home of one of our members," Dania said. "They have a nice big house, and their son and daughter are at university in Sweden, so they have a lot of room. Our three children are not yet out of the house."

"That's very nice of them," I said.

"They are honored."

We drove down a few side streets before pulling up outside a large home painted white with a green front door and shutters. I couldn't tell what color the roof was under its snow cap. The door soon opened, and we were introduced to our hosts, Anika and Jon. After Hunter and Aki unloaded our cases Dania and Aki left, citing the big day ahead.

Anika and Jon were older than Aki and Dania but seemed younger in their outlook. They also spoke excellent English. We sat in front of a blazing fire and drank warm gløg, which is red wine and vodka spiced with cinnamon. Delicious and very warming. Soon we were shown through to the dining room, where Anika was busy bringing dishes from the kitchen. I'd been hoping and praying that there wouldn't be mutton and skyr, and my prayers were mostly answered. There was a roast leg of lamb (which must have been frozen as it was too early for fresh), a large fish of some kind with skyr mixed with dill to one side, potatoes, and greens—I'm not entirely sure what they were. A white wine accompanied the meal, and everything was delicious. A pudding made with blueberries followed.

Anika vehemently refused offers to help clear away. We sat around and drank some aquavit before we all decided to have an early night.

Breakfast the next morning comprised a selection of hard bread, a dark loaf and wonderful butter, cheeses, and cold cuts. And coffee, of course. Hunter ate an embarrassing amount of cold cuts with his bread. Missing his steak, I suppose. At ten, we left for the hof, which was just outside the city.

When I got out of the car, I suddenly felt at home. I turned in a circle with my arms wide open.

As Dania mentioned, the temple had been built into a hill and was surrounded by forest on the sides, but had a panoramic view of the sea. Anika led me over to a group of three rocks.

"We chose this site because these rocks are considered sacred, relating to the life and powers of Odin. On the day we seek to free him from his stone prison, we will stand close to them."

I leaned over and set both hands on each rock in turn, closing my eyes and thinking my way through to their essence. I felt a low hum of energy in their core, almost like a fluttery heartbeat that vibrated through my veins. When I straightened, I knew Odin would come to this place, drawn to it like a magnet.

We moved inside a majestic edifice with an inverted glass dome that Anika said was aligned with the stars. We stopped at statues of each of the major deities. I noticed Hunter standing in front of Odin's statue, his head bent. I wondered if he was communicating with his brother. I hoped he got through. I stopped in front of Freya's, looking up into eyes that burned back into mine. She knew all about our mission. I heard wind whipping up the sea foam and hail slapping the dome. I looked over at Hunter. His hearing should be up to my level now. I pointed to Freya's statue. He nodded and strode over.

"The statue of Freya must be destroyed immediately," he said. "She bears ill will toward you and this place."

There were hundreds of people inside now that the weather had turned bad. They called out, some in alarm, some in protest. Freya had always been a popular figure, as she had once deserved.

Hunter took charge. He asked them to listen and told the whole sad story. We hadn't planned to divulge our godly heritage, but he told them he was Odin's brother, Hoenir, and described his journey and Freya's betrayal. All the while, the weather got fouler, but he knew it was imperative to persuade them. He finally got to the date and time of the worldwide call for Odin to be free. He was so unexpectedly articulate that everyone was transfixed, including me. When he stopped speaking, several husky men rushed at the statue. When they grasped it, they let go immediately, yelping in pain. I touched it and yelped myself—it was red hot.

Hunter went into action without hesitation, hoisting the statue over his head as he headed for the doorway, which a couple of people opened for him.

"Find me a hammer," he yelled over his shoulder.

I could tell from his face that he was in pain, but he had a job to do. Aki rushed up with a hammer and a mallet. I grabbed them and joined Hunter, who had thrown the statue to the ground. We pounded away until Freya's statue lay in pieces. The wind dropped, hailstones melted, and the sun shone. I took Hunter's hands and turned them palms up. The blisters were terrible. I blew on them and blew, watching as the blisters dried and subsided. When I raised my head, we were surrounded by a quiet crowd.

"We will join your call to Odin," Aki said. "Now, let us consecrate our sacred space and give thanks to our Lord Odin and his Lady Frigg.

We all filed back and sat in the carved pine chairs set out in precise rows in front of the altar, whose pine top looked as if it came from one piece of wood. That must have been a spectacular tree. To my surprise, a masterful rendering of Yggdrasil in basalt took pride of place. A musical trio settled themselves by the altar—flute, oboe, and violin. A unique mix, which worked quite well, given the surroundings.

We had much the same sort of service that everyone else described, just more of it. At the end, Aki called out, "We dedicate this sacred hof to our Lord Odin and our Lady Frigg. May they soon be free from their shackles of stone."

Cheers erupted among shouts of praise for Odin and Frigg. The din died away as people resorted to chatting excitedly among themselves as they moved to a couple of side rooms for wine and cake. I was about to join them when a little light caught my eye. A square table stood in a niche that I hadn't noticed before, lit from above by a crystal sconce. On the table stood dozens of tiny statues in silver. A tongue of fire snaked out from one of them, and the silver glowed orange. I smelled the wood burning underneath it. A sudden flash and the whole table was consumed, except for that little figure, which stood a few feet away. "Fire!" I yelled. Hunter! Bring water! It didn't take long before the fire was extinguished, as they had a supply of buckets in the kitchen in case of an emergency—this building was mostly built of stone, but plenty of wood had been used, too. Aki also assured me that there was a strong sprinkler system, but was glad it didn't activate and ruin the celebration.

"Where is that little figure?" I asked Hunter. "It obviously depicted Freya, but it was so small and hard to tell. We circled the great hall, looking into every nook and cranny, of which there was a surprising amount, given the modern and clean-cut appearance of the building. Then it struck me. The altar. She'd want to be an object of worship. It made sense—I hoped.

I prodded Hunter, nodded toward the altar, and put my finger to my lips. I motioned him to go around the back while I approached from one side. I got there first, and sure enough, there she was, half-hidden behind Yggdrasil, still glowing orange, and giving the edge of the beautifully embroidered runner a nasty brown singe to restart the conflagration. Poor Hunter, another hot potato. I pointed, and he grabbed and ran for the door. How would he dispose of this one?

Once outside, he dropped the figure and stomped it. He shouted unrepeatable curses in our old language, which I hoped was far enough from Icelandic to be intelligible to the crowd that again watched a drama ignited by Freya. He grabbed a small garden statue of a frog that sat by a flowerbed and turned it upside down.

"Good, hollow," he grunted.

Hoenir tossed in the figure into the empty frog, and stared at it, the veins in his forehead popping out like grapevines. Muttering and fuming until the silver melted and filled the space, he took a bucket from one of the men who had prudently kept it with him and poured the water over the silver to cool it so it would harden.

"Let's see how you like life in a stone frog, my lady," he said, calmer now. The crowd broke into applause. "Are there any more statues of Freya?" he asked them. They assured him there were not. "You see how wicked she has become?" They murmured assent.

We went back inside and enjoyed the celebration. I slipped away to look at the runner Freya had tried to burn. Anika joined me.

"So many of us worked on that for months," she said.

I inspected it closely. There were bears and trees, foxes and flowers, children and babies. "It's a marvelous accomplishment," I said. "The most beautiful things, and she almost destroyed it. I'm so sorry we didn't find her quickly enough to prevent that burn mark."

"That's all right. We won't change it. It is part of the story of what took place here today. It will become part of our history."

We linked arms and went back to the celebration. What a good time we had amongst those people not so far from our culture in many ways, eating and drinking, making jokes, dancing with each other and with the children. And, the strangest part, I realized we had both been speaking Icelandic all day.

We spent another week there, visiting the stones most days. It is a sacred spot, and I know Odin will visit and feel at home beside that hill.

Lin stood up, her face pink and happy with those memories. "I must go back. They are the closest thing to my people on earth."

"But your people were gods, nothing like these people," I said.

She thought for a minute. "I suppose I mean the people I used to visit on Midgard at that time to do the work my Lady Frigg asked of me. Yes, those people. The good ones, that is. We will go back. All of us, including Agna."

10

The big day arrived. We had all called the groups of Norse god worshippers we'd visited to confirm the details. We needn't have worried. They were too all excited by our validation and the prospect of releasing Odin from his stone prison to have forgotten. Rose and I moved into the wing we shared with Auntie the night before.

"Where will we stand for the ceremony?" Hunter asked at dinner the night before.

"Around Yggdrasil, surely," Auntie said.

"Yes, absolutely," Lin said.

Agna, Margareta, and Sven agreed, too. I thought it fitting.

Lin said, "Mary, you haven't said anything. What do you think?"

"I definitely think that standing around Yggdrasil is the place to be. It's just that I didn't think it was my place to comment."

"You went to plead our cause in Maryland. Of course, you are part of this."

"Do you think Dora and Stan will come, too?" I asked.

"Oh, yes," Lin answered. "I already checked. Neither of them are strangers to the old worlds, albeit different from ours.

The afternoon was blessed with sunshine, fortunately. Snow would have been a real pain. As usual, there was a chilly breeze coming off the Bay, but we could wrap ourselves up against that.

We filed out of the house and encircled Yggdrasil. Hyndla, Rose's fox, came out of the woods and sat right under the tree. Lin held a stopwatch.

"Now," she called.

We all called out the rehearsed mantra: "Odin, come to us, Odin, we believe in you, Odin, come to us, Odin, we believe in you," and so on. We called out until I couldn't anymore. I was so hoarse. Rose did her share, too. I hoped she wouldn't mention any of this to her school friends. Our voices died away. Our eyes raked the heavens. Finally, the sun seemed to expand until I thought it might burn us. The air warmed, and the clouds exploded outward. The light whitened to the point that I had to close my eyes. When I half opened them, I found the light yellower and kinder. A man and Hunter stood in an awkward embrace. Awkward, because the stranger was so much taller. Not a man, of course. Odin.

We all gathered behind them as if drawn by a magnet. Odin broke the embrace and spread his arms.

"My dear ones, I must thank you. You are true and faithful. I have already explained to my brother Hoenir that I do not ask for worship or sacrifices, or even giving up any existing religious ties you may have. I only ask that you embrace the goodness of your religion's teachings and shun the harmful. These harmful beliefs are inserted into religions by men for their own purposes and are not part of the foundation, nor part of most of the belief systems I have witnessed over the eons. I only ask that you believe in Odin's Word. The path to good. The way to peace and harmony.

"And, dear ones, please embrace our nine ancient noble virtues: courage, truth, honor, fidelity, discipline, hospitality, self-reliance, industriousness, and perseverance.

"Now, please forgive me, for I must visit all the disciples who called me back to life. I will watch over you, always. And, Mary, you will be surprised by what your future holds, your very long future."

I felt his kiss on my brow before he vanished. I realized he had not spoken aloud, but flowed into our minds. He had not approached me, yet he had kissed my brow and addressed me personally. I moved next to Rose, who had been standing next to her father. She looked happy, almost exalted. She took my hand.

"Odin told me I will become someone special. I don't know what that meant, but his voice made it sound like something nice. And he kissed me here." She pointed to her right cheek.

"It was a wonderful thing to experience," I said. "But it is our family secret. Remember that."

"I know, Mama. All our best things are secrets."

We all went back inside. I wondered how long it would take Odin to visit all those places that had called him. I supposed it worked much the same way it did with Santa Claus. A compressing of time and distance. Not that Santa is real, but ... oh, never mind.

We all sat around nursing cups of hot cocoa.

"Rose heard different things from what I heard," I said. "It seems that Odin spoke to us all individually. He told me that I would be surprised by what my future holds and that it would be a very long future and Rose that she would become someone special.”

“He told me I am truly his kin,” said Sven.

“He told me the same thing,” said Margareta.

“He told Hunter and me that our immortality will be strong once more. I hope that means no more rebirths,” said Lin.

“He said I would be free of the bonds of Zeus and become one with his kin,” said Dora. “I will welcome that, but cannot think of leaving my family. This family, that is.”

“He said he would free me from old age and pain,” said Auntie. “And I do feel better.

Funnily enough, her wrinkled brow looked smoother, and her eyes shone brighter.

We turned to Stan, who looked more relaxed than I’d ever seen him. “I will become one with his kin. My mind is clearer now than it has ever been, no longer filled with the cries of the dying and wounded. I feel whole again.”

Eir frowned and said, “He told me to be ready. There would probably be a great need for my skills. That is a little troubling.” She went outside to the terrace and sat on the stone wall after brushing off a dusting of snow.

Agna also looked troubled. “I am tasked with assisting Odin in the battle against Freya. She is a dangerous opponent, as you know. Her madness could destroy Asgard and even Midgard if she prevails. She will try to destroy me and ensure that Frigg will never be released from the stone so that she can take Odin as her husband. It is certain that she would then try to destroy Odin and his close kin to consolidate her power. And she can reach me with her mind and witchcraft, as you know. I might not be as distant from her as I thought. I must lock myself away and prepare. There is a battle ahead, a fight to the death.”

Well, that threw a wet blanket over the party. Agna rose to go to her room. At the door, she said, "Lin and Hunter, may I stay here until the battle is won or lost?"

"Of course," they chorused.

Agna did not come down for any meals the next day, or the day after that. Since the next day was Sunday, Rose spent most of her time playing outside with Hyndla. When I realized I couldn't see her out of the living room windows, I looked in the kitchen, where she often went to wheedle cookies out of Dora. Dora wasn't there, but Rose was fast asleep in the big saggy armchair, with Hyndla spread across her small lap, also asleep. The fox opened one eye and looked at me for a couple of seconds before deciding I wasn't going to be a problem and shut it again. I tiptoed out.

Lin spent most of the day taking phone calls from the groups we'd visited. We had given out her phone number to consolidate the findings. Every group had been visited by Odin. All reported a happy and uplifting experience. All had renewed hope and belief. I heard Lin ask them to keep Odin's visit to themselves, although it would be wonderful if they could spread his message: Odin's Word.

Well, it didn't take long. On Monday morning, there was a visitor at the gate. Special Agent Bates of the FBI. A curious phenomenon had been reported in the sky on Saturday afternoon, and it seemed to have come from the Thoren's property. What did we know about it? Lin invited him in.

"Yes, we did notice it," she said, leading him into the living room. "A very bright light, so bright it seemed to be shining down from the sun itself. And the clouds were acting strangely, as if there was a strong wind very high up. We wondered about it, but it didn't last long. What have you heard?"

"That's what I hoped to find out from you. A couple of neighbors are sure it was over your property."

"Well, our neighbors are not very close by, and it's easy to misjudge distance, especially close to the water. It was over our property in the sense that we could see it above us, but it seemed very spread out. And don't forget, there's a military base across the bay."

"No, ma'am, I had not forgotten. Hence our concern."

"Well, you are welcome to look around. We have a man working here by the name of Stan who takes care of our grounds and cars and does odd jobs. He will show you the garage and shed."

"Thank you, Ma'am. I think I will do that."

Lin called Stan, asking him to come and take the captain around. "He will be here in a few minutes."

"Where is your husband, Ma'am?"

"He had an appointment in Washington this morning."

"Did he notice this occurrence?"

"Oh, yes, he was quite worried at first. But, as I say, nothing else strange happened and things soon got back to normal."

Stan and the captain left by the front door. We watched them crossing the grounds, back and forth.

"Hunter will go mad if he knows we've come to the attention of the FBI. At least he pays his taxes on time."

"Do we have to tell him?" I asked.

"We'd better. Suppose they come back and realize we've kept it a secret? It will arouse suspicion."

"You're right. But he's going to start obsessing about it."

"I know. And I'm not moving out of this house. This is our final place on Midgard. No more flitting around from pillar to post."

"What will you do about your appearance if you stay in one place?"

Lin frowned. "I hadn't thought about it. It's early days, yet, and we don't mix much with the outside world. There are delivery services, don't forget. We'll probably just have to shut ourselves away for a generation and then pose as descendants of the original inhabitants. It'll be a real nuisance when we need services like cleaning or repairs. The house will be quite old by then."

"You can have Dora and Stan pose as caretakers. They can have those things done."

"Yes, but people will remember them, too."

"It's all so complicated. I think you'll just have to repair things as you can and have a big renovation done when you emerge again. Your lawyers can deal with you inheriting the property and make the title transfer. You'll need death and birth certificates. And new credit cards. And what will you tell the lawyers?"

Lin sighed. "I suppose you're right. If you spread enough money around, most problems can be solved. Anyway, you and Rose will have the same problem."

"Whatever do you mean?"

"What do you think Odin meant by the surprise in your long future? You, Auntie, Rose, Margareta, Sven, Dora, and Stan, are either immortal now or soon will be. Dora always was immortal, but she's one of us now."

I flopped down into the nearest chair. *Immortal?* It was hard to get my head around. On the one hand, I was glad not to go through sickness and dying. It was exciting to think of all the new things to do and see in the future. I wouldn't lose the Thorens, and especially Hunter. Rose was secure. But thousands and thousands of years? Would I become tired of it all? And maybe Earth's future would not be a happy one.

"Just go with it, Mary. Take it one century at a time." I guess Lin meant that to be reassuring. But it was all too much to take in.

I heard footsteps clattering down the stairs. Must be the kids. No, Stan had driven them to the airport yesterday. I rose. A middle-aged, robust woman in navy pants and a white blouse walked into the room. Auntie? I sat back down.

"You look well," I croaked.

"I am a new woman," she said, her voice vibrant. "Literally."

Lin laughed. "I'm so happy for you. You deserve it."

"Wait until Rose gets home. You started to change right away, and I could see a difference yesterday, but this is so sudden."

"I took a long nap this afternoon, and this is how I woke up. Who knows what tomorrow will bring? I have to go shopping."

Something alarming occurred to me. "How far back will this take us?" I asked Lin.

"I have no idea. There is no precedent."

"There is, actually. What happened when Odin made Loki his blood brother?"

"He stayed the same. But he was different, one of a breed that was very long-lived already."

"My god, they could take us back to babyhood."

"I doubt it," said Lin. "You've only changed a little.

"Have I? But Auntie did, too, at first."

"Odin would not do anything harmful. Stop fretting and wait and see. I suspect you will be happy with the results. How old are you now? Thirty? I predict that you will just end up looking like a twenty-year-old."

I wished I shared her optimism. Auntie looked downcast. I pulled myself together, so as not to spoil her newfound delight in freedom from the discomforts of old age.

"You're right, Lin. Odin would not cause us any distress. I will simply be grateful for this gift."

And I was, sort of.

11

gna decided to return to London. It was March, and she'd been away since the new year. Lin, as I expected, was a little down about saying goodbye to her best friend. We sat together in the living room after lunch one rainy Saturday afternoon. Everyone else had gone off to their own pursuits. I wanted to get home, but Rose had taken herself off to Hunter's study to read and cuddle Hyndla while he did some paperwork. They treasured their time together, and I didn't want to spoil their afternoon.

"I'm so used to having Agna around," Lin told me, sounding depressed. I felt the usual twinge of jealousy. "It's not that I don't value our bond, Mary, but Agna knew Asgard. She knew our gods and our ways. She knows."

"I understand completely," I said. I'd let down my guard, and she'd sensed my feelings. And I did understand. But Lin was closer to me than my own sister, with whom I'd lost touch. I felt guilty about it because I hadn't made much effort to keep the channels open beyond sending birthday and Christmas cards. Last Christmas, I'd sent nice gifts and had received only a perfunctory thank you note in return. She'd written nothing on her card beyond the names of her family. I should visit. I must visit. I slumped a little and clenched my fists into my lap.

"Yes, visit your sister, Mary. Family is everything."

"You are my family now."

"Think about what I just said. She knows your upbringing, remembers your parents, your school, your lives."

"I know. But she's always so weighed down with babies and housework, she seems to have lost interest in the world around her. After I went away to university and she got married, our paths led in different directions. Whenever I came home, I found we had absolutely nothing to talk about."

"How long is it since you've seen her?"

I looked at my rigid hands. "About six years."

"Has she had more babies?"

"I don't think so."

"So there are no more diapers, and they are probably in school now. Maybe she's come up for air. Give her a chance."

Her words stung. Give her a chance. I hadn't been in her shoes when I had Rose. I'd had my new family and no money worries. Lin leaned over and put her arm around my shoulders.

"I think I'll go to London with Agna. Why don't you go visit your sister while I'm gone?"

I sat up and said, "I will. I'll call her and book myself into the local motel."

"That's the spirit," she said. "I'd better book my plane ticket and tell Hunter I'm going with Agna. I'm glad he's got you to keep him company so he won't mind my absence."

That was the sort of remark I never knew how to respond to, other than with a weak smile. She went to find Hunter, and I picked up my phone.

"Lizzie? It's Mary."

"Oh, hi," she answered with a notable lack of enthusiasm.

"I've been thinking it's been too long since we've seen each other, and you've never met Rose. I'd like to come and see you next week. I'll book myself into the Renaissance Inn near our old house. Would it be convenient?"

"Sure. The kids are still in school. We could go to the mall or something."

"Yes, that would be fun. And I could take you to lunch. Is that restaurant we used to love for special occasions still there?"

"Yeah. It's a bit expensive, though."

"My treat."

"Well, you seem to have done very well for yourself."

I ignored the resentful tone. "Not so bad. I'll tell you all about it when we meet." Well, not *all* about it.

"Okay. Let me know when you're coming."

"I'm looking forward to it."

"Yeah. Bye."

It was a start. The resentment started after I went away to college. Lizzie had wanted nothing more than to get married right after graduating high school. It had been a sweet wedding between those two hopeful young kids. By the time Christmas rolled around, I could see the disillusionment setting in. Her husband Keith was a nice young man, but not yet skilled enough to earn much, and the same went for her. So there was a dingy little apartment, plenty of cooking from scratch, and not much going out. Keith came home exhausted from his job in construction, and she was numbed by boredom in her assembly line job in a factory. And there was I with tales of high jinks and parties, and my parents' pride in my good grades. Then came the babies and their unceasing demands, both physical and financial. Six months after the second child arrived, Lizzie worked in the factory three days a week, while Mom took care of them. But then Mom got sick and couldn't do it anymore. After graduation, I did my best to help, but had to help Mom, too. Keith got a promotion to foreman a few months before Mom died, so they were able to manage without me. I couldn't wait to leave that gloomy town where I drowned in sickness and crying babies and rank diapers. Auntie Peggy's house in Salton was a haven, as was her motherly comfort.

I'd have to square Rose's absence for a week with the school. She was an excellent student, so it shouldn't be a problem. The real issue was instilling in Rose the things she must absolutely not talk about. She knew, of course, how discreet she must be, but there would probably be some form of interrogation, especially about her father. And she was smart enough to raise Lizzie's hackles by being too forthright.

Maybe I wouldn't take her. She had Auntie, Dora, and Hunter to look after her. I'd just take pictures. School would be the perfect excuse.

After lunch on Monday, Hunter drove Lin and Agna to Dulles Airport. I set off for Pennsylvania shortly after. The drive started out pleasantly enough, but the third hour took me through some pretty depressing townships. Lizzie's looked a little better than it used to, with some newer houses and more interesting shops. I'd decided to look for a place to stay in her town, Painton, which would be more convenient. It's not as though I had any particular fond memories of our old stomping grounds.

I checked into a Holiday Inn that was basic, but clean and offered a comfortable bed, before driving to Lizzie's house. She'd moved out of the apartment into a small house just like all the others on her street. The front yard was ablaze with color. I'd forgotten what a green thumb Mom had.

Lizzie must have inherited it. I'd just cupped a magnificent purple azalea blossom in my palm when the door opened.

"Hello, Mary."

"Lizzie! I was just thinking you must have inherited Mom's green thumb." She looked pleased. "This is a stunning display." She even smiled.

"Come in, Mary. I put the coffee on. I baked a lemon pound cake, too.

Lizzie took me down a narrow hall, its walls scarred by things being dragged along it, to a living room with a dining ell.

"Sit down, Mary. I'll just go to bring the coffee and cake."

I looked around. The walls had fared better in here and were a pretty shade of cream. The green sofa and chairs looked comfortable. There were a few prints on the wall, making for a cozy atmosphere. An interesting coffee table was placed in front of the sofa. I went over to look at it. It had a polished top that looked like a cut from a massive branch, given the tree rings. The legs curved outward before they bowed in and had carvings of leaves and acorns on the arches.

"Keith made that."

"What talent! It's marvelous. He could earn a fortune selling things like this."

"He has sold one or two. Most people around here couldn't afford them."

"He should take pictures and sell them through the internet."

"We're not really up on all of that."

"I could help."

"We'll see."

"I'll buy one."

"You can ask him." She handed me a mug of coffee and a small plate with a slice of cake.

"Thank you." I took a bite. "This is delicious. I love lemon."

"I remember." She seemed stiff and ill at ease again.

"The kids will be home from school soon. Keith won't be late, either. He leaves for work very early, you see."

"I'm looking forward to seeing the kids. They will have changed so much. I'm sorry I didn't bring Rose. I realized that I shouldn't take her out of school."

"That's all right. It can be hard when they fall behind. Ours have grown a lot. Jay, ten now, is doing well at school. He's very good at math, in particular. And Jessie is good at reading. She's eight. I'm sorry not to meet Rose. What's she best at in school?"

"She's pretty much an all-rounder. I'm not surprised she's good at reading and spelling, but math? She certainly didn't get that from me."

"Maybe her father?" She looked me in the eye. "Are you married?"

"No, I am not. I had a lover for a while, but it didn't work out. We broke up before I realized I was pregnant. I didn't tell him, because I didn't want him in my life. The family I was living with made me very welcome and paid me well for writing their memoirs. They moved into a larger place and let me use their old house, which is on the Chesapeake Bay. Auntie Peggy lives with me now. Rose even calls my employer's husband Papa. They are very good to her, as are their own children."

"Whatever do you do for money?"

"I'm still writing for them, as well as for myself. We only live a ten-minute drive away from each other."

"Well, well. You certainly have nice clothes."

I hoped the interrogation was over, and mercifully the ruckus of children barging through the back door made sure of it.

They put on the brakes when they saw me.

"Children, this is your Aunt Mary. Mary, this is Jay, who is ten, and this is Jessie, who is eight. Say hello."

"Hello, Aunty Mary," Jay said. Jessie just stared. They could have been twins if it weren't for the size difference. Jay towered over Jessie, but I got the feeling Jessie ruled the roost, the way he glanced her way every few seconds.

After the introductions, they sat around politely while I made the usual annoying adult inquiries about school and so on. Jessie answered for both of them. They obviously had places they would rather be. Lizzie let them off the hook after twenty minutes or so, and they raced upstairs to change before going out again to be with their friends.

"Lovely children, and so polite," I said.

"Thank you."

"You must both be very proud of them."

"We are."

They were attractive children but didn't strike me as articulate or even curious. I thought they might be a little interested in meeting this long-lost aunt, but they were not at all. Who knows what their mother had told them?

Anyway, that conversation had clearly run its course.

"Did you ever meet the people who bought Mom and Dad's house?" she asked.

"Only at closing. I didn't like them much. They were not very clean, for a start. I doubt their house looks anywhere as nice as yours does. And they hardly said a word."

She preened a little. "I like a clean house. I asked because I've heard things."

"What kind of things?"

"People going in and out at all times of the day and night. Did I tell you that Keith joined the police department a few years ago?"

"No, you didn't. Good going!"

"Well, he told me they're keeping an eye on the place."

"That's a little sad, don't you think? Mom worked hard to keep the house clean and tidy, even after she got sick. I bet it's a real dump now."

"I drive past there sometimes. The front garden is ruined, full of junk. All Mom's roses have died."

"No! They were her pride and joy."

I felt tears well up and blinked them down as best I could. Lizzie regarded me coolly.

"I'm surprised you feel that way. You sure got out of town fast enough after the house sold. Not a backward glance."

That was so unfair. I clutched my cup and stared at my lap. "What else could I do? I went to stay with Auntie Peggy to get my bearings. It was a very stressful time, nursing Mom at the end, then having to clear out the house. I needed a break, and Auntie took care of me. It's not as though I had a job. While I was there, I read this ad in the local paper. It's amazing how it all turned out. They are very good to Auntie and me."

"Well, I'm glad it turned out. Things have looked up for us, too."

"I can see. Your house and gardens are quite lovely. Anyway, what about tomorrow? Lunch and shopping? A movie? What do you think?"

"That sounds great. I don't shop much, except for groceries. We still have to be careful."

"That's fine. I don't really need anything, but we can look around to see if anything catches our fancy. Or would you rather go to a matinee?" It occurred to me that she wouldn't want to feel embarrassed by me buying her things, which I would have loved to do.

"We don't get to the movies much, so I'd enjoy that."

"Okay, lunch and a movie it is. Well, I'd better go and unpack. I have a few things to type up. What time shall I come by tomorrow? Do we need to make reservations at the Blue Jay?"

"Are you sure you want to go to that expense?"

"Of course I am. It's a celebration."

"Of what?"

That was a bit of a downer. "Of us getting together all this time, of course."

"Oh, yes. I will come and pick you up. I'll make reservations for noon, so I'll pick you up at eleven-thirty."

"Sounds like a plan."

We both stood awkwardly outside the front door. I am a little taller than Lizzie, so I bent down and kissed her rigid cheek.

"See you tomorrow."

She nodded. As I walked down the path, I noticed Jessie peering at me from behind the hedge. I waved, and he disappeared.

I didn't have anything to type up, but wanted to let Lizzie take it all in and, hopefully, mellow out. She could have invited me for dinner. On the other hand, she would have wondered if I would want that or not. Best let things go slowly.

The next morning, I waited outside the front entrance for my sister. A light rain fell, and I was glad of my warm coat, wool pants, and cashmere sweater. She pulled up in a sedan that had seen better days.

"Not as fancy as your car, I'm afraid," was the first thing she said as I climbed in.

"It's just fine."

"I made the reservations. "

"You look nice." She'd put up her hair and applied some make-up. She was still a pretty woman.

"Not as nice as you."

"You know, Lizzie, all these comparisons are not healthy. I've worked for what I have, but a lot of it has been dumb luck. You and Keith have worked very hard for a long time what you have. There is great virtue in that. So, let's drop it."

"Sorry. You're right. It's just so hard to get ahead. You get a bit put by in savings, and then the washing machine conks out, or one of the cars breaks down. It's a constant struggle, day after day."

"Are you and Keith happy together?"

"Yes, we are, actually. We went through a rough patch when the kids were very young. It was so hard. They took so much out of me. And Keith didn't lift a finger when he got home. Said he'd worked hard all day and needed to rest. What did he think I did all day?" It obviously still rankled as she hurled the car around a corner.

"They haven't a clue, have they?" I felt I should show some empathy.

"No. Then, I had terrible pains one night. Such terrible pain. I stuck it until morning and told Keith he'd have to take the kids to daycare and take me to the doctor. It was appendicitis, so I had the operation that same day. Keith had to take time off from work—for which he got no pay—and take care of the kids. Then he knew what I did all day."

"Poor you. Did it take long to recover?"

"I wasn't back to normal for a couple of weeks. We went through a really tough time financially, what with both of us losing so much pay. That's when a friend of Keith's suggested he apply to the police department. And he got in. It's saved us. Regular pay, health insurance, even a pension."

"Great move. Does he like it?"

"It can get boring sometimes in a small town like this, although there has been an uptick in drug trafficking recently. But he enjoys the company of the men he works with. They're a pretty good lot."

We drew up outside the restaurant.

"I'm not used to these fancy places," Lizzie said, hunching in her seat. "I don't want to make a fool of myself."

My heart melted for her. "I felt the same way the first time the Thorens took me to a fancy place. But it was fine. I just watched what they did. It's just lunch. Nothing strange."

I led the way in and gave the maître d' Lizzie's name. We were seated at a table next to the window.

"Not many folks out and about today," I said. "Pity, I love people-watching."

"Me too," she replied.

I placed my napkin in my lap, and she did the same.

We discussed the menu. I really fancied the escargot but thought I should give it a miss. We both decided on wild mushroom soup followed by trout almandine. It sounded like a non-controversial choice, although given the restaurant's reputation, the quality of both choices should be outstanding. And they were. We didn't chat all that much, as Lizzie was clearly rapturous, first as she tasted the creamy soup, then the buttery trout. She loved the glass of chilled Sancerre I ordered for each of us, too. I'd become accustomed to drinking white wine with my meals, thanks to Lin.

We sat back as the plates were cleared. "Room for dessert?" I asked her.

"Just about."

I ordered a Grand Marnier soufflé. Lizzie laughed in wonder as it was flambéed at the table. It was delicious, and we finished every bit.

"You see," I said as we rolled out to the car. "There was nothing to worry about. You were just fine."

"Thanks so much. I've never had such a marvelous meal. I don't think I'll eat again for the rest of the week."

"Me, too. I feel ready to pop!"

We giggled, and it felt good.

The movie was a romantic comedy I barely remember. Lizzie enjoyed it though, which made me happy. She drove me back to the hotel.

"Do you really have to go back tomorrow?" she asked.

"I really must. My employer is taking Rose to school and picking her up while I'm gone, and I don't feel I should impose. Tell you what, why don't you bring the kids over for a few days in the summer? My house is right on the beach. Do they like the seaside?"

"Oh, yes, they love it."

"Well, let's do it, then. And let's call each other from time to time. We mustn't grow apart again. We're sisters!"

She flung her arms around my neck and we rocked back and forth for a few minutes. She looked happy. I don't suppose she looked happy very often.

I drove home after the rush hour and arrived with time to spare before Rose got back from school. When I'd called the previous evening, Hunter said he wanted to pick her up from school, so I went straight to the castle. Lin was out, and Auntie was drinking coffee with Dora in the kitchen.

I heard the car and went out front to greet them. Rose ran into my arms.

"Hello, Mama! I missed you. Papa and I have a project to finish in the study."

Hunter pecked me on the cheek, laughing as Rose dragged him down the corridor. Had she missed me at all, at least a little?

The early April sunshine was warm enough for Lin, Auntie, and me to enjoy afternoon tea on the terrace. I'd thought of sitting on the smaller terrace facing the beach, but that wicked breeze still blew off the Bay. The house sheltered us from it on the main terrace. Rose sat reading on the swing seat with Hyndla asleep across her lap. It was so peaceful, with nothing otherworldly intruding into our lives. I'd noticed increased strength and speed in both Rose and me, but nothing that would make people look at us funny. We were all waiting for Dora to give birth, as she was at least a couple of weeks overdue. Rose was especially impatient.

I'd just popped the last of a little jam tart into my mouth when I saw Dora sprinting across the lawn toward the woods with Stan in hot pursuit. Her protuberant belly led the way, so that she leaned back as she went, but still made good time. I stood up, as did Lin. "How can she run like that when she's pregnant? What the heck is going on?"

"I think we'd better go and find out," Lin said, almost across the lawn before I'd noticed her rising from her chair.

I glanced over at Rose, who looked up from her book, shrugged, and went back to the adventures of Mr. Toad. Auntie shoved her knitting back into her bag.

Lin, of course, caught up with Dora before the rest of us. By the time I got there, Stan and Lin were holding onto her, each gripping one arm. I leaned over to catch my breath. I'd moved so fast that I'd become disoriented.

"What's going on?" I asked.

"She's in labor. She's insisting she has to give birth up a tree." Lin's frown and huffy tone suggested a high level of irritation.

"Dora, the baby could drop to the ground and be killed," I said.

"I tried to tell her," Stan said, shaking his head wildly. "She won't listen."

"Now then, Dora, I've called Dr. Ayre. She'll be here very soon and will take care of everything. Just wait." I hadn't noticed Auntie arriving. She must have been running fast, too. I had a sudden thought.

"Dora, didn't Dr. Ayre give you an ointment to rub over yourself when you go into labor?"

"Yes," she panted. "When the contractions are every five minutes. Ooh, ouch." When she bent double, Stan and Lin loosened their grip. She darted out of their reach and leaped onto the first big branch. The tree shook slightly as if trying to shake her off. Lin tried to join her, but Dora jumped out of her reach to the next branch, and then the next. She moved like a mountain goat.

Lin followed, trying to grab her, lost her balance, and slid down the trunk. "Shit!"

"Leave her," Auntie said.

"How can we leave her? She's crazy, she's putting our baby in danger." Stan had tears in his eyes.

"Dora," I called. "We won't come up after you. Find a comfortable place and use the cream. That last contraction was five minutes after the last one, right?"

She peered down at me, her face framed by oak leaves. "If you promise."

"Promise. Lin, you promise?"

Lin promised.

"Why does she think she has to give birth up a tree?" Auntie asked.

"She's a wood nymph, remember?" Lin said, impatiently.

"But wood nymphs don't have babies, do they?" I asked.

"No, of course not. They just are. But I guess she is feeling some old pull to be with her kindred spirits at this time," Lin said. "We should be her kindred spirits by now."

"Odin told her she was one of us. She's forgotten."

A jar dropped from the tree, knocking a squirrel to the ground. It ran for its life.

"I've done it," Dora called down.

"I hope this is going to work," I said.

"It could go the other way. She might get more attached to the tree." Lin looked worried. "I guess I can always go and carry her down if she's not too difficult about it."

Dr. Ayre joined us while we waited. We explained the situation. We all stood around the bottom of the tree, staring up into it. Dora began to sing. It was a lilting, gentle song, in a language I didn't recognize. I didn't speak the old Norse, but I knew what it sounded like, and this wasn't it.

Lin listened intently. "She's dedicating the new life to the tree. I can't make out all the words. It's been eons since

I spoke ancient Greek. She said something about embracing the tree's life, the baby belonging to it, serving it."

The tree began to sway and shake. Stan moaned. "It's going to shake her out. We've got to get her down."

I didn't like the way this sounded. I whispered to Lin, "Do you think the tree wants the baby as a sacrifice?"

"By the gods, I didn't think of that. I'm going up."

Lin climbed the tree like a monkey. The song grew louder and less musical. Dora started singing in English.

"The trees are my family, the trees will save us, long live the trees." Then back to Greek.

We were soon greeted by a very strange sight. Lin held Dora under her left arm, a big pregnant belly poked out below her arm and swollen breasts hung over it. Dora's arms and legs were being scratched up, but it was the only way to get her down. With a belly like that, Lin could hardly have used a fireman's lift. Dora's dress had ridden up enough to show us that she had removed her underwear in preparation. Her water had clearly just broken as the fluid cascaded down her legs. Her arms were flung out to each side as, eyes closed, she sang like a drunk. Lin lowered her into Stan's arms.

"Good gracious," Auntie murmured.

"No time for the hospital. Back to the house. Right away." Dr. Ayre took off across the lawn.

"Stan, take her to one of the guest bedrooms in the main part of the house. It'll be easier to take care of her."

"No, we have everything we need in our home," he said, striding toward the garage, which led to their apartment above.

Dr. Ayre called back over her shoulder, "Mary, you can stay to help. Lin, kindly fetch my bag from the terrace and bring it up. Everyone else can go about their business."

"I guess I'm not needed," Lin muttered mutinously as she handed over Dr. Ayre's bag.

"No. I don't like a crowded labor room."

Lin snorted and flounced away.

I didn't feel like attending someone else's birth, but Dr. Ayre's tone was stentorian. I followed her meekly up the stairs.

"Do you have a tarp or a rubber sheet?" Dr. Ayre asked Stan.

"I have some disposable plastic tarps in the garage."

"Get one for the bed. Put her on the sofa for now."

As soon as he returned, we stripped the bed, lay down the tarp, and covered it with a sheet. Stan picked up Dora and carried her to the bed.

"Should I boil water or something?" I asked.

"No need. My instruments are already sterilized. Stan, give Mary a towel and put a baby blanket on the chest. You have a baby blanket, I assume?"

"Yes, ma'am."

"And bring me some towels to clean up with afterward."

The contractions went on for some time. The waters must have broken when Lin grabbed her. Stan's pacing, alternated with kneeling by Dora's side and holding her hand, began to get on Dr. Ayre's nerves, and she ordered him out.

Dora was only half singing by this time, sometimes chanting, and sometimes babbling something in her own language, but she didn't seem to be in any pain.

"Ah, it's crowned."

Against my better judgment, I took a look. The head pushed out a little more. I couldn't take my eyes off it. Suddenly, the baby slid out.

"It's a girl," Dr. Ayre proclaimed. "Here, Mary, hold her in this towel. Rub her to clean her and warm her while I cut the cord."

I stopped looking at this point. Placentas look like an outsize lump of liver at the butcher's. The baby opened her mouth wide and let loose. I didn't expect such a loud noise from such a tiny creature. Rose was pretty feisty, but this one bellowed to beat all. I had tears in my eyes as I rubbed her and rocked her.

Stan poked his head around the door.

"Come in," Dr. Ayre called. "You have a daughter."

He tiptoed in—as though he might wake the baby—and gazed down at his daughter's puckered red face. I handed her over, although I didn't want to let that warm bundle go. She stopped wailing and gazed up at her father. He started to sing to her in another language I didn't know.

"Do you have a name?" I asked him.

"Penelope is Dora's choice. A queen who symbolizes strength and survival. We'll call her Penny."

"Lovely name," I said.

"Dora is coming back to herself," Dr. Ayre said. "Another fifteen minutes, and she can hold her baby. I will remain here for a half-hour, and stay up at the house for another two so that I may check up on her again. In one week, I want to see her in my office, and the baby should see a pediatrician at around that time."

"Why, is something wrong?" Stan asked, his voice shaky.

"No, of course not, or I would have called an ambulance. The baby must be seen regularly by a doctor and get her immunizations. And don't forget to register her birth. I will fill in the necessary form. Mary, help me clean her up."

I didn't much care for that part—washing and drying, putting on a pad and panties, then changing the sheet. I bundled up the tarp and threw it in the trashcan before throwing the soiled sheet and towels in the dryer. I suppose nurses get used to it, but I felt newfound respect for the things they have to do—and this wouldn't be the worst of it.

Dora called from her bed, "Stan, what happened? Did I have the baby?"

We went to her and watched as Stan handed her the little one. "Penelope, meet your lovely mother."

I couldn't stop the tears this time. "She's beautiful," I told Dora.

"You did very well, Dora. The baby is fine. Congratulations."

"Thank you, Dr. Ayre." Dora didn't take her eyes off the baby.

Dr. Ayre and I walked through the connecting door to the castle kitchen.

"Tea?" I asked.

"Something stronger. Let's go into the living room."

"Good idea." I felt as though I'd run a marathon.

We found the others in there and told them the good news.

"I'll take them dinner tomorrow," said Auntie.

"I have a sister!" Rose jumped up and down, her face the picture of excitement.

"You could say that," said Hunter. *And where were you while all this was going on?* "I had an online meeting with someone and didn't come out until you were on your way to the apartment. Lin told me what was happening when she got back."

I looked at him, startled. He winked and smirked.

You read my mind!

It's not that hard.

"Penelope. That's going to be hard for a baby to say," Rose said.

"They're going to call her Penny," I said.

"Penny is easy. I like that."

So, your godly powers have certainly gotten stronger.
You bet.
I like my privacy.
Okay, I will turn it off. And never forget, you have godly powers, too.
I'll draw a curtain over my thoughts.
There you go.
Before I do that, I would like a gin and tonic.

I imagined drawing that curtain and felt the space in my mind clear. Lin looked from Hunter to me, a barely concealed giggle escaping her lips. I'd have to watch out for them all. Hunter handed me my drink.

"Come on, young lady, let's get some cookies and milk," Auntie said, taking Rose by the hand.

After they'd left the room, Lin said, "Let me tell you a story about another birth."

I got my phone out of my pocket and fiddled with it as if checking for messages, but setting it to record. Hunter still had no idea about the memoirs I was writing for Lin.

Tape 4, Volume 4

I was visiting a handsome young naval officer in Portsmouth. It must have been around 1916. He had a couple of days' leave before having to report back to his ship, docked there for minor repairs. We'd met at a friend's party in London and hit it off at once. He was practically drooling. Hunter was still a kid, so there was nothing happening there. I was up for a romp.

Ronald had to leave early the next morning, as he had a few things to do in Portsmouth the day before his leave ended. I arranged to get a later train down there and meet for a fond farewell. It wasn't guaranteed that either of us would arrive when we hoped to. The trains weren't reliable, and if a lot of troops were to be ferried down to the coast, you hadn't a hope of getting a seat.

Anyway, our trains left more or less on time, and I met up with him at around tea time. We flirted over a stained tablecloth in a rundown tea shop on the front that offered bread with a smear of butter and weak tea. A dry-as-dust sponge cake topped off the meal. We hardly noticed the poor offering. The next trick was to get me into his lodgings without his landlady finding out.

The house was a semidetached a couple of streets back from the sea, with the staircase facing the small hallway. A little glassed-in porch protected the front door from drafts. The postage stamp-sized front garden was rigidly neat with its rows of cabbages and little field of potatoes. No one gave space to flowers by then. The plan was simple. Ronald would enter while I stayed to the side, out of sight. If the landlady wasn't in the hall, he would leave the door slightly open for me and go through to the living room and kitchen looking for her. He'd let her know he was home and that he was going to take a nap. While she was thus occupied, I'd run up the stairs and into his room, second door on the right.

It went as planned as far as leaving the door open. It seems he didn't find her in the living room or the kitchen. He looked out of the kitchen window. She wasn't in the garden, either. Her handbag sat on the kitchen table. Horrified, he ran upstairs, expecting the worst. His room wasn't the second door on the right, it was the second door on the left. The second door on the right was the bathroom and fully occupied. Now, a bathroom in old houses in Britain had a handbasin, a tub, and an airing cupboard. The toilet was always in a separate room, which makes sense when there is only one bathroom in a houseful of people. The woman was in the bathtub, with her eyes focused on an open book on some sort of rack in front of her and a glass of what looked like gin and something on the ledge. Fortunately, the mirror was steamed up, so she couldn't see my reflection, and I had opened the door stealthily since this was a secret mission. I closed the door as quickly and quietly as I could.

"Is anyone there?" The querulous voice was accompanied by a good deal of splashing, so I gathered she was getting out of the tub to check. I darted into the lavatory, hoping that was Ronald's room.

"It's me, Mrs. Buckley," he called out. "Just going to take a nap."

"Oh, good. Captain Rivers, you gave me quite a fright!"

"Sorry, Mrs. B."

More splashing as she lumbered back into the tub. I opened the door and followed Ronald into his room. The poor chap was pale and panting. I locked the door.

At about seven, I heard Mrs. Buckley stomping upstairs.

"You all right, Captain? Don't you want any tea?"

"I'm fine, thank you. I had tea out. I'm really tired, so want to get in a good night's sleep before reporting for duty. Good night!"

"Good night, Captain."

Well, anchors aweigh. Not much sleep, but it didn't really matter, as it turned out. At around two in the morning, I heard the sound of one of those awful German airships that dropped incendiary bombs on England during World War I. They sounded like a hissing freight train. Of course, ports were a primary target. It got closer and closer and I heard a sort of clang, which told me that a bomb might have been launched. I grabbed my clothes and bag, opened the window, and jumped out, frightening a big old tomcat into streaking up the street. I followed and soon overtook the creature. In fact, I ended up about two miles away in a minute. I'd run so fast that no one could see me, but had to find a few trees to hide behind while I got back into my clothes. Humans are funny about that sort of thing.

The explosion was deafening, even at that distance. I went back, more slowly than I left. Half of Ronald's street was reduced to rubble, as were streets in front and behind. It was a sad sight. Mrs. Buckley's bathtub perched on top of a pile of bricks. The bed I'd been enjoying only a few moments before lay in a mangled heap in the street.

An arm protruded from somewhere underneath, one that wore Ronald's watch, one his father had given him for his twenty-first birthday, and which he'd shown me with great pride in the tea shop. He'd aspired to great things in the Navy. Perhaps this was better than a fate he might have met at sea. I turned away and walked back to the station.

I wasn't the only one escaping the ruins, so I realized there had been more than one raid. I don't know where they were all going. They all looked a bit ragged, so if they'd lost their home, where could they find shelter? It wasn't until later that I realized that the station was the shelter. There were places to hunker down dotted around town, but this would have been the closest for many.

Anyway, I heard cries of distress coming from a corner of the waiting room, and men sidling away from the area with looks of extreme discomfort. So were most of the women.

"No better that she ought to be." I heard one woman say with a derogatory sniff.

A very pregnant woman, who looked to be about twenty, sat with her back wedged in a corner, holding her belly and crying, sometimes bellowing like an animal. Right, she was about to give birth. I'd heard this could be a protracted and messy business. I think I told you once, Mary, that I just pop them out without fuss or muss.

"Does anyone have a blanket?" I asked. No answer. They all turned their backs.

"My hubby's been away more than a year," the woman sobbed. "They don't understand. I didn't want to do it. He made me."

"Who did?" I asked.

"Landlord. Put up the rent as soon as my man left. Said he'd have me out on the street if I didn't pay or give him what he wanted. Couldn't pay, and nowhere to go. And our stuff was in the house. He said he'd keep it. Aaagh."

"Likely story," said a woman with a prune face leaning over my shoulder.

"It happens more than you think," I told her. I asked the girl. "What's your name?"

"Geraldine."

I turned to the room at large. "Now, do we endanger the life of this child, or do we help?"

"I'll ask in the ticket office if they've got anything," said a younger woman. "My landlord tried to take advantage of me, too. Only my brother came and sorted him out. Me with a little girl sleeping in the same room, too."

Others in the waiting room seemed to be listening now. A small blanket was found, and a couple of dingy towels. I put the larger towel under Geraldine and slipped off her panties. More like bloomers, actually. It really was messy. After an hour of moaning and sobbing, accompanied by assorted bangs and blasts outside, I could see what I thought was the baby's head, although it was a bit hard to tell which was what. With a big contraction shortly after my sighting, the whole baby slithered out. It really needed a bath, but I rubbed it down with the spare towel as it squalled in protest before wrapping it in the blanket and handing it to my sympathetic helper, who announced that we had to get hold of some scissors.

"Whatever for?" I asked, horrified.

"To cut the cord, of course," she said, laughing.

She went off to find some. I wondered if I should put the girl's panties back on, but there was still blood coming out. And then a god-awful swoosh of something that looked like liver. What was I to do with that?

"Here's some newspaper. Wrap the afterbirth in that," said the prune woman. "One of the men can put it in the rubbish bin outside."

I looked at Geraldine to see how she was doing. She was smiling at her baby, cooing and singing, oblivious to the unpleasantness below. I wondered how her husband would feel about keeping the baby and how she would respond to being asked to give it up. I hadn't looked, so had no idea what sex it was.

"What will you call the baby?" I asked her.

"Margaret, after my Mum."

"That's a lovely name."

"Thank you for helping me."

"As soon as this air raid is over, we're going to see your landlord. Do you live nearby?"

"Almost next door."

"There's a wheelchair kept here for wounded soldiers," said one man, who looked like a retired boxer, given his cabbage ears and crooked nose.

"Thank you, I'll use that."

He brought it to the corner. I folded the least-stained towel on the seat and lifted her into it, to the surprise of all paying attention.

"By golly, you're a strong one," he said in admiration.

"Yes, that landlord is going to find out how strong."

"I'll come with you. Men like him need to learn a lesson or two."

"Thank you."

"Well, I think the raid is over, so let's get it over with."

We must have been a strange sight, trundling up the road with a bloodstained and wheelchair-bound woman holding a newborn. I was beginning to regret agreeing to the man accompanying me because I'd have to restrain myself. And what was to stop the landlord from taking it out on her once we left? I'd have to stay awhile.

I rapped on the door, which was opened by a man with a belly bigger than Geraldine's had been. The logistics involved with him fathering a child distracted me a little. A cigarette dangled from his mouth.

"What'cher want? What's wrong with 'er?"

"You are what's wrong with her," I said, wheeling her in as he jumped aside.

"Here, you ..."

"Here you," my companion said. "This young woman gave birth to your baby in the station. Where were you?"

"I've got a shelter at the bottom of my garden. She were making a fuss, so I told her to go to the station. I don't 'old with no fusses. Got enough on me mind."

"Well, there's a baby here that's going to make a lot of fusses, so get used to it."

"She'll 'ave ter go, then."

"She's going nowhere," I said, gripping him by the collar of his filthy shirt and forcing him back against the wall. "You're going to do right by her, or I'm going to the police."

"My word against hers. Me brother's a solicitor."

"And mine is a London barrister. You don't stand a chance. I'll be staying a while."

He brought an arm up as if to chop me on the back of my neck and found himself with said arm twisted behind his back. He howled.

"Behave yourself," I said. My companion released that arm, only to twist the other one behind his back.

"Me and my wife live in the next street. One of us will be checking on Geraldine every day after this nice lady leaves. So don't be getting any ideas. I've won more boxing matches in my day than you've eaten sausage rolls. And I can still pack a punch."

"And I'll be checking on her, too." We turned to find the prune lady standing on the doorstep. "I'm going to my daughter's house. It's quite near. I know she's got some baby clothes she can spare. I think she's still got all the nappies, too."

"You are all so kind," Geraldine said tearfully. "I'll never forget any of you."

The landlord snorted.

I supported Geraldine while she climbed the stairs to her room. I found towels and a couple of blankets in a cupboard in the hallway and helped her change her clothes. Fortunately, she had plenty of sanitary pads. I took the bottom drawer out of her dresser and made a snug bed for the baby. I got her into bed and put the baby, now wrapped in a clean towel, into her arms. The next day, I'd see what I could do to get her some help. Social services, maybe get her husband home on emergency leave and deal with the issue early on, find her somewhere else to live, etc.

To make a long story short, we couldn't track down her husband, so I took her home with me after a week. My nanny had her hands full with Hunter and could do with some help. Geraldine couldn't be a huge help at first with a newborn, but she could do a few things for us until her husband came home, which was nearly a year later. I sent him a ticket for the train up to London and invited him to tea. I should have realized that he'd be intimidated by a big house like mine, but I did my best to put him at ease.

He sat in an armchair, and Geraldine sat next to me on a sofa with the baby in a portable cradle next to her. After I'd poured the tea, I left, telling them to spend as much time as they needed to talk things over. I went next door to the library. It wasn't long before I heard a slap, a cry, a baby's wail, and the front door slam.

"You're better off without someone who behaves like that," I said.

"I'll find a job as soon as I can," Geraldine said, sobbing as she held her red cheek.

"You are welcome to stay as long as you like."

As it turned out, six months later, my nanny's father had a stroke and her mother needed help. I arranged for Geraldine and her baby to go up north to help nurse the poor, sweet man. The mother loved the baby, and Geraldine stayed on until the old lady died. With her daughter's permission, she had willed Geraldine a small rental house she owned in the same village. Geraldine's child was at school by then, and she got a job in the local general store/post office, eventually becoming postmistress. She married again, too. So it all ended happily ever after, as they say.

"That's quite a story. I remember the story you told earlier about your English nanny in those days. Was she happy about all of this?"

"Absolutely. They became the best of friends."

in ran into my room early one May morning.
"Mary, wake up."

Her tangled hair and wrinkled nightie made me think
she'd experienced a tussle of some sort during the night.
Maybe with Hunter. I pushed that thought aside.

"What's happened?"

"My lady Frigg has escaped the stone. She came to me in
my dreams. She will visit me today. My lady is coming here.
To me! Agna arrived late last night. She said she sensed a
battle was close."

"That's exciting," I said.

"You don't sound very excited." She pouted like a little
girl and sat on my bed.

"You just woke me from a deep sleep. And it's early."

"Sorry, but I had to tell someone."

"What about Hunter?"

"He's in such a deep sleep I couldn't wake him. It's possible he's communing with Odin."

"Should we do something special? Cook something?"

"I hadn't thought of that. I'll leave that to Dora."

"Dora should rest more. Penny is still tiny and needs a lot of care."

"Oh, she's as strong as a horse. Don't worry. Flowers. We need lots of flowers. That's the best tribute."

"We can go to the flower shop when it opens."

"No, you go. I don't know when she'll come. I have to be here."

"What shall I get?"

"Anything that looks pretty. And a lot. Better pick up a few vases, too. I think I've only got five or six. She likes wine. We have plenty of that. And cakes. Dora can make some. Maybe Auntie can help." She was bouncing up and down on my bed now.

"Okay, you go and get dressed. I'll get ready, too. The flower shop probably won't open until ten. I hope she doesn't come early."

Lin darted out of my room. So, her idol, her goddess would be with us. I wondered how she would look. Beautiful, of course. Huge like Odin? Petite like Lin? Would she be stern or soft, uncaring or kind? I could only hope she would be all Lin wanted her to be. Our memories are so often rose-tinted, and Lin hadn't seen her mistress in eons.

I took my shower and laid out Rose's clothes so that getting her ready wouldn't take too long. I'd let her and Auntie sleep longer. I went downstairs expecting to find a flurry of activity. The kitchen and living room were empty. The coffee wasn't even made, so I started with that.

The wind suddenly picked up, whistling down the chimneys and around the house. I went over to the sliding glass doors. The tree branches thrashed around as if fighting off demons. It was only May, so the leaves were still firmly attached, and not all had unfurled. I went to another window to check on Yggdrasil. Our noble tree had folded itself over like an umbrella blown inside out. Its branches clung tightly together, while the whole swayed with the tempest. The wind screamed now, and I felt like crawling under the table. Rose, I had to find Rose. I needed Hunter. Where was everyone?

I ran back to our wing to find Rose's bed empty. A whimper came from my room. Rose had climbed into my bed and covered herself with the duvet. I climbed in next to her and held her tight. As the wind screamed louder, I felt like whimpering myself. What on earth was going on? A mighty crack came next as a flash of light penetrated even our dark blinds. Lightning, and it had hit something.

"Mary, are you all right?" I still couldn't get used to Auntie's young voice. I peered over the duvet.

"Such a terrible storm, Auntie. I think something just got hit by lightning."

"Yes, I heard that. We should get up and look around the house to make sure everything is in good shape. Come along."

The day had turned dark gray, and sheets of wind-driven rain whipped the house, thudding against the windows as if demanding entry. Rose held my hand tightly. We examined every downstairs room except the garage and Dora's apartment, where I assumed she and Stan had hunkered down. Nothing had been breached.

"Do you think we should go upstairs, Auntie?"

"Yes, of course. This is a very strange storm. Very sudden and wild."

"I wonder if it has anything to do with Frigg." I told Auntie what Lin had told me earlier.

"Sounds like mischief-making to me," she said. "Upstairs. You can be sure Agna is keeping busy with this one."

We went up, Auntie ahead of me, climbing fast as if she'd never heard of arthritis. She didn't even hold the handrail.

We walked toward Lin and Hunter's room. The door was wide open. Hunter and Lin stood in the middle of the room, watching Agna, who writhed on the floor, crying out what must have been incantations in the old tongue. Wind eddied around her, pulling her this way and that as she flung out her arms, time and again. Rose hid behind me. A flash of lightning hit the floor close to Lin, and it started to smolder. Lin stamped it out. Another hit Hunter's shoulder, causing him to cry out. His tee flamed out and the sickening smell of burning flesh filled my nostrils.

"Water," Auntie Peggy yelled.

"There's a kitchen nearby. Rose, come with me."

I wanted to leave Rose in the kitchen, as this was a dangerous situation I didn't want her anywhere near. I filled the kettle and picked up as many bottles of mineral water as I could carry.

"Rose, I want you to stay here. It's quieter and safer for you. This is a nasty storm."

"All right, Mama. I'll be scared without you."

"I know, honey. But think how proud Papa will be of you when I tell him how brave you've been."

"I know. I heard him shout. Is he hurt?"

"Oh, no, he was just angry at the storm."

Thank goodness she'd been hiding behind me when lightning struck her father.

"Shut the door behind me, now. I've got too many things to carry to do it myself."

I got back to the bedroom as fast as I could, only to find Lin, Hunter, and Auntie stomping around the carpet as if performing a clog dance. Agna lay still now, her eyes closed as her lips moved, no doubt still uttering chants and spells. I handed out water, leaving a couple of bottles on the floor by the door. The wind didn't sound so loud now. I breathed a little easier until a loud crack and flash set the duvet on fire. I picked up the bottles and poured water over the flames before Lin jumped on the bed and did some more stomping.

"Damn her to hell, I liked that duvet," she whispered. "I'll cut her to pieces and make a quilt out of her, you see if I don't."

"Who?" I asked.

"Freya, of course. This is her doing. Frigg has escaped, and she is still trapped. She wants to destroy us all."

"I hope Frigg can still come," I said.

"I am here," said a gentle voice.

She was tall, slim, and curvy. I'm not sure about the color of her hair. Sometimes it looked golden brown, at others, almost white. Her face made me think of the stars because light seemed to radiate from it. Her eyes changed with the light. We all stood transfixed for a few minutes as she looked into our eyes, one by one.

"My dear family," she said. She took Lin into her embrace before lifting her hand, thereby raising Agna from the floor. Auntie went to support Agna, who was so weak she could hardly walk.

"Put her on our bed," said Lin. "She has exhausted herself for us."

Hunter, shirtless now, kneeled before Frigg and kissed her hand. Frigg touched his burned shoulder. The puckered red skin stretched and calmed itself to a healthy tone. She looked at Auntie, then at me. "I believe you are part of Lin and Hoenir's family now. Therefore, you are my family, also." When she smiled, I felt a sense of well-being that has never left me, no matter what tribulations come my way. "Where is the child?"

"She is nearby, my lady," I replied. "I will bring her."

I found Rose with puffy eyes. "There is a very special lady who wants to meet you. You must call her 'my lady,'" I told her.

As we entered, Frigg turned her bright gaze on Rose. "Come here, child."

She picked Rose up and kissed her cheek. "I know that was a terrible storm. But all is well now. Do not be afraid anymore."

"No, my lady. I am not afraid of anything anymore."

"No, my dear, you are one of us now."

"My lady, shall we go downstairs to a more comfortable space? I wanted to greet you with flowers, but the storm prevented us from finding any."

"No matter, Lin. It is enough for me that I see you and Hoenir again and meet your family. It also will be enough for me to sit on something soft." She laughed.

I looked across at Hunter, or Hoenir, as I should probably think of him now. He blew me a kiss.

"Papa?"

He blew Rose a kiss, too. She ran over and he picked her up. I went over to the bed to check on Agna.

"Agna will recover in a few hours," Frigg said. "Do not worry, no harm will come to her, despite Freya's evil intentions."

Lin and Frigg led the way to the living room. Auntie peeled off to the kitchen. I had no idea if this goddess drank coffee—would eat or drink anything, in fact.

Hunter asked, "My lady, what of my brother Odin? Is Freya trying to harm him?"

"Not just now," she replied. "She needs to destroy me first. Her plan is that once Asgard is fully reborn, she will destroy him so that she might rule."

"But if Asgard is reborn and the other gods are also reborn, won't they oppose her?" I asked.

"She will have woven her spells into the very soil and every creature. If we let her get that far, we are finished."

"She tried to kill Hunter when he visited," Lin said.

"I know. She controls the small clouds and some of the plants, the young trees and the pebbles that live on stream beds. She must be destroyed before she gets any stronger. My lord Odin finds it more and more difficult to keep her out of his mind. She must never escape the stone."

"I will visit again soon," said Hunter. "I know how strong she is. I must help my brother."

"Do not go alone. Take Lin and Agna. I know how arduous your first journey was. You have no need to climb Yggdrasil now. Just use your mind."

"Yes, my lady. Can we offer you refreshment?"

"No, I will leave now. I do not like to leave my lord for too long. She will use my absence to probe his mind more aggressively. Let us go to Yggdrasil. You saved the tree, Lin."

"Yes, my lady. I kept a sprig and planted it everywhere I've lived. It never grew until Loki died. His destruction was largely due to Eir, by the way. She is still a physician."

"I want to see her again. I know she strayed, but all is well with her now."

We walked out of the house to a jumble of broken tree branches strewn across the grounds. A couple of old oaks had come down, too. We all gasped when we came to Yggdrasil. The trunk had been split down the middle, the outward-bowed edges charred. Thousands of brown leaves lay under it.

"No!" Lin and Hunter cried in unison.

Frigg went to the tree and wrapped her arms entirely around it, so easily that it took me a minute to register what I was seeing. She pulled the trunk together. I looked at Auntie and Rose. Auntie looked shocked, but Rose only nodded at Yggdrasil and smiled. She went up to the tree and stood next to Frigg, patting the trunk, and saying, "Poor tree, get better, we all love you."

The trunk began to straighten as Frigg released it, pulling itself together in slow motion. The edges started to knit as the very heart of the tree rumbled slightly. Branches rose toward the heavens and, while still without leaves, a green maze of buds studded them.

"Yggdrasil lives! Asgard lives!" Frigg cried and disappeared.

After a moment's silence, Lin said, "I need my coffee."

We all did. By the time we got to the kitchen, Dora had everything started. Penny gurgled happily in her day crib in a corner. We drank our coffee and nibbled croissants and said nothing beyond the usual pleasantries. I noticed Stan standing in the middle of the lawn, hands on hips, looking around as if wondering where to start.

"I will go to help Stan," Hunter said. "That is a big job out there."

"I think I'll help, too," said Auntie.

We all did. Even Rose bagged a lot of leaves. We ate a good lunch of macaroni cheese and salad. Dora announced there would be roast lamb for dinner.

After lunch, Hyndla came limping out of the woods. Rose flew to him and sat next to him. "He's hurt his leg," she cried.

Hunter went over and felt his leg. "Nothing broken." He held the fox's head and gazed into his eyes. "A branch fell on him. He hurt his paw pulling out from under it. He just needs to rest it."

"Papa, could you please carry him to the terrace? I'll get an old towel to make him warm and comfy."

Her father carried the little creature and laid him on a loveseat up against the house, sheltered from the wind. Rose came out, carrying something that looked larger than a towel. When I went inside later, I realized that it was one of Rose's blankets. They both lay on it, and Rose had folded it across them. They both fell asleep, Rose with her head on Hyndla's back. I couldn't be mad. It was all so sweet. I'd leave being mad to Dora. She did it better than me.

14

I was sitting on the beach at our house, enjoying an unusually hot Sunday for the middle of May. Lin and Hunter had decided on a last-minute trip to Paris to meet friends. They had a fair number of mysterious friends that they never talked about. Rose had a friend over and they were making an elaborate sandcastle that involved three turrets and a moat fed by the incoming tide. They knew the castle would be obliterated in a couple of hours but worked hard at it anyway. *Everything changes* is a Buddhist saying that I had decided to adopt as a sort of New Year's resolution. It helped me to accept the metaphorical tsunamis that seemed to overcome me on a regular basis.

My phone rang. "Mary, can you come over this evening?"

"Lin! I thought you were still in Paris. Is something wrong?"

"Yes. Hunter has lost touch with Odin."

"For how long?"

"Since we've been gone. A week. He communes with him every morning as soon as he wakes up. They talk about how Asgard and the gods are coming back to life. But now silence. We have to go."

"Do you think Freya is behind it?"

"Probably. I just hope he's still alive. And my lady, too." She sounded teary. "After all this, we can't lose our heaven."

"Of course I'll come. Rose has a friend here and they'll be having dinner before she goes home. Will a couple of hours be soon enough?"

"Sure. And bring Auntie. Agna came back with us."

I told the girls I was going up to the house to put their dinner in the oven. It would be ready in half an hour. I'd made a macaroni cheese ahead of time, so all I had to do was make the salad. Auntie was sitting on the patio knitting. I told her about the problem. She just nodded and carried on. She didn't need to pack anything, after all. We all kept toiletries and clothing at the castle.

They were both disappointed when it was time to tidy up and carry their stuff off the beach. I took a picture of their castle.

"It's the most beautiful castle I've ever seen," I told them. "I'll print out a picture for each of you. The waves will take it away with them, but you'll have the picture forever."

That cheered them up. They toted all their stuff up to the house. I'd rinse the toys and chairs later. Right now, I could hardly think about anything other than Asgard. A heaven I had never seen. Would I ever? I felt a moment's resentment about being locked out of so much of Lin and Hunter's lives. It would always be so, and I must lose them or accept the status quo.

Another worry was that I didn't know how Hunter and Lin planned to get up there. Odin said they could think their way up there. I hoped it would work and they wouldn't have to make that awful climb.

Hettie's mother came to pick her up at the appointed time. After she'd left, I told Rose we would be spending the night at the castle. She never minded going to see her Papa and Hyndla.

"I have to take my homework. It's already packed in my bag. I'm so glad they came back early. Will Papa take me to school tomorrow?"

"I don't think so. He might have to go away again for a bit."

"He should stay home where he belongs."

"I'm sure he wishes he could."

We got to the castle by eight. I was surprised to see Dr. Ayre there. Rose went to call Hyndla, who came running out of the woods at once. She gave him a lamb bone Dora had given her, left over from dinner. They sat on the lit terrace while he devoured it, and she stroked him and kissed his head. I called her in as it was too cold by now. She never wanted to leave Hyndla, but was "persuaded" by Auntie, who said, "Come along," took her by the hand, and marched her off.

"So, what's going on?" I asked Hunter.

"My brother has become silent. I am afraid that Freya has caused him some harm. Lin cannot find Frigg, either."

"So you commune with Frigg? I didn't know that," I said to Lin.

"We just started recently ... once she became strong enough. Freya tries to break in sometimes, but we manage to block her. They have both been silent since we left. We will try again in the morning, in case it was because we went far from Yggdrasil, although that seems unlikely."

Lin had twisted a tissue until it fell to scraps in her lap. She reached for another. I patted her hand and picked up the pieces.

"So, if you don't hear, what will you do?"

"We will have to go. We might need to save them. Eir will come in case her skills as a physician are needed. And Agna's powers might be needed to thwart Freya's evil spells."

"Will you have to make that awful climb?"

"No, we don't need to anymore. We are once again strong enough to will ourselves to Asgard."

"Thank goodness for that. I hope all will be well."

"We'll tell you all about it when we get back."

If you get back, was my unspoken thought.

"Yes, a big if, Mary," said Hunter.

So he was reading my mind again? I must have let the curtain slip. Maybe he was reading my face.

We all went to bed around ten. Hunter crept into my bed shortly afterward, and I held him tightly, unwilling to let go. He disengaged my arms gently after a few hours and kissed my cheeks. "I will be back, my love. I can't leave my Mary and my Rose."

But you are leaving us. I eventually fell asleep, half-waking with a start several times after tortured dreams.

The next morning, I got Rose dressed and took her into the kitchen for breakfast. Auntie was making coffee and had Rose's orange juice and cereal ready.

"I've packed her lunch," she said, pointing to a lunch box adorned with pictures of woodland animals, the biggest one a fox. It had been Sven's inspired Christmas gift, full of chocolates that hadn't lasted long.

I drove Rose to school. "Where is Papa?"

"I don't think they're up yet."

"He came to say a long goodbye to you last night. Why didn't he come into my room?"

I had to remind myself to close my mouth. How the heck did she know? She'd been fast asleep by the time I climbed into bed.

"He thought you were asleep."

"I was asleep. But I know things in my dreams."

How much did she know in her sleep, for heaven's sake? "I'm sure he'd have come if he'd known."

I kissed her and dropped her off, watching her sturdy little figure swinging her lunch box and bowing slightly under the book bag on her back as she strode confidently into school. Raising a goddess has its drawbacks.

When I got back, Auntie was still sipping coffee.

"Where is everyone?"

"Dora came in briefly and told me they left already. She's tired and went back to bed. I think the baby kept her awake last night."

"I wish they'd waited."

"I guess it was urgent, as they obviously hadn't heard from Odin or Frigg."

"I suppose we just stay here and wait? Did Dr. Ayre go, too?"

"She did."

We stayed at the castle for a little over a week, Rose constantly asking about Papa and Linnie, Dora droopier than a half-dead daisy, and Auntie Peggy knitting something infinitely long and garishly pink. My nerves were at a breaking point by the time the four warriors stumbled into the kitchen, looking as if they'd been fighting their way through a prickly hedge. I'd never seen Lin looking other than perfectly groomed. Her hair was tangled and even looked broken in places. She had red welts over her arms and legs, and her clothing was ripped. I found her appearance disorienting. After relieved embraces and greetings, they went upstairs to shower and rest.

Rose and I went back to my house the next morning, a Sunday, although Auntie decided to stay at the castle to lighten Dora's load. When I came back from taking Rose to school on Monday morning, I found Lin sitting on my living room sofa. Her hair looked shiny and perfect, and her welts had disappeared. I knew that disarray couldn't last for long.

"I had to come and tell you all about it," she said.

"I was hoping you would. You all looked as if you'd been through hell," I said.

"Oh, we had. But we prevailed."

I went to a drawer upstairs in my bedroom to retrieve the tape recorder. I knew she'd want to put up her feet for this one.

Tape 5,
Volume 4

We tried to contact Odin and my lady early in the morning, to no avail. I armed myself with a sword I'd found after Ragnarok. Hunter gathered a few things. I'm not sure what. The four of us went out to stand by Yggdrasil with our eyes closed. A stiff wind started up, but when Agna shouted an incantation, it dropped. We held hands and chanted in Norse, "Asgard, Asgard, welcome us, your children, take us into your arms."

We opened our eyes to find ourselves standing within a ring of clouds. They slowly began to roll toward us, hissing and spitting as they came. One touched Hunter and he ripped it to shreds, tearing it with his hands and teeth. The hissing got louder as they began to spit hail that cut into our faces. Agna shouted another incantation and the sun appeared overhead, its heat dissolving the vile vapor. Another loud chanting started up as a blanket of angry black clouds started to lower themselves over our heads and masked the rising sun. Hunter punched at them, but they just squelched in and pushed back out again. Agna went to work once more. Lightning split the clouds, thunder roared, and sparks ignited long grass on either side of us that I hadn't noticed before.

"Run!" she yelled.

We ran, zigzagging to avoid lightning strikes and hopping over blazing tufts before coming to the portico of a massive palace. Behind it, the sun was still rising.

"This is the place where I first found Odin," Hunter said. "Freya is also here. Frigg, too. Be careful."

We walked up to the open doorway. The threshold rose and closed the door with a clang. Hunter threw himself against it, to no avail. I noticed a keyhole. But we didn't have a key, of course.

"Leave it to me," Agna said. She stared at it and clenched her fists. This went on for a while. Just when I thought whatever she was doing wasn't going to work, we heard a key turn and unlock the door, which swung open.

"Don't overtire yourself," I whispered to her. "You know how you get." Casting spells wore her out. I remembered my alarm when her legs gave way during a battle with Loki and his horrible handmaiden a couple of years ago.

"You've forgotten. Odin gave us back our lost strength. We are better than ever."

I had forgotten. How else could we have willed ourselves up there?

We entered a long hall where statues stood on either side, stretching as far as even we could see.

"That is strange. They were all seated when I came last time," muttered Hunter.

The first two bases on our left were empty. "This is where Odin and Frigg sat," said Hunter. "We will look for them."

We wandered the length of the hall. I recognized a few of the statues, but not many. Sweet Baldur was one. Hunter kissed his cheek. I patted his bottom.

"We will try the corridors leading off the main hall. But be very careful. Freya is down one of them."

I looked back the way we came but saw no doorway. I remembered how Hunter had gone adrift, thanks to Freya.

We went down one dim corridor in a diamond formation—Hunter striding ahead, me looking to the right, Eir to the left, and Agna bringing up the rear, looking out of the back of her head. Yes, Mary, she can do that. There weren't any statues in this corridor. We went back to the main hall and searched the next corridor. Again, empty. The next one was really dark. About halfway down, something long and muscular whipped itself around my neck. It smelled as horrifying as the wandering strands of souls in the under-world—a stench of despair, decay, and misery.

"Hello, Lin. How lovely to see you again. And your handsome Hoenir. And is that my traitorous handmaiden, Agna? Do you really dare to come into my realm?"

"This is the realm of the gods of the Aesir, and Odin is their leader," Hunter thundered.

"Oh, so fierce. Look, your little wife is having trouble breathing."

I could see well enough in the gloom, withdrew my dagger, and cut off Freya's arm as far up as I could reach. The hand scrabbled at my neck, but Hunter ripped it off. She screeched, the cacophony bouncing around the walls like ricocheting bullets. Agna had backed up against the oppo-site wall. Suddenly, the corridor became as bright as day. Freya sat on her throne, encased in stone below the waist, but her top half free. Her once beautiful face had become hard and twisted, and her hair had turned a nasty yel-lowish shade of white. She held what was left of her right arm with the left, which was extraordinarily long. The wound dripped a viscous green liquid, which formed little balls that rolled away to wriggle against the walls. She muttered spells, her voice rising and falling. The arm seemed to regenerate. But after a few minutes, only a black hand protruded from the elbow.

She pointed her stubby black hand at us one by one. "You will die for this."

Agna approached her now, screaming spells. Freya did likewise, spitting and writhing, her long arm stretching even farther, trying to snare us, trying to poke Agna. We dodged this way and that, while the air filled with flying creatures, bats, I think, that tried to cover our eyes with their wings, while other creatures scuttled across the floor, tripping us and biting our ankles. We all struck out blindly, trying to avoid getting anywhere close to Freya. I managed to dispatch a few creatures with my sword. It was a sword I found in the charred wood after Ragnarok just before stumbling into Hunter. I don't know whose it was, but could only hope it carried some enchantment.

I handed it to Agna. "It might be enchanted. I don't know."

"It is the sword of Freyr, brother of Freya!"

"Give it to me," Freya screeched as she thrust out her intact arm that stretched and stretched toward it. Agna dodged around the snaky fingers, leaped at Freya, and cut off the arm at the shoulder.

The bats disappeared, as did the rats, if that's what they were. I've never seen blue rats, though. Everything went quiet while Freya looked down at her arm, which twitched as it lay against the opposite wall. It began to roll back toward its former owner. Hunter stomped it. It jumped like a snake, then lay still. Freya didn't take her eyes off it. It began to undulate. Scales formed, and soon a triangular head and slit eyes. It slithered toward me and reared, fanning out its hood. It flickered its tongue. I couldn't tear my eyes away from those yellow orbs with their black pupils. I felt myself weaken.

Hunter grabbed the serpent behind its head and held it high. I came to my senses. Freya screamed again, and Hunter threw the thing into her face. Enraged, or perhaps startled, it bit her neck before tumbling to the floor, a severed arm once more.

Freya's head dropped forward. "Odin, you are mine," she whispered. "It is all mine."

The stone seemed to grow around her, like a rising water table. Soon, she was a statue once more, an armless, stooped old woman.

We were exhausted.

"We should crush her statue," Hunter growled.

"Might that set her free again?" I asked.

"No," said Eir. "She has gone. I tried to get at her to inject this, but I couldn't get close enough." She held up a syringe. "I always arm myself for perilous situations. I will inject it into the stone. That will make sure."

I didn't know how a syringe would get through stone, but this was Eir, after all. She aimed the needle at the nape of its neck and jabbed. It went through the stone as if it were butter.

"And there's an end to it," she said, as the statue turned to dust, covering the floor and a lot of our clothing.

I ran out into the hall and brushed myself off with my hands. I didn't want Freya anywhere near me, dust or not. Hunter wasn't far behind, coughing.

"She got in my throat," he rasped.

"You're lucky that's all she got into," I said.

"Now we must find Odin."

"Let me sit down for a while," said Agna, finding an empty base to rest on. "There was a statue here recently. And now it is free."

So there were others who had been reborn. We searched the rest of the corridors but found no sign of Odin or Frigg. Or any other gods, for that matter. Agna joined us when we were ready to leave.

We found the door easily enough, now that Freya couldn't ply her magic to disorient us. The sun was beginning to rise into a powdery blue sky, and the scent of brightly colored flowers was almost overwhelming. Huge old trees, fully in leaf, shaded the avenue outside the palace that seemed to stretch beyond the horizon. Our fighting had continued from the last sunrise to this one.

We walked and walked until the sun relinquished the reins to the moon. We lay on the soft green moss and slept, only afraid of what might have become of Odin and Frigg.

The next day, we wandered into a small orchard on the side of the road and plucked golden apples for our breakfast. Their juice quenched our thirst and their meat filled our bellies. Their magic renewed us.

"Why do you think we still feel hunger and thirst?" I asked the others.

"Perhaps because we do not wish to give up the delights of filling those needs," Eir replied.

On the road once more, we finally came to a modest dwelling set in an emerald-green meadow. Hunter went ahead, pushing open the door. "They are here!"

Odin and Frigg lay together on a wide bed, sound asleep. Hunter shook Odin's shoulder.

"Brother Odin, wake up. Freya is no more. We are all free. "

Odin stirred, opened his eyes, and tried to sit up. Hunter helped to prop him up.

"Spells," he mumbled. "Wicked spells. So weak. Near to death. And my lady."

He tried to reach out to Frigg, but could hardly lift his arm. I lifted Frigg in my arms. "Awaken, my lady. It is Lin. We have destroyed Freya."

She fluttered her eyes. "Lin, feed me."

I looked at Agna. "What shall we do? Why are they still under her spell when she's dead?"

"She cast a sleeping spell on them. They have been immobile for long enough that they have become very weak and would have died had we not found them. You know gods must move to stay alive."

"No," we all chorused.

"Even I didn't know that," said Eir. "Of course, we sleep now, but like any human, we move while we sleep and after we get out of bed, even if it's to the couch or to get food. Even if we read, we turn the pages. No one stays completely still for days unless they are in a coma. Interesting."

Something suddenly occurred to me. "How come Odin goes into his Odin Sleep every now and then to rejuvenate himself and awakes renewed?" I asked Eir.

Agna answered. "That's different. He initiates that to begin a process that renews every last cell. It's an active process. Freya's spell cast them into a coma so deep that nothing could renew itself.

Agna's dispassionate explanation didn't solve the problem of how to revive the couple until I thought of the perfect food. "The golden apples," I said. "The ones we just ate. They will give them back their strength." I ran back down the road and gathered as many as I could shove down the front of my shirt, into my pockets, and clutched in my arms. I was soon back. We cut them open with a scalpel Eir had in her pocket and trickled the juice into the ailing pair's mouths. They managed to swallow the juice of at least three each. They could sit up, leaning against the wall, by this time. We cut off small cubes of the flesh, being careful not to make them choke. They ate a surprising amount, moving their heads and arms more as time went on.

"Now then," said Eir. "They must walk."

"Too weak," said Odin.

"We will help. You must move a lot to recover."

On TV programs, I've seen how people drag overdose victims around while waiting for help to arrive. That's how it was. Hunter draped Odin's arm over his shoulder and walked him up and down the room, while Eir did the same with Frigg. After a tedious hour or two, the couple seemed to be almost back to normal.

"I built us a new palace," Odin said. "I wonder if she destroyed it."

"Where is it?" I asked.

"Near here somewhere," he said. "I don't quite remember."

I glanced at Eir. That didn't sound encouraging.

"Well, never mind," Eir said briskly. "It's not as though you can go to bed. You must keep up and moving for at least a week. Build a new one."

"Oh," Odin murmured, "I'm so tired."

"You may not wake up again if you go to sleep again too soon."

"Odin, Eir knows best. We must do as she says. You know it as well as I do."

"Yes, my dear Frigg, I suppose you are right."

Good grief, they sounded like a human married couple. I hoped they would get back to their godly selves soon. We stayed another couple of days, making sure Odin and Frigg kept up and about. One way we handled it was to search for the new palace. We never did find it, so when we left, they were sketching plans for another.

15

We led a quiet and—for a change—normal life during June. The weather warmed up, although the wind over the Bay still cut into the balmy evening air more than I'd have liked. Rose adored baby Penny. She claimed she was her sister, and I chose not to disabuse her of the notion. I'd been worried at first that she might get under Dora's heels, but she learned how to take care of things fast. Rose even successfully changed poopy diapers without seeming to be grossed out. She never left the house without kissing Penny goodbye and received the babe's first gappy smile, too, or so Dora told her. That really puffed her up.

Since Rose had told everyone and anyone that she had a new sister, I received a few congratulations from her school friends' mothers when I went to pick her up. "My, you are back to normal quickly. Lucky you," was the gist of several comments. I hastened to tell them that the baby was not, in fact, mine, but that of a family friend. That always made Rose pout. "She is, so, my sister!"

I was looking forward to the end-of-school play, in which Rose had the starring role. One of the teachers had written a play that was a version of The Velveteen Rabbit. She had to rewrite it to create enough roles so that everyone who wanted to be in the play had a part. I'm not sure if that was legal, but since they weren't selling tickets to the public at large, I doubted anyone would make a fuss.

Hunter visited Asgard every ten days or so since he could make the trip in seconds now, sometimes accompanied by Lin. Once, Lin stayed up there for a week, while Hunter returned to tend to his investments. Auntie, ever tactful, moved over to the castle.

We barbecued and walked and picnicked on the beach. It was blissful. He and Rose built an enormous sandcastle, and she basked in his attention, for once willing to abandon Penny in favor of her darling Papa. When she fell asleep, we'd watch a movie or just talk. The first night, he was full of news. I had left my phone in the kitchen, unfortunately, but typed up his tale from memory the next morning after he left to check the stock market.

Tape 6,
Volume 4

"Frigg and Odin are obsessed with their new palace. I do not know why, really. I suppose they foresee a day when they will host feasts and other celebrations there. But that will not be for a long time. Most of the other gods are still not released from their effigies, although some have emerged from their various confinements. Odin visits all the statues most days, talks to them, and entreats them to use willpower to overcome their fate. I was with him when he tried a hammer on Thor, which resulted in a mighty roar of pain that reverberated through the heavens. The stone cracked down the middle, and half of Thor was revealed. The visible half of his face scowled at Odin.

"Have I not been punished enough, brother?"

"I am sorry, Thor. I was trying to free you from the stone. I did not mean to cause discomfort."

"Discomfort! You do not know your own strength."

"I am sorry, brother. I have heard the same thing said of you many times."

Thor grasped the edge of the stone around his face with his free hand, trying to crush it. "I have lost my strength. I will be forever imprisoned."

"No, Thor. The only thing that can release you is your will. Think yourself free. Or I can help with the hammer once more."

"I think not. And that looks like my hammer. I shall want it back. Leave me now to think."

We walked around the hall to other statues while Odin gave his pep talks.

A voice came from behind us. "My dear father."

We both knew that sweet voice and slowly turned, hardly daring to believe it. Baldur stood before us. Odin embraced him for many minutes. I embraced him only briefly because he did not smell too good. Hel is not the most fragrant place, and if one spends long enough there, I suppose one cannot help but absorb its miasma of decay and misery.

"Bathe yourself in the waters of a running stream, my son, then make haste to visit your dear mother. She mourns you still and tried her best to release you from your fate."

"I know, father, as did you. But we are all back now."

This touching scene was interrupted by an almighty crack and crash coming from Thor's direction. We ran over to find him standing free of stone. He stepped off the plinth and fell flat on his face, which elicited an inventive stream of curses that set us all laughing and laughing, which resulted in more curses aimed at us this time. Thor got to his knees and shook off Odin's helping hand as he stood once more, reeling slightly.

"You are weak, my brother. You have not moved for many ages. Go slowly."

"My hammer, if you please."

Odin handed it over.

"Where did you find it?"

"In the dwelling where Frigg and I slept after Freya cast a spell on us. Hoenir, Lin, and Eir saved us after they killed the witch. I will tell you the story later. First, you must join us for a feast. It will not be a feast as you remember them. We will have wine and fruit by a gazing pool. Our palace is not yet completed, and there are many gods still to be released before we can rebuild Asgard in its former glory. As you can see, Baldur is with us once more. Oh, happy day."

Odin walked with Baldur to find a good stream and then Frigg. We walked in the opposite direction, as we knew the reunion would cause a huge outpouring of joy that deserved privacy, at least at the beginning. Thor, still unsteady, cut a branch off a tree next to the path to use as a cane. He was beginning to get back to his old self as his face—that could have been carved from wood—assumed its usual confident and often arrogant mien. I hoped his confinement had tempered him, at least a little. He tended to be a bully.

"So, Hoenir, were you in stone?"

"No. I was badly wounded. Lin found me and carried me to Hel, where we stayed while I healed and until Midgard rose once more and have lived there as man and wife ever since. We live human lives, at least as far as possible. Lin and I have had many children, but they were not immortal, and we outlived them. I hope that will change now. I have three children in this lifetime."

"You have human habits, I suppose."

"Yes, we eat and drink, sleep, feel pain—or at least we used to—and, until now, have to be reborn at regular intervals. Our powers weakened after Ragnarok. Lin met Freya's handmaiden, Agna, too. They are like sisters."

"Will you kill her?"

"No, no need. She is with us. She helped us destroy Freya."

"Do any humans know you as gods?"

"A few. One is my lover, whom Lin is very fond of. I will ask Odin to make her and my daughter by her immortal. Her aunt, too, who is loved by the whole family. He has already bestowed some godly powers upon them, so I am hoping he will grant my wish."

We sat under a tree whose leafy branches offered shade from the sun that had suddenly become extraordinarily hot and bright. Soon, we could hardly hear each other from the birdsong that swelled from all directions. Deer, squirrels and foxes came out of their hiding places, chattering at each other in their own languages, jumping around in great excitement.

"Frigg has reunited with Baldur," Thor shouted.

We laid our heads back on the trunk and closed our eyes until the world calmed down. It was time to find the feast.

We discovered Odin, Frigg, and Baldur sitting beside two statues. The stone figures sat with their elbows propped on their knees, chins cupped in their hands.

"Who are these?" I asked, slapping the shoulder of one. To my surprise, the statue twitched. Odin laughed.

"They are my twins Vidar and Vali. This is truly a happy day."

"They do not seem trapped in the usual way. And that one did not feel hard."

"No, they are not imprisoned in stone. They survived Ragnarok and fell into despair. They have been sitting like that ever since. Look, Vidar is trying to sit up."

The creature's hands slowly lowered to his lap, causing his head to drop. His neck had not enough strength to hold up his head. I straightened his head and held it for a while. It gradually sank once more. He moved like a sloth. His brother had not tried to move.

"Leave him," Odin said. "Now they know Asgard will be once more, they will revive. It will take time. We have a lot of time."

We sat for a long time in that place ... until shadows lengthened to the point where we settled down to sleep on a soft moss carpet. Small clouds rolled over to serve as cushions and blankets. I would rather have gone without the comfort, given my previous experience."

"What's the matter, Hoenir?" Frigg asked.

I told her about the clouds that tried to kill me.

"Oh, that was Freya's doing. They answer to me now."

We all slept until the sun rose once more. Frigg produced fruit juice from an ewer I had not noticed the night before. Probably because it was not there. The juice was very like what the Greek gods we once visited called nectar. I felt it course through my veins, giving a sense of well-being.

A sucking sound behind me made me jump. Vidar was sitting up now, his head straight and his mouth open. His fingers twitched on his knees.

"The poor darling is thirsty," Frigg said. She filled a goblet and gently poured some into his mouth, a few drops at a time. His eyes opened. One hand extended, palm up. Frigg balanced a piece of fruit on it. He clasped his fingers around it and brought it to his mouth, pushed it in, and chewed. This all took place in agonizing slow motion while we watched in fascination. His brother had not moved. The palm was extended once more, and the procedure repeated. Next time, Vidar turned his head to his brother. His hand reached and rested on top of Vali's head.

"Vali," he croaked.

There was no reaction. Vali was the one I had touched, so I knew he was alive.

"Time. It will take time," Odin said.

"Time! They have had all the time in the universe," Frigg declared.

She marched over to Vali and slapped his head. "Wake up at once." His eyes snapped open. "Vidar has begun to move, and it is time you did, too." She turned to me. "He was always even lazier than his brother."

A tear rolled down his cheek. "Well, I am waiting." She lifted his hands above his head, which knocked Vidar's hand down. Vila's shoulders creaked horribly as he emitted a low wail. "Oh, my poor boy, I am sorry. You must take your time." She kissed the top of his head. A look of distaste crossed her face as she wiped the dust off her mouth with the back of her hand. "But not too much time, or I will be very cross with you. You, too, Vidar." She started to bend toward Vidar before quickly straightening up. She caressed his face instead.

"Let them be," Odin said. "We will visit the statues again. The twins must do it in their own time."

"Just think what they could have achieved waiting for our return," Frigg said.

"How do you think they could have withstood the attentions of Freya? She would have killed them."

The truth of this sank in as we walked peacefully back to the great hall. I left shortly after.

"I'm confused," I said, looking up at Hunter. "I thought Odin conferred immortality on us when he came down. Look at Auntie Peggy and how she has changed."

"He granted you powers that fall short of immortality. You have not realized all of yours yet. It has happened slowly, so you do not realize how much stronger you are. And we can read each other's minds, you must have realized that. You had better pay attention, or you will get yourself into trouble. And watch out for Rose, too."

"I don't know how I feel about immortality. I hate the idea of getting old and dying, but you and Lin seem to find it tedious."

"No, we do not expect to be surprised very often, that is all. But there is always something interesting to know or see. The world changes … people change, although not as much as they think. Pleasure is still pleasure, love is still love, joy is still joy."

"Do you think I will be allowed to visit Asgard?"

"Yes, I will try to take you. And if you are made immortal, you will definitely go."

"And Rose?"

"When she is a little older, I will take the three of them."

"I wonder what she will make of it."

"She will be enchanted."

We went upstairs to bed.

When I got out of the shower, Hunter said, "I forgot to tell you. The Grunewalds have invited us to visit them next month for a couple of weeks. Have you been to Austria?"

"No, never. How exciting! Who is going?"

"All seven of us. You, Rose, Auntie, Sven and Margareta, Lin and me.

"That's a lot of people to foist on them."

"They have a very big estate."

We had met the Grunewalds a couple of Christmases ago in Denmark, where Lin and Hunter had been instrumental in rescuing their daughter Gerda after she was kidnapped. Before that, we had all spent quite a bit of time together as the girls had become inseparable, and the adults enjoyed each other's company. It would be nice to see them again.

The next two weeks went by quickly. Sven and Margareta had completed their academic year, so returned home. We all descended on Rose's school for the play, which would begin at three in the afternoon. Dora had left Penny with Stan, declaring she wouldn't miss it for the world.

Rose was every bit the actress I expected her to be. She never flubbed her lines and was very natural as the little girl who would love her rabbit to life. The applause was heartfelt, and not only from us.

In the car home, she said, "Second grade next year. I wonder what play we'll do then. By the way, Mama, can I have ballet lessons? I really want to after seeing that lady dancing on TV last week. I've been thinking about it."

"I think that will be all right," I said. "I'll have to get recommendations for a good school. Ballet has to be taught properly. It's quite a bit of work, not all twirling around in beautiful costumes until you've mastered the technique." At least she'd forgotten about riding lessons.

"How do you know?" she asked.

"I tried it once. I wasn't very good."

"Ah, I see. Well, I think I will be good. And I will work hard."

"That sounds like a good idea," Hunter said. "I look forward to seeing you dance."

The next morning, I realized I hadn't spoken to Lizzie for a couple of weeks. Our two calls after our little reunion had been brief and awkward, centering on mundane matters. I thought I should let her know I was going to be away for a couple of weeks in Austria, and that I would love for her and the children to come to stay for a few days.

"I'll call to firm up a date when I get back," I said.

"Have fun." That note of resentment was back. Oh, well.

16

One Friday morning, I thought I'd have coffee at the castle. Auntie had been staying there for several days, helping Dora and enjoying the baby. She made all kinds of silly cooing noises when she thought no one was looking. She'd always been a loving aunt to me, but her words and actions had always been pretty much down to earth, even when punctuated by a hug or two. I found it highly amusing, but touching, too.

I found Lin and Hunter in the living room, reading different sections of the Washington Post—as might be expected, Lin the style section, and Hunter the business. I heard Auntie chatting with Dora in the kitchen. Penny must have been asleep, as there were no peeps from her.

Lin looked up. Hunter blew me a kiss before retreating back to the paper.

"Hello, Mary. I just read something very interesting in the Metro section. There's been a murder."

"Oh, Lin, there's always been a murder up there," I said, a little miffed by Hunter's absorption in stocks and shares.

"This is the murder of a young follower of our gods. Apparently, there is a hof in Great Falls that I'd never heard about. I wonder why no one told us?"

"Maybe they were so secretive that no one else knew about them. So, what happened?"

"Molly was a college student who shared an apartment with two other girls in Arlington. The other two girls had jobs, so they left for work in the morning, while Molly slept in. The first one home found her in the foyer stabbed to death. Only one of them knew about her hof membership, and she told the police. She didn't know the address of the hof, but knew it was somewhere off the Georgetown Pike. She said Molly used to grumble about the forty-five-minute drive in the winter."

"That could be way out in a rural area."

"Most of those rural areas are now suburbs. But property is still a little cheaper out there. Of course, I don't know any of their members, but I somehow doubt they're awash with cash."

"Unless one of them inherited a property," Hunter said, peering around his paper.

"I must look into it."

"The cops won't like that," I said.

"Joe might know something."

"Why don't I ask the Maryland group leaders if they know anything about the hof?"

"Would you? It's possible they've heard something."

Auntie came in bearing a tray of coffee for us all. "I thought I heard your voice, Mary," she said. "I just baked some chocolate chip cookies."

"Hello, Auntie," I said, getting up to kiss her. "I guess Penny's asleep."

"No, she's been very fussy, so Stan is walking her around the grounds in her stroller. Poor Dora was up half the night. Teething again."

"Poor Dora," I said. "I remember those days. Rose wasn't too bad, fortunately."

"Her godly parentage," Hunter said.

"Well, Penny has godly parentage, too, doesn't she?" I asked.

"Not really. Nymphs are different. Not to mention leprechauns." Lin accompanied this remark with something between a sniff and a snort.

"Well, I'd better get moving. Give me a call when you've spoken to your contacts, Mary."

"You mean you're going up to town now?"

"Of course. We can't have our followers being done in. There must be consequences. I'll go to our condo and call Joe from there."

Lin left to pack her bag. Hunter finally lowered his paper. Auntie looked bewildered and asked what the heck was going on, so I told her.

"Oh, so she's getting into the thick of things again, is she?" was her only comment as she cleared the coffee things away and bore them off to the kitchen.

"Sorry I have not come around this week," Hunter said.

"I was a little surprised, given the coast is clear," I said.

"I actually had to make a flying visit to Asgard to deal with a problem."

I turned my phone to record.

Tape 7,
Volume 4

"Lady Frigg had some trouble with the wife of one of the Vanir who was slain at Ragnarok. They were both encased in stone. Frigg spotted them in a dense forest while she was gathering herbs. She released the goddess from the stone, but not could not free the god. She claims Frigg left her husband imprisoned deliberately to prevent him from taking his rightful place as leader of the Vanir and the Aesir and her as queen."

"Why couldn't Odin handle it?"

"He has been in Iceland for a week, helping solve a problem at the hof. Did Lin tell you how Freya tried to set the place on fire?"

"She did."

"Well, I trapped a small figure of her in a garden ornament shaped like a frog and melted it so that it filled the head. Even though Freya is destroyed, the frog acts as if it were alive. Jumpy, spitting out small flames and frightening the congregation. I wish I could have seen it. I hope Hunter does something spectacular to it."

"That's the last remnants of her power," I said. "Let's hope Odin destroys it, however he manages it."

"Oh, he probably already has. He likes it there, so I think he's delaying his return. Anyway, I went to see the angry lady, who berated me and the Aesir gods as power-hungry and callous."

"Isn't that what Freya called you? Power hungry."

"Good point. I didn't like her tone and thought she could become a problem. We've had enough problems. It occurred to me that perhaps Freya had somehow corrupted her and her husband. Freya was half-Vanir, after all. I have not come across any Vanir statues or restored Vanir gods, so at first, I thought I'd leave it to Odin. His son, Baldur tends to be too tender-hearted sometimes."

"So Frigg has to deal with it until Odin gets back?"

"No. I invited the lady to show me her husband's statue, as I had not yet had the honor of greeting him. We walked through the forest for a long time before arriving at a small clearing where huge trees blocked the sun. The statue was standing, unlike most of the others I saw when I first arrived. The goddess went straight to it, stood on the ped-estal, and embraced her husband's cold figure with passion.

I heard a sort of growl in my head. "Set me free, Hoenir. I am a godly king. Give me my due."

"What is your name?"

"Norg."

"I have not heard of you."

"I am the son of Lady Freya's sister. You will hear much of me when I am released from this stone jacket."

"Freya is no more."

"My dear aunt was so sweet and beautiful. She should have been queen of the Vanir."

"Unfortunately, she wanted to be queen of the Aesir and tried to destroy our lady Frigg. She failed. Your world was destroyed, Norg. Asgard is only now being restored. You will have to live among us, and we are ruled by our lord Odin."

"Your lord, not mine."

"There can be only one leader in Asgard. Do you not agree?"

"Yes."

"I knew from the tone of his answer that he did not accept Odin as his lord. I gazed and gazed at his wife, imagining her encased in stone, until my mind swirled. With a faint cry, she tried to back away from her husband. She could not, and is forever entrapped in their embrace."

"How sad. I guess she really loved him."

"I think she did. But her manner was unpleasant and disrespectful, as was his. Norg was stupid to be so arrogant toward someone who could perhaps have freed him. If he were to become a troublemaker, he would have to be dealt with after causing all sorts of problems. And then there would be his wife to carry on his work. No, it is too soon in Asgard's rebirth to admit such thorns. It was better this way."

Lin came back. "I'm leaving now. I'll keep in touch. Remember, Mary, to let me know what you find out."

The Maryland group was astonished that there was a group that they'd never heard of so nearby. Very odd.

Lin returned a week later while I was doing a school run. I'd already read about it in the paper but was eager to hear her side of the story. The article only mentioned a lady who'd been present at the arrest but had disappeared shortly thereafter and could not be traced.

I'm back. See you tomorrow morning.

I picked up a chocolate cake on my way home.

Tape 8,
Volume 4

Joe was happy to get my help, especially with the Norse god worshippers. He felt I could gain their trust and took me along to their next meeting. After a long drive down narrow roads, then lanes, we arrived at a house that looked typical of the area—large, white, and columned. We entered and were met by a man who had clearly expected us. Joe introduced me to him before tactfully withdrawing.

Ted Ferguson was an impressive figure who looked vaguely familiar. He wore a dark suit, blue tie, and shoes polished to the point they'd wear through if he kept it up. When I looked around, I saw that all the attendees were well dressed and coifed, sipping white wine and making the modulated sounds of polite nothingness you hear at most Salton soirees.

"It's very nice to meet you, Mr. Ferguson."

"Ted, please."

"I'm Lin. I have visited a major hof in Iceland and my colleagues have met with several throughout the United States, but we have never heard of you. Why is that?"

"You know how it is around here. You live in Salton, don't you?"

"I just have a condo now. We moved to Southern Maryland. Do I know you?"

"I am your husband's stockbroker."

"Oh, yes, I think we met once quite a while ago."

"Well, as I was saying, we are all professionals who would probably lose most of our clients if they knew about our religious affiliation. Pagans have no credibility in this land of evangelicals. Hence the secrecy. I hope you will be discrete."

"Of course, because Hunter and I are one of you."

He looked shocked. "Really?"

"Yes, really. The fact is, we are gods. I would like to explain the situation to your congregation if you would be good enough to give me the floor."

He looked wary, a small frown wrinkling his brow. "Certainly. You may face some skepticism.

"Of course. I will find a way to persuade them. Perhaps you would like to hold your service first? I am working with Joe Paglietti to find Molly Blackstone's killer. I'm sure you want to say a few words about her."

He frowned for sure this time. "Indeed, a very sweet young woman."

"How did she come to know about your group?"

"Her boyfriend. Unfortunately, he died in a car accident last year. Run over while he walked down an unpaved road not far from here. Hit and run. They never caught the driver."

"How sad. Did you tell Detective Paglietti about this?"

"No, I didn't think it was relevant."

"Don't worry, I'll mention it. Every little bit helps."

That was interesting. Maybe a religious zealot?

The congregation was hanging around us by now, curious to hear what we were talking about. Ted didn't introduce me to anyone but showed me to my velvet-covered seat in the front row. The altar was attractively laid out. A mahogany table with a white runner embroidered with colorful wildflowers held a couple of huge matching vases filled with sunflowers. A statue that I supposed to be a rendition of what the sculptor thought Odin looks like stood in the center. It was pretty accurate, to my surprise. I'd have to ask Ted who made it.

I closed my eyes and asked Hunter to make a sudden appearance when I gave the signal. It was too much to expect Odin to show up.

Side tables lined the walls, filled with glasses and silver buckets containing ice and wine bottles. Other tables held platters of canapes covered in plastic wrap. I noticed that most people topped up their glasses before sitting down. There must have been around thirty present.

Ted took his place in front of the altar and rang a small bell. The room quietened as everyone found a seat.

"We have a special guest this afternoon, whom I will introduce later. I believe she has an important message for us. First, let me dedicate this short prayer to our dear friend, Molly Blackstone, who departed this life in terrible circumstances."

The room murmured until Ted raised his hand for quiet.

"Dear Lord Odin, please accept the soul of this faithful servant Molly, and lead her to eternal life."

The congregation repeated it after him. I heard a few sniffs. Well, let them think that mortals ascend to Asgard if it brings them comfort. That's not the way it works, unfortunately. Dead is dead. Mortal is mortal.

They sang a hymn in English that sounded more Celtic than Norse. It praised one god after another in rather a tedious fashion. I'd have to tell them to stop them praising Freya. There was another prayer before Ted introduced me.

"I would like to introduce Lin Thoren. She and her husband, Hunter Thoren, are known to me. We can rely on their discretion. She has a message for us."

I got up and stood in front of the altar.

"Thank you, Ted. First, let me say how sorry I was to hear of Molly's passing. I am a private investigator and will be assisting the police with the inquiry into her case. If anyone knows anything about her that may help, however insignificant, please let me or Detective Paglietti know.

"I and some of my friends visited a few hofs last January. I visited the one in Iceland, that I'm sure you are aware of. Others visited groups in Maryland, California, Pennsylvania, and Florida.

"We had a message for them. My husband and I are Norse gods."

The congregation gasped as one.

"My husband is Hoenir, brother of Odin. I am Lin, former handmaiden to the goddess Frigg. After Ragnarok, I cut a sprig of Yggdrasil, the sacred tree of life, and carried it with me through the millennia. I planted it everywhere I lived, but it never thrived. But it didn't die, either."

I had them in the palm of my hand by now. Sophistication had melted away, and they sat rapt like kids being told an adventure story.

"It was only in the last few years that I learned that Loki had also survived. He had continued his evil acts down the ages, most recently running a sex-slave trafficking ring locally. I broke up that ring, and he vowed vengeance. After many dangerous encounters, he met his end. At that point, Yggdrasil started to grow in our backyard. It grew so fast, we knew we had to replant it, which we did on a large piece of land we own. Eventually, it stopped growing. At great risk to himself, Hoenir climbed Yggdrasil to see what remained of Asgard."

I told them about the call to Odin in February and how he appeared to the people who supported him. I described how gods were trapped in stone and Odin's and Frigg's release. I told them about Freya, which elicited various dismayed utterances.

"So, Odin is with us once more and Asgard is undergoing rebirth. Odin does not ask anyone to worship him, only to do good, to eschew hatred and intolerance. He will appear at an event in Southern Maryland to speak to his followers and others who are curious. I hope you will be able to attend.

"I hoped my husband would be able to attend today to talk to you."

I shut my eyes and thought, *now*. More gasps told me that Hunter had arrived.

"Good evening," he said. "I am Hoenir, god of the Aesir. I understand that my wife has told you of recent events regarding Asgard. I will ask my lord and brother Odin to visit you when he can. I have urgent business to attend to now, so must leave you."

He walked through the center aisle of chairs and out to the hallway. After a few minutes, I heard his car start, but too far away for mortals to pick up. He'd obviously driven over and waited to make his appearance easier. Slacker!

The meeting dispersed. Everyone smiled at me, but no one came near except Ted.

"Well," he said. "Well, well. There's a turnup for the books." He seemed too overcome to come up with any meaningful remark.

"I must go, too," I said. "Detective Paglietti is waiting for me."

"Of course," he said. "We will certainly try to attend your meeting. September, you say?"

"Yes. I'll let you know."

Ted walked me out. I texted Joe, and he arrived in seconds. He must have parked around the side.

"How did it go?" he asked.

"Very well. I got Hunter to make a surprise appearance."

"I thought I saw him walk across the lawn."

"He drove over and parked before manifesting in front of the attendees. He made quite the impression. At least it made them believe my story."

"Good. Any leads?"

"Only that Molly had a boyfriend who introduced her to the group. He died in a pedestrian hit-and-run close to here last year. The police never found the driver. Too much of a coincidence?"

"Well, that is interesting."

"Can we talk to Molly's parents?"

"I called them. We can go now."

"Oh. Okay. What did you tell them about me?"

"That you are a consultant to the police. They didn't ask too many questions. Probably too numb to think straight. The father, at least. The mother seems pretty composed."

We pulled up outside a brick house in Upton that looked to have been built in the 1960s. That harsh, dark red tone of brick seemed to have been popular with builders then, as did the boxy design.

A portly middle-aged man with red-rimmed eyes opened the door. His gray cardigan was done up wrong.

"Detective, please come in." His flat tone sounded like despair.

He showed us into a living room with dark green upholstered furniture and a plethora of knick-knacks on every available surface. There was a line of them on the mantlepiece. I was tempted to topple an end one and watch it take down the rest like a row of dominos.

A small-boned, angular woman with a pointed nose sat in an armchair near the dead fireplace, knitting ferociously. She didn't stop as she raised her head to acknowledge our presence.

"Detective. And this is your consultant?" She said consultant like she might have said, floozie. I could hear the quotation marks around the word. In spite of her loss, I somehow didn't feel sympathetic.

"How do you do," I said. No answer.

"Please sit down," said Molly's father.

"I am very sorry for your loss," I said. "I believe Molly's boyfriend was killed in a hit-and-run last year. Any news on that?"

"None," said Mrs. Blackstone. "He's the one that got her into that pagan setup. He'll rot in hell." Her voice was low and vicious. Now I thoroughly disliked her.

"I'm sure his parents are as devastated as you are, Mrs. Blackstone," I said.

"His parents died when he was a baby. He was brought up in an orphanage. See, no one wanted him, even then. Bad stock."

"Now then, now then," said Molly's father. "That's not very nice."

"Introducing my daughter to paganism isn't very nice." The needles clicked even faster.

The doorbell rang.

Mr. Blackstone went to answer it. A gaunt figure in a dog collar loped into the room.

"Pastor Dan, this is Detective Paglietti and his consultant."

"Good evening. Are you saved?"

"I believe so," I answered, before Joe could. "In our line of work, we do most of the saving, of course."

"That is not what I…"

"A godless lot, most of them," Mrs. Blackstone broke in.

"Jesus saves. He will forgive the repentant," Pastor Dan intoned like an automaton. My kids used to recite their times tables like that.

"We are investigating Molly's sad passing," Joe said.

"Sad indeed. She will be suffering the torments of hell," Pastor Dan cruelly pronounced.

A sob escaped Mr. Blackstone. "How can you say such a terrible thing? She was a good girl who never harmed anyone."

"She rejected our savior," Pastor Dan insisted.

"If he's your savior, he's not likely to be mine," I said. "Is this your idea of comforting grieving parents?"

"Well, I'm sure I …"

"Molly repented before she died."

"How do you know?" Joe and Pastor Dan chorused.

"Because I know my daughter. As soon as the knife went in the first time, she would have realized her wickedness and asked god's forgiveness. The knife cleansed her."

Mr. Blackstone rushed from the room.

"Molly's father will come to acknowledge the truth. I hope her mother is right, and that the knife cleansed her soul." Pastor Dan was unrelenting in his hateful assault.

"Come, Lin. I don't think we have any more to learn here," Joe said as he rose, his voice almost growling.

When we got to the car, he sat breathing heavily, his hands gripping the steering wheel.

"Bastard. I feel sorry for the father."

"He can always stand up for himself. But I'll bet he never has. Old habits die hard."

"True enough. She's a despicable woman, and as for that so-called pastor, he's a snake."

"I think he's a suspect," I said. "Maybe you should look at that hit and run again. Did the police notify body repair shops?"

"Yes, they did. Even visited most of them around here. Of course, it could have been someone from out of town."

"Or it could have been someone who never got their car fixed."

"Could be. I need to look at that pastor's car."

"It only needs a quick pass. I'll do it."

"But he's seen you."

"He won't see me this time."

"Ah."

Joe looked at me and grinned.

"Did you find the knife?"

"No. The post mortem stated it was probably a kitchen carving knife."

"We need to get into the Pastor's kitchen."

"I suppose you're going to do that too?"

"Why not? I'll need the address."

"Okay."

Joe drove me home. Shortly after, I received a text with the address. Pastor Dan had made me really angry. Why wait? I searched the church online and found they had a service at seven on Sunday nights. I knew that people like Pastor Dan like to declaim their opinions at length, so I should have plenty of time. I'd have to be careful, though, as it was still light outside. And if he returned early, I'd just knock him out before he saw my face. It's not as though I have any fingerprints to leave behind. Actually, I would have liked to let myself go on his nose and teeth.

The awful man lived near the Blackstones in a little house adjacent to a clapboard church. It was all very modest. I tried the back door, which, as expected, was locked. A small window was open, but it would be a tight squeeze. I couldn't try the front door because it was too exposed. Thank heavens I'd finally managed to acquire a skeleton key set—the good ones are not as easy to find as you'd think. One of the few things you can't get from Amazon.

The house was devoid of personal touches. No photos, no mementos. Minimal furniture, and plain white blinds at the windows. I left the kitchen until last. What a disappointment that turned out to be. A couple of frying pans, some cutlery, plates, two glasses, and two mugs. A kettle. In the fridge, three bottles of vodka, one half-empty, and cans of orange juice. Hah! But no knife set. Nothing sharp. I didn't even find a computer. Maybe that was in an office at the church. I went back to the living to look again.

Footsteps were coming up the front path. Two sets. I rushed to the back door and left. There was no time to lock it. I decided to hide under the window so as to hear who was with him. They came to the kitchen.

"Are we going to have a party?" a teenage girl asked.

"You might say that. Let me get you a drink."

"The bottle says vodka. I thought you said that was wicked?"

"No, my dear, not for me. I am the pastor and I know how best to use things and do things. What I do is always in God's service. You should know better than to question me."

"Yes, pastor, sorry pastor."

"Drink a little at a time. You will feel better. I know your father leaving you and your mother made you very upset, but if you try this and submit to my bodily prayer, things will get better."

I knew he was a bastard. I'd wait it out. I needed pictures. Actually, I needed Joe. I texted him.

[Outside the pastor's house. Teenage girl with him. Giving her vodka. Telling her about bodily prayer. Don't use sirens, come around back.]

Fifteen minutes later, Joe appeared by my side. "I knew you'd come during the service," he whispered.

I put my finger to my lips. "He's taking her upstairs. This door is unlocked."

Soon, the protests got loud enough for Joe to hear. He went inside and crept up the stairs. I followed after unlocking the front door, my camera phone ready to shoot. Joe quietly opened the bedroom door to find a naked Pastor Dan attempting to remove the girl's underwear. She was putting up quite a fight. He was furious with lust.

"Don't fight God's will," he panted.

I took a picture, and he suddenly realized they were not alone. He deflated fast, both physically and mentally.

"Trespassing!" he yelled, trying to pull on his boxers.

The girl picked up her clothes and fled downstairs. I followed to make sure she didn't leave.

"You are safe now. Stay here."

"He's a pastor. I didn't want to, but he said it was God's will. Like a prayer." She cried bitterly.

"He's not a proper pastor," I said. "Proper pastors don't do things like that. He's a very bad man."

"Will I go to jail? Or hell? I drank vodka. He made me."

"I know. You're not in any trouble. He is."

Joe came downstairs with the pastor in handcuffs. I found it a cheering sight. "God's will, huh?" I said.

"You Jezebel, you broke into my house."

"We most certainly did not. Look, you were in such a hurry to get into her pants, you forgot to lock the door. Look. We came to interview you and heard her crying for help. Not a thing wrong with that."

"You just unlocked it."

"I came straight down to help the girl." I turned to the girl. I still hadn't asked her name. "Did you see me unlock it?"

"No," she whimpered.

Well, that all ended well. No more Pastor Dan, just Conman Dan. The church will probably disband, and all that disgusting fire and brimstone can simmer down, I hope. The only thing was, we hadn't found our killer. Dan had had the same car for eleven years, and its many dents and scratches were not compatible with a hit-and-run.

"What about renting a car?" I asked Joe a couple of days later.

"He doesn't have a credit card, believe it or not," Joe told me. "And I'm not sure you can rent a car without one. I doubt he has the cash to do it. We can check the congregation to see if anyone lent him one. But I don't think he did it. His faith wasn't real. You see, he wouldn't have cared about a girl choosing a pagan faith. It was all for show. This isn't the first time he's been caught molesting young girls. It happened in Ohio about four years ago."

We went to see the Blackstones again.

"She doesn't want to see you," Mr. Blackstone told us. "She doesn't want to see anyone, even me."

"I'm sorry. The pastor's arrest must have come as a shock."

"She doesn't believe he's done anything wrong. Says the police have it in for him."

"Why on earth would the police have it in for him?"

"Lord knows. Not talking sense to her. She just goes on about evil, and pagan forces, and so on."

I had a sudden inspiration. "Mr. Blackstone, do you each have a car?"

"Yes, two old Fords. Why?

"Have you had any trouble with either of them?"

"Well, someone dented my wife's car last summer in the Giant parking lot. She was very upset when she got home. Said she didn't see who did it. She wouldn't even call the police. It's right there, outside. She just got back from her sister's. We've only got a one-car garage."

Mrs. Blackstone suddenly appeared at her husband's shoulder. "Get out of my house, you godless pagan lovers!"

"Not before I've had a look at your car," Joe answered.

"No one is going to interfere with my car. I know my rights." Her face was practically purple with rage, her mouth horribly twisted and wet with drool.

"Is that your car?"

"No."

"I can soon get a warrant."

"No need for that," Mr. Blackstone said. "She's not been right since she found out about Molly going to that pagan church."

"May we come in?"

"Please do."

Joe made a phone call, asking for more officers, scene of crime personnel, and a tow truck. Mrs. Blackstone rushed upstairs.

"I'd like to see the kitchen, please."

A knife holder was almost full. Joe looked in the dishwasher. Empty.

"There seems to be a chef's knife missing."

"She said it broke, so she threw it away." Mr. Blackstone looked as if he were about to faint. He could see where this was going. "Surely you don't think ... her own daughter?"

"I think she is unbalanced," Joe said.

The backup crew was soon there, so I made a hasty exit through the back door. I could do without the exposure. So religious fanaticism led to a mother murdering her own daughter. It happens. Religion can be a dangerous weapon.

Lin leaned forward and cut herself another slice of cake. I hadn't finished my first slice yet.

17

Acouple of boxy black vans picked us up from Vienna's international airport and drove us to the Grunewald's estate. Auntie, now back to her seventy-ish state to match her passport, had a little trouble climbing into the high vehicle. As usual, I gazed out of the window, determined not to miss anything. We traveled through the city past impressive old edifices, as well as unimpressive contemporary creations, before gradually emerging from heavy traffic onto quieter roads. Now, I practically drooled over picturesque houses adorned with riotous window boxes, wide grassy meadows dotted with herds of cows, all backed by rugged snow-capped mountains purpled by the haze of distance.

Rose was in the car behind us, sandwiched between her brother and sister, with her father sitting opposite. Lin and Auntie Peggy rode with me. One car would have sufficed for seven passengers but for the mountains of luggage. Lin had warned me not to pack light. It might be summer, but it was not the sort of summer heat we were used to in Maryland, and I would find the mornings and evenings chilly. In addition, the Grunewalds may well take us to places that necessitated formal dress. When we'd emerged from baggage claim into the bright sun and a chilly breeze early in the morning, I was glad of my warm jacket.

When we turned through the ornate iron gates onto the tree-lined driveway that supposedly led to their mansion, I wondered where on earth it was. All I could see was parkland. My question was answered when the driveway took a sharp bend to the left, and there it was ahead—a mansion that some might call a palace. The façade comprised windows set deep into stone walls with intricate carvings above each, a massive brass-studded front door that looked as if it could withstand a canon's onslaught, and a flight of worn stone steps leading to a wide terrace. Those steps would test Auntie's stamina. It looked impressive, but cold—not only metaphorically, but literally. Those stone walls could never absorb enough heat during the day to do anything but radiate chill. I shivered in anticipation of a frigid sojourn. The children wouldn't care, wouldn't even notice. Lin and Hunter wouldn't, either, as gods could survive the harshest conditions. It was Auntie and I who would suffer.

Herr and Frau Grunewald waited for us on the terrace, their faces full of welcome and delight.

"Where is Gerda?" Rose asked when she joined me by the cars. She'd been so excited about seeing her friend again.

"I expect she's inside," I said.

Sven rushed over to help Auntie up the steep stairs. Rose's little legs struggled, so Hunter carried her. Thankful for the railing, I toiled up, trying my best to look agile. The mansion was clearly very old, so I couldn't help thinking with sympathy of those ladies of yesteryear who had mounted these same steps in tight corsets under heavy, voluminous ballgowns and capes.

"Welcome, welcome," Herr Grunewald cried.

His wife greeted us warmly, clearly very happy to see Auntie, whom she took by the arm. "Come, Peggy, you must sit by the fire." They chatted in German as they walked down the hallway. We all followed to enter a huge living room—salon, I suppose—bedecked with blue and cream brocade-upholstered antique furniture and heavily framed oil paintings. The most welcome amenity was a fireplace tall enough to stand in, that hosted a roaring fire.

Auntie was seated in an armchair next to the hearth. I sat in one opposite, stretching my hands toward the blaze. Rose rushed over and sat in my lap. She looked sad.

A maid rolled in a trolley of pots of coffee and cake. Frau Grunewald said something to Auntie, who turned to me.

"Gretchen said there is hot chocolate as well as coffee. Some cakes, too."

The idea of Rose drinking hot chocolate on such fine furniture sent chills up my spine. I looked around and saw a sturdy table and chairs by the window.

"Rose, would you like to sit at the table and have some nice hot chocolate?" I asked her.

"I want to sit on your lap."

"I'm afraid that's not possible. If you spilled your drink on the chair, it would spoil it."

"Come on, Rose. I'd like some hot chocolate, too. Let's sit over there together. Just us two." Margareta took her by the hand and led her over there. Margareta had a commanding presence, and Rose seldom bothered to argue with her.

"Where is Gerda?" she asked Herr Grunewald on the way.

"She is with her tutor. She is learning English. Perhaps she can practice with you, Rose. She will be here in twenty minutes or so."

Rose laughed and clapped her hands. "I will be so happy to see her again."

"*Ja, ja.* She is also looking forward to playing with you." He rocked back and forth on his heels, hands clasped behind his back. Half-moon glasses perched on his nose, adding to his grandfatherly appearance.

We all drank our warm beverages and enjoyed pastries oozing with cream or chocolate, or sometimes both, before being shown to our rooms.

"Walk around the house or gardens as you prefer," Herr Grunewald told us. "Or rest in your rooms until lunch at one o'clock. We have a visit planned to the Belvedere this afternoon, where they have a marvelous collection of Klimt paintings." He spread his hands as if in apology. "Forgive me, I have planned nothing for tonight. I know that jetlag will make you get tired early. But tomorrow, the opera!"

I'd seen a few pictures of Klimt paintings and liked them well enough. But opera didn't thrill me, and the idea of Rose sitting through a performance quietly was the epitome of wishful thinking.

I said, "That is very generous, Herr Grunewald. Rose is rather young to sit through an opera, though. I hope she won't spoil it for everyone."

"Oh, we didn't think it would be to her taste. Our nanny will stay with the girls. She has quite good English, I think. We have some movies they might like. And please, call me Hubert."

I hadn't met the nanny and hoped she was up to the challenge.

"Most kind," I said. I guess the mention of a nanny made me act formal.

We all went upstairs. Rose and I had a lovely, big bedroom overlooking the park. It was furnished with an old mahogany bed, chest, and wardrobe. The drapes and bedcovers had cream backgrounds strewn with roses in all shades of pink, nestled in abundant leaves. We even had a fireplace. Rose kneeled on the padded window seat and looked out while I unpacked.

"There's a Bambi," she cried.

I went over, and, sure enough, a deer grazed not far from the house and was soon joined by four or five more. A black dog chased after them, barking furiously until it finally obeyed the harsh commands of its master and turned back.

"That's a bad doggie," Rose said, frowning.

"It's natural for a dog to chase other creatures in its territory."

"Sam wouldn't do that."

"Unless he was scared of the deer, he probably would. Haven't you seen how he barks at dogs, rabbits, or even crows he sees on the lawn through the glass doors at home?"

"Yes, I suppose so."

"I'm nearly unpacked. Have you used the bathroom?"

"I have, Mama. It's lovely in there, isn't it? I can't wait to have a bath."

The bathroom walls were tiled with vivid portrayals of fantastical creatures and florid garden scenes from floor to ceiling. The claw-foot tub was intended to accommodate the largest of men or an amorous couple. Too bad I couldn't indulge.

After freshening up, we put on our coats and ventured downstairs.

"Rose, Rose, *kom her!*"

Gerda was waiting by the front door with a young woman who looked like a bodybuilder. She was clad in athletic gear so tight that her arm and leg muscles forced definitive bulges in the stretchy fabric. A wide smile transformed her rather masculine face to a softer appearance as she prepared to greet us, before settling back to its severe mien after fulfilling her social duty.

The girls rushed toward each other and hugged and danced around in an ecstatic reunion. It was strange considering how little they actually knew each other. Rose didn't speak German, or Gerda English—unless the tutor had worked wonders.

"I am Anna, Gerda's nanny," she said, holding out her hand to me. We shook hands.

"I am very pleased to meet you. Your English is excellent. I'm afraid I don't know any German."

"Thank you. Now then, young ladies. Time to take our walk. Come along. *Auf gehts.*" Her tone brooked no dissent. Yes, she'd be up to the challenge.

Margareta came downstairs as Anna opened the door.

"Going for a walk?" she asked. "May I join you?"

"Of course," said Anna without much enthusiasm. What was her problem? Maybe the fact that Margareta was a beauty and she, while attractive, couldn't compare.

We moved down a concrete path to the side of the terrace, which led to a winding ramp that took us down to ground level. I was relieved not to have to carry Rose down the steep steps.

"That's nice that we don't have to use the steps," I told Anna.

"Yes, they are too steep for the little ones. Herr Grunewald's mother lived here until she died last year. She was in a wheelchair for many years, so his father, who is also dead, had this ramp built."

We set off at such a brisk pace that I wondered if the girls would keep up. They fell back at times, then ran to catch up, giggling and holding hands all the way.

"I am pleased to meet you," Gerda told Rose, again and again.

"I am pleased to meet you, too," Rose answered.

They seemed to find this hilarious. After a while, we did, too.

Margareta said something in German to Gerda. Then, "I am glad you are my friend."

Gerda finally got it right.

"Now say, 'I am glad you are my friend, too,' in German." She said the words slowly, with Rose repeating them until she got it right.

Rose was delighted. "I can speak German! Anna, will you help me speak some German?"

"Of course. We will have our first lesson tomorrow morning. You will learn German, and Gerda some English. I do not know why Herr Grunewald brings that tutor. I can do just as well."

Margareta and I exchanged a glance, amused by this fit of pique. Anna's English was very correct, so she had a point. We had almost reached the shore of a small lake where a wooden rowboat bobbed and strained at the rope that tied it to a stake by a short jetty.

"I like to swim here," said Anna. "Gerda is not allowed because it is too cold. She should not be so spoiled, but it is her mother's wish. Her father is less indulgent." Her tone was contemptuous when speaking of the mother, softer when referencing the father. I wondered about her ambitions and began to like her less.

"Are there a lot of weeds?" I asked. "They can be dangerous to swimmers in freshwater."

"Nothing of consequence. They have never bothered me."

A few ducks swam toward us, clearly hoping for handouts.

"Mama, can we feed the ducks?" Rose asked.

"I'm afraid I didn't bring anything. I didn't realize there was a lake."

"Tomorrow, duckies, we'll bring you something tomorrow," she told them. They squawked and quacked while paddling away.

The sun finally emerged and started to do its job. I took off my jacket and tied it around my waist. I enjoyed the peaceful landscape while Gerda and Rose amused each other, and Margareta and Anna chatted, switching between German and English. They seemed to be on good enough terms after a few awkward exchanges of the "Where are you from" variety. By the time we got back to the house, the girls were flagging, and I was more than ready for lunch.

Anna took the girls upstairs to have lunch in the nursery. We sat around a formally set dining table and enjoyed pea soup, a peppery hare stew, and a fat apple tart with thick cream. I thought the stew was very tasty until I found out what it was. In my mind, a hare was like a rabbit, and bunnies were nearly on the same level as cats, and eating cats was abhorrent. I couldn't finish my portion. The dark bread rolls slathered with sweet butter were fragrant and delicious, though, so I ate a couple of those. I sat next to Hunter.

"Lin is very quiet," I whispered to him.

"She feels uneasy. I do not know why."

"Very odd."

"Indeed."

After lunch, I reconnected with Rose upstairs. We got ready and put on our coats. Anna would also come so she could take the children outside if they got restless. The ride back to the city was on a slightly different route, one that passed houses less quaint than on the roads we had ridden on before. They were certainly neat and clean, with beautiful gardens, but not the sort of quaint my touristy heart craved.

The Belvedere Museum turned out to be a baroque palace surrounded by gorgeous gardens and elegant sculptures. I caught a glimpse of a round ornamental pond in front, in the middle of which two stone figures were either flirting or killing each other—I wasn't close enough to make out which. Hubert explained that it was once the summer residence of Prince Eugene of Savoy. We would only go to the Upper Belvedere, the palace with the green roof, as also visiting the Lower Belvedere—the one with a red roof— would probably prove too much for the little girls and Peggy. I didn't dare look at Auntie. She would not have appreciated being lumped in with little girls. The chauffeur dropped us off at the entrance. More stairs.

We tramped around for an hour before we came to the Klimt collection, which enchanted me. I think most people have seen reproductions of Klimt paintings on birthday cards, calendars, and cocktail napkins, but the real paintings look quite different. They shimmer. Lin stood by me as I gazed at "The Kiss."

"The real paintings look quite different from reproductions. I love them," I said.

"Yes, they are very beautiful," she answered in a flat tone.

"What's the matter with you?" I asked. "Don't these paintings move you at all?"

"Yes, they would if I were not so disturbed by our host."

"Whatever do you mean?"

"I'll explain more fully later. But I knew his great-great-whichever grandfather. He was an evil man, a psychopath. I didn't remember until we got to the house. I wondered why Hubert seemed so familiar when we met in Copenhagen but couldn't quite pin it down. Of course, the ancestor had a beard, like most men of his day, but otherwise, they look very much alike. I hope they are not alike in character. And there's a portrait of the old man in the hallway. It quite took me aback."

Hubert strolled over. "Are you ladies admiring our most famous painter? You were having the most serious discussion, and all in whispers."

"The guards in these museums get so awfully cross if you talk too loudly," Lin said, flashing him one of her devastating smiles. "Yes, we were admiring the Klimts. Mary was just telling me that she's seen so many reprints, but standing in front of the real thing is another matter entirely."

"Oh, yes," I said. "They have an aura about them that captivates me."

"I am glad you are happy with our little expedition."

He smiled and strode into the next room. His smile seemed sinister, but I'd probably been swayed by Lin's revelation.

"Lin, where are the girls?".

"I think Anna took them down to the gardens. They are very extensive, you know."

"When we've seen all the Klimts, let's join them. Where's Hunter?"

"I think he went out, too. Oh, no, here he is."

"Look at this painting. How it glows under the light," I said.

He stood with one arm around each of us, looking at the painting, his head tilted to one side. "It is romantic in the most extraordinary way," he said. "I like it very much."

We wandered around to see the others, chatting happily. Hubert did not reappear. We went out, down a flight of marble steps, and started to walk around.

"I have a pamphlet that should show us where the prettiest flowerbeds are," I said, digging into my tote to find it. "I wonder where Auntie got to?"

"She and Gretchen went to the Klimt rooms first, I think," Lin said. "My guess is, they found a pretty place out here to sit and chat."

We didn't have to go far to find them. There were two benches opposite each other, so we sat down, too.

"Rose and Gerda are nearby, just over there," Auntie said, pointing at some tall hedges. "I hear them squealing from time to time. That young lady with them is quite the martinet."

"That she is," I said. "I was wondering about her being able to deal with Rose, but I needn't have worried."

As if on cue, I heard squeals and laughter as Rose sprinted around a tall hedge, closely followed by Gerda. They both collapsed on the grass, giggling. Where was Anna?

"Mama, Herr Grunewald came and found us. He said if we didn't run fast enough, he'd catch us and cook us for dinner."

Gerda clearly told her mother the same thing. Her mother was not amused. I could see her point. Neither Hubert nor Anna had appeared.

Lin's sudden intake of breath reminded me of what she'd just told me. I hadn't packed the tape recorder, so we'd have to use my phone. I really wanted to hear the story, but would we have enough privacy? It wasn't something Rose should listen to. I thought it might be best to keep a close eye on my daughter while we were here. She went to sit next to Auntie for a cuddle, and Gerda did the same with her mother.

After another ten minutes or so, Hubert and Anna rounded the corner, strolling nonchalantly as if nothing was wrong. Maybe it wasn't. They both looked impeccable.

"We were taking a look at the roses," Hubert said. "Their collection is quite magnificent. They have a few I have not yet heard of. I will order some.

"I am also fond of roses," Auntie said. "Especially the scented ones."

"I will take you to my walled rose garden. They have excelled themselves this year."

Another intake of breath from Lin. I had to get that story.

"I would love that," she said.

"You know, you seem familiar somehow," Hubert said, standing in front of Auntie. "It has been nagging me since we met last Christmas in Denmark."

"I don't think so. It was my first trip to Denmark, and this is my first time in Austria. Where could we have met?" Auntie looked up at him with a faint smile and a puzzled look.

Was she lying? She was artful enough that I couldn't tell.

"Did you ever work for your government?" Hubert persisted.

"Well, yes, but only as a secretary in the Department of Agriculture," she replied. "Nothing special."

"Ah, well. Perhaps it is time to go back to the car. I think you are all getting tired. Perhaps a little nap before dinner?"

"How thoughtful you are, that sounds perfect," Auntie said in a gushing manner. "I get tired so easily since my stroke." *You were lying.*

Just after I put Rose to bed for a nap, Lin knocked on the door and slid inside without waiting.

"Is there anywhere we can talk?" she asked.

"Rose fell asleep almost immediately. There's a little alcove that should prove private enough."

The entryway to the bathroom was a strange comma-shaped space with a small table and two chairs set before a window in the widest part. I thought it a strange place for anyone to choose to relax, but it suited our purposes admirably.

"Turn on your phone."

Tape 9,
Volume 4

This happened a couple of hundred years or so ago. I forget exactly when. Hunter had run off with a young girl he met in Paris. I knew she had family in this area, so I came looking. I stayed in Vienna for a few weeks, and socialized with the aristocratic set, thanks to the aristocratic title I'd invented for myself. It didn't take long before I met a woman who knew this girl's family and took me to a dinner at their townhouse. Since I seemed the right sort of person, they invited me to their home in the country, where they would be hosting a ball. I was eager to go, as I hoped the girl would be there. She was not in town. As it turns out, she was not in the country, either. I made polite conversation with her mother about our families, and she told me she had one son and one daughter. Her son was an army officer, and her daughter was away at present. When I asked if her daughter would be away for long, she confided in me the real story. The girl had been promised to a distant cousin and was suddenly refusing the match because she had formed an attachment to a stranger she met in Paris. Just the week before, they had sent her to a convent in the mountains until she came to her senses. Poor Hunter! Either he'd gone back home to London, tail between his legs, or he'd go after another adventure. About twenty at the time, he could be hard to keep track of.

Anyway, I met the former Herr Grunewald at the ball when he joined a few guests in my circle. He mentioned that his wife was unwell and, sadly, could not attend. I found him charming. We danced and chatted quite a bit before he asked me if I would like to visit. He would like to show me his art collection, and his wife would enjoy taking tea with a guest. It sounded innocent enough.

Later that evening, I joined a group of older ladies, who sat in a cluster of chairs in a corner just off the dance floor. They were kind enough to switch to English for my benefit—I chose not to tell them I'd become quite proficient in German while in Vienna. They spoke in hushed tones about the disappearance of a number of local girls over the past few months, most of them maids. No one had seen a trace of them after they disappeared, supposedly after going to bed. At first, they assumed they'd sneaked out to meet an admirer, but after the first two or three stayed missing, they feared the worst. I wondered if I should try to solve the case, then immediately squelched the thought. Now that the Hunter problem was cleared up, I was here to have fun, not to chase after errant serving girls.

A vast buffet dinner was served on silver platters that shone under the chandeliers and sconces. I loaded my plate in a way that invited critical glances—it wasn't ladylike to eat like a starving laborer. Since I would be unlikely to see these people again, I didn't care. The house was so full of lively people, all chattering like magpies, and very overheated on this July evening. I decided to take my food into the garden, where a number of stone benches were scattered around, cooled by a gentle breeze.

It wasn't long before Hubert—for that was also his name—appeared in front of me.

"May I join you, Countess? After a few hours, I find these affairs a little too noisy for my taste."

"Of course," I said. I knew he must have been watching me and liked the idea. "It became too hot in there, and, as you say, too noisy."

"If you have had enough of the ball, we could visit my art collection now."

"Now, so late? Wouldn't that inconvenience Frau Grunewald?"

"Not at all. She retires early and takes a powder to help her sleep. We can stroll around the collection and be back here in no time."

"Very well. I am a little tired of this. The old ladies are talking non-stop about some missing maids. They seem to think they've been lured away and murdered."

Hubert laughed. "What nonsense. They probably got a better job somewhere else. They'd have to run away because they wouldn't have been allowed to leave."

"Let's go, then. I'm in the mood for a little art." I smiled widely, which usually reels them in.

We got into his small carriage, which waited conveniently close by and sat close together as the coachman whipped the horses into a canter, arriving in only five minutes. We entered the house by a side door on the lower level, which Hubert opened with a long iron key he fished out of an inner pocket. I assumed he wished for privacy. This was a dark place of shadowy corridors, lit only by the occasional sconce. Hubert plucked a torch from one of the holders and led the way.

"I have a special room down here where I keep the most precious pieces in my collection. They are too valuable to be left in the open."

I began to feel a little uneasy. Hubert had started to breathe heavily and looked feverish. After a few twists and turns, we came to a piece of furniture that looked like a Chinese cupboard, given the jade figures adorning the doors and sides. He pushed it to one side without effort—clearly, the wheels had been oiled recently—and pressed a slight indentation in the wall. A door swung open, and he beckoned me to enter. The first thing I saw was a raised bed with wrist restraints. The second was a shelf containing jars of something I couldn't quite make out, some suspended in a murky liquid, while others floated in a clearer solution.

The door shut quietly behind me—it felt more like a slam, given the circumstances. Obviously, I had walked willingly into a trap. Well, as long as he didn't disable me with some sort of anesthetic, which would weaken me dangerously, I could deal with him.

"So, there is no art collection?"

"Not down here. I have some good pieces, but they are all in the public reception rooms."

"What are those things in the bottles?" I strolled over to look more closely.

"They are human hearts. I am interested in how the heart differs from one type of woman to another. Is a common girl's heart smaller or bigger than that of a noblewoman? Does it make any difference if she is in love? It is very interesting, you know."

"I imagine it is. I suppose you have enough examples of serving girls here. How many of these are noble?"

"None. There is too much fuss made when one goes missing. I have not yet managed to entice a noble heart here."

"Until now."

"You seem unnaturally calm."

"I am a noblewoman. That is our way."

I turned to face him. "What do you do to them, exactly?"

"I make love to them. At first, some of them are flattered, others are scared. I usually end up having to secure them to the bed. As I come toward climax, I strangle them. Watching their eyes bulge, then glaze over, is the ultimate thrill. This room is soundproof. No one can hear their outbursts—or mine. Of course, they are dead by the time I open their chests. The first one I didn't dispatch first, but it was too messy with all that spurting blood."

"Yes, most inconvenient. Where do you dispose of them afterward?"

"In the lake, in a sack filled with stones. My coachman helps move them."

"You are a very evil man. Insane, certainly."

His face twisted with rage, and he lunged at me. I jumped to one side, and he pivoted to find me behind him. He tried to punch me and screamed when I snapped his arm. He darted toward the hearth, no doubt to grab the poker. I got there first and clobbered him with it. He muttered a little, as he wasn't completely out, but offered no resistance when I undressed him. After dumping him on the bed, I locked the wrist cuffs and discovered shackles for the ankles, too. I briefly considered castration, but he'd already pointed out how messy cutting into living flesh could be. I planned to go back to the ball, so getting splotches of blood on my gown was out of the question.

He was a tall man, so I had to bend his knees to position them properly. I knew there must be a key to unlock the restraints, so I searched the pockets of his clothes. I found several keys and pocketed all of them. I'd dispose of them later.

The door opened easily, as the knob on the inside was not concealed. I heard a moan as I left. I closed the door by pressing the outside indentation and moved the cabinet back in front.

"Where is he?"

I cursed my carelessness. The coachman emerged from the shadows, which loomed a lot larger than he did. A tall, thin man, his weasel-like face looked brutish.

"Where is my master, woman?"

"How dare you address me like that! Your master is busy in his room. Please drive me back to the ball."

"No, I do not believe I will. What are you up to?"

I sighed. "You are being rather a bore, you know."

He didn't see the blow coming, which broke his neck. I had to open up the damned room again and roll in the coachman. Such a nuisance.

"Help me, I'll give you anything you want," came a feeble cry from the bed.

"Your coachman has joined you. He is dead. You will join him in a couple of weeks. It's known as atonement."

Hubert started to weep like a toddler. I locked up and left. The carriage was still by the side door we entered through, so I drove it most of the road back to the ball and ran the rest of the way. I walked nonchalantly in from the garden and mingled again. I don't think anyone noticed I'd been missing because there was such a crowd.

After everyone left, my hostess remarked how Herr Grunewald had left without taking his leave.

"You talked with him a good deal, my dear. Was he unwell?"

"I filled my plate but did not see him in the dining hall. I was feeling a little overheated and took my food to the garden to cool off. It was so lovely out there that I stayed quite a while. You know, the scent of your roses is quite intoxicating. I came in for a cool drink and chatted with those older ladies sitting by the edge of the dance floor. They were talking about some missing maids."

"Oh, yes. Nasty business. Another went missing only a couple of days ago."

"I hope they are found alive and well."

"I doubt it. That sort of girl doesn't have the brains to keep out of trouble. They need to be kept on a tight leash."

That cut to the quick. Of course, I can get out of trouble more easily than most, but had proved naïve, even with all my experience of the world. I left the chateau a couple of days later. By that time, a great hue and cry had been raised about the missing Herr Grunewald and his coachman. I wonder if they are still there?

I sat without moving, lost in thought. I found myself pondering these thorny issues of justice served all too often after listening to Lin's stories. She saved more girls from harm, but she killed the coachman without compunction and left the murderer to endure a horrible, lingering death.

"You are shocked, Mary. You know he would have killed again and again. He had to be stopped. The wealthy were not easy to prosecute in those days. And if he had been found guilty, he would have been executed. Now, I have to know what's in that room."

"Be careful, Lin. You don't know if this Hubert is dangerous."

"I think he may be. Just a feeling I have. And if that room no longer contains the jars and skeletons, it means someone else knows about it. And those stories of girls going missing again. I have to find out."

"Knowing you, you'll do it, no matter what I say. Will you at least tell Hunter?"

"I haven't decided. He can be clumsy, but useful. Maybe I'll have him lurk in the hallway as my lookout."

"You know, he asked Auntie if they'd met before. She acted all innocent. But I know her. She was lying."

"Let's ask her."

"Mama?"

I got up to go to the bed. "I'm here, darling, talking to Linnie."

"Is it dinnertime?"

The first gong sounded. "I guess it is. We'd better get dressed."

I still felt a little shell-shocked after hearing Lin's story. I don't know why, because she'd told me hair-raising stories before. But this new reminder of her otherness, not only in terms of her godly powers but of her and Hunter's approach to solving problems, jolted me.

And now I was one of them.

18

We enjoyed a pleasant dinner that evening, less heavy than lunch. I guess that was their way, and perhaps healthier, too. The girls ate with us this time. The occasional giggle erupted from their end, only to be squelched by a stern glance from Anna. Rose got the picture and minded her manners in a way she had never been required to before. I noticed her observing the adults when they picked up a certain utensil, and how they laid them on the plate when finished. The girls spoke only when spoken to. This was the stiff kind of etiquette I wouldn't care for in my own home, but it was good for Rose to be exposed to it and know how to behave in a more formal environment. I must admit, the same went for me, too.

Anna took the girls upstairs after we'd finished. She told me they'd be allowed to play in the nursery for half an hour before she gave them a bath and put them to bed. Rose could show her where her nightie was. I hoped that Gerda's bathtub was as fanciful as ours, as Rose was fixated on it. Well, we'd be staying for a week, so there'd be plenty of time.

We spent a pleasant evening chatting and listening to music. Hubert had installed a fabulous sound system with hidden speakers in several areas of the room. It sounded as if we were sitting in the middle of an orchestra. He favored Schubert, to my relief. When he started to talk about his newest toy, I feared an evening riding with the Valkyries.

Both Auntie and I retired early, at around ten. The others stayed on. We were both still jetlagged, Auntie more so than I. We climbed the stairs carefully and slowly.

"Auntie, there's a private little nook in my room where we won't disturb Rose. I need to tell you something that Lin told me."

"All right."

We tiptoed into my room. Rose was fast asleep. Anna sat on a chair beside the bed, reading. She closed her book and rose when we entered.

"Rose was afraid to be alone. I could have put her in bed in Gerda's room, but I thought you might not like that."

"It is so kind of you to stay with her. I would have come up sooner if I'd known. I'm so sorry it took up your entire evening."

"It does not matter. I would have only been reading, anyway." She left the room.

"I think I should buy her a gift before we leave," I told Auntie. "It might offend her if I give her money."

"Good idea. Let's sit down."

We sat in the little nook outside the bathroom. I told her everything Lin told me. She didn't bat an eyelid.

"You don't seem surprised."

"No, this one has blood on his hands, missing girls or not. He spied for the Russians during the Cold War. I trapped him once in Berlin, but he escaped. That's why he thought he'd seen me before. After that incident, he disappeared. We didn't know who he really was. He had a heavy beard in those days, and was young and agile, too. As soon as I saw that portrait of his ancestor in the hallway when we arrived, I knew. But we got his fingerprints. I alerted my former employer, and they are investigating."

"They are so kind to us. It feels bad to accept all this hospitality under the circumstances. Do you think his wife knows?"

"She is clearly a lot younger than him—and look how young his only child is. They probably haven't been married more than ten years."

"Lin says she is going to investigate that secret room in the basement. I hope she doesn't get caught. I also hope she takes Hunter."

"She'll be all right. I just don't want him spooked before my people do what they need to do."

"I'll tell her in the morning."

But the next morning, Lin did not appear at the breakfast table. Gretchen seemed ill at ease, as did Anna, who spoke unnecessarily sharply to the girls on more than one occasion. They looked at each other in surprise and kept quiet for the rest of the meal. I raised my eyebrows at Hunter in a silent question. He pretended not to notice. I knew Lin had gone ahead with her plan. Auntie's bland expression made me wonder what she knew. I ate more fragrant dark rolls with creamy butter and what must have been local strawberry jam than I should have. No one was taking any notice of me, after all.

Hunter disappeared immediately after breakfast. I was tempted to go up to their room but thought better of it. They might have things to sort out, and I'd only get in the way. Anna took the girls upstairs to play as rain pummeled the dry gardens. Auntie looked at me and indicated with a little tilt of her head and a jerk of her chin that I should leave. I decided to go to my room and wait. At least I had my

Kindle and was in the middle of a spy thriller that was perhaps exciting enough to take my mind off things.

I reclined on the bed and propped myself up with pillows to read. Predictably, I dozed off, only being awakened by the first gong for lunch. Nearly one o'clock already. Time to freshen up quickly and head downstairs.

Gretchen sat at the head of the table with admirable dignity, given her puffy eyes. Auntie sat next to her. Where were Sven and Margareta? And Lin and Hunter? Worry gnawed at my gut.

"Auntie, where are the others?"

"Sven and Margareta took one of the cars into Vienna. They wanted to see an opera, so will try to get tickets."

"Oh, the opera. I completely forgot we were supposed to go last night. What happened?"

"I'm afraid Hubert has disappeared. He went to bed as usual, and when Gretchen woke up, he wasn't there. She hasn't seen him since."

"Good heavens. I'm so sorry, Gretchen. You must be very worried." Auntie translated. Gretchen tried to smile and nodded her head as tears rolled down her cheeks.

"There will be other events shortly," Auntie told me quietly. Gretchen didn't notice.

We ate sparingly, even though the lamb was so tender and delicious. Tension can wreck the appetite.

We had just finished our crème brûlée when the maid entered, followed by a couple of heavyset men in suits, one close to retirement age and a much younger fellow. Gretchen rose.

There was a terse exchange in German before Auntie entered the conversation. Gretchen looked shell-shocked.

"They are looking for Hubert," she told me.

"I assumed so. But do we know where he is?"

"No. We must find Lin and Hunter."

"Ask Gretchen if she knows about that Chinese cupboard."

Auntie asked her and said something to the men. They all moved toward a door in the hallway, just before the kitchen, and I followed.

"You will stay here," the older man rasped at me.

"I must help my aunt. She is elderly and had a stroke recently."

"Very well."

Auntie looked daggers at me. She detested that being brought up. Besides, her current frailty was only temporary. I'd meant to ask her how she did it, and how she planned to roll back the years once this was over. This was not the time to raise such questions.

We descended the worryingly narrow stairs and took several turns until reaching a dark corridor with doors on each side. I found a light switch to the right of the bottom step. After a few minutes, we came to a small square hall, where a beautiful Chinese cupboard sat against a wall, as did Lin and Hunter, along with a young woman wearing a simple cotton dress. They all stood up.

"Where is Herr Grunewald?" asked the same man. I guess the young man was so junior that he wasn't encouraged to speak.

"We will show you," Hunter said.

He swung the cupboard away from the wall and pressed the indentation Lin had described. A concealed door opened silently to the sound of a very angry man, no doubt cursing in German. We all filed in. Hubert lay on the bed, restrained as Lin had described. He rattled his shackles as he struggled. The two agents moved to face him. His white face was a picture of horror after the senior officer spoke to him.

Lin produced a key and set him free, upon which the officers applied their own handcuffs. Poor Gretchen sank to the floor, sobbing uncontrollably.

I looked at the shelves, which were lined with glass jars with things floating in them.

"I suppose you killed those girls?" I asked him. "Just like your ancestor. What bits of them did you save?"

"What is this?" asked the young officer.

Lin answered this time. "The male line of his family seems to have a tradition of kidnapping and murdering young local girls. I believe you will find their remains in the lake. These trophies give new meaning to the concept of family heirlooms," she said, gesturing to the jars.

Hunter said, "By the way, Herr Grunewald's chauffeur is further up the corridor. He is dead. Broken neck. He tried to attack my wife, so I punched him. His head smashed against the wall."

The two agents looked at each other, clearly at a loss for words.

I went over to the jars. "These are not hearts," I said. "I don't know what they are."

"Wombs, you stupid woman. It is very interesting to see how they differ from one cow to another. I only used women who should never reproduce because they are too stupid. One of them is yours, Gretchen. It's the big one because it got stretched by Gerda."

Gretchen, hysterical by now, yelled something at him. Auntie told me later she revealed that Hubert had forced her to have a hysterectomy after Gerda was born. One of his friends performed the operation. I felt deep pity for her degradation at the hands of this animal.

After one of the agents warned us to leave the room alone so that the police could thoroughly examine it, Hubert was led away, stumbling and trembling.

We followed, a straggle of dispirited witnesses to the evil of this once noble family—well, maybe noble wasn't quite the right word. Lin held the young woman's upper arm in a firm grip.

Anna stood in the front hall, holding the children's hands. Gerda's mouth gaped when she saw her father in handcuffs.

"He will never hit us again, Gerda," Gretchen said (as Auntie told me later).

The child smiled, which shocked me. "*Auf Wiedersehn,* Papa," she said happily and waved him out of the door. He turned his head away from his daughter.

Before they went down the steps to the army jeep, he turned back to Anna. "Tell them how you found the girls for me," he shouted—in English, for some reason.

Anna dropped the girls' hands and made a run for it. Lin gave chase, as did the silent officer. Hunter grinned and didn't bother to join in. Anna didn't have much hope of making her escape. Sure enough, Lin rounded the corner at a run, dragging Anna in a headlock while the young agent trotted behind, casting embarrassed glances at his superior.

We all went back inside and sat in the living room, Gerda snuggling up with her mother on one side, and Rose with Auntie on the other. Auntie rang the bell and ordered afternoon tea, which didn't seem to faze the maid. She conversed softly with Gretchen, who was beginning to perk up.

"Gretchen wants you all to know that she had no idea Hubert was bringing those girls here. He made her take sleeping pills some nights. Now she knows why. He was a cruel man who hit her often and taunted her about her looks and stupidity. He'd started to hit Gerda lately, too."

A female police officer soon arrived to take charge of the young woman, who had almost been Hubert's latest victim. She'd been sitting with us in the salon on an upright chair in one corner without uttering a word, gazing straight ahead, expressionless, hands clasped on her lap. She was probably in shock ... and no wonder.

It wasn't long before a stream of police officers in white overalls and various kits paraded in and out. I showed them the way the first time, before leaving the door ajar and letting them get on with it. I guess a different team dragged the lake. Hunter and Lin whispered to each other occasionally but otherwise kept quiet. I didn't see the chauffeur being removed. Perhaps they used the side door.

"*Der hund*," Gretchen said, suddenly. Auntie translated. "Hubert has this big black dog that he keeps in one of the stables. He never lets her near it. It is very fierce. But it needs food."

"She can show us where after tea," I said. "Rose is very good with animals."

A gardener hovered around the stable door while the poor dog whined inside. It wasn't much of a life for a dog, being locked in a dark stable and only being let out now and then.

"What's the dog's name?" Rose asked Gretchen.

"It is Tor."

"Tor, boy," she called. "Are you hungry? Can I come in?"

A little yip sounded. Hunter lifted Rose and shot the bolt to the upper stable door, opening it gradually. "Hi, Tor. Can I come in and feed you? He's wagging his tail, Mama. Please open up, Papa. He won't hurt me."

The gardener brought a big bowl of dog food. Hunter opened the lower door a crack and placed the bowl just inside before opening it wide enough for Rose to enter. My heart thumped like a washing machine off its moorings as Hunter and I peered through the upper opening. The Great Dane stood in the middle of the stable, wagging his tail and making funny little noises. Rose walked up to him, put her arms around his neck, and kissed his snout.

"Come along Tor, here is your dinner." They walked together to the bowl, and she sat with her back to the wall, talking to him about her friend the fox, and how he must be missing her. Tor slurped up his food and lay beside her with his head on her lap while she stroked him and sang him a song. After a while, she got up and opened the door, holding his collar as they walked outside.

"Let's go to the little house over there. You should have a ball to play with. I'll buy you one."

I knew what would happen next. She'd demand to take Tor home. And that's just what happened. The vet was consulted, as was the American Embassy. Vaccinations were arranged and a passport issued. Yes, the dog got a passport. He would travel over to Washington with Gretchen as soon as she was allowed to leave.

Sven and Margareta came home from the city late that evening to a very different household. Gretchen had recovered from her shock sufficiently to make a number of snap decisions. She would move into the city, where Hubert owned a townhouse, and file for divorce. She would put the mansion up for sale, then visit us in Washington for an extended stay. Gerda would miss a fair amount of school, but becoming proficient in English should make up for it. And what did it matter if she had to do an extra year of school?

We stayed the rest of the week.

As I suspected, it turned out to be a little more complicated than that. All these arrangements took time. But she allowed Gerda to come home with us. Going to school, either locally or in Vienna, would have been difficult for her because all the other children would know about her father by the time September rolled around. I phoned the school, told the headmistress an edited story of the child's situation, and she agreed to admit Gerda. She could go to school in September with Rose and I'd tutor her in the English language for the rest of the summer. Gretchen would come as soon as feasible and have a break while deciding where to settle. We warned her that the United States was not overly generous with visas.

And I made sure to get Lin's story of the capture of Hubert before I left.

The morning after Hubert's arrest, Gretchen decided to walk the grounds and took the children with her. That left Lin and me free to record her experience with this Hubert. We sat in the nook outside my room's bathroom again so that the maids wouldn't overhear us.

Lin took a sip of her coffee and smoothed her skirt.

Tape 10,
Volume 4

As you now know, I decided there was no time to be wasted because I knew the security people would come knocking in a short while. Thank goodness I decided to include Hunter. I had never told him the old story before. I was so annoyed with him when I got home and found him on the *chaise longue* slurping beer and guzzling a mound of food with his hands, that I hardly spoke to him for a month. He was peeved that I hadn't told him the story before, but when I reminded him of his own mistakes at the time, he stopped arguing and started agreeing. We had to investigate.

It was around two in the morning when I heard a carriage pull up by the side of the house. Humans wouldn't have picked it up because the horses' hoofs had clearly been fitted with cloth coverings, but they let out a whinny or two. I nudged Hunter awake, and we tiptoed downstairs. I hadn't planned for Hubert to be present while I investigated the secret room, but I suspected that there was a girl to be saved.

We got to the hallway in time to see the chauffeur (who closely resembled the coachman in my previous experience down there) carrying a girl whose wrists were bound and her mouth gagged with a red scarf. Hubert pushed the cupboard aside and opened the door. They went inside. After a while, the chauffeur came out and pushed the cupboard back into place. He started off toward the door, but froze when I said, standing right behind him, *"Guten morgen."* I'd thought of trying to say something nasty in German but came up empty. He wouldn't have understood much English. He pulled back his arm to deliver a knockout punch when I delivered one of my own. The blow drove his head into the stone wall. I examined him quickly to see if he needed to be hogtied, but his neck was broken. Just desserts and all that.

Now for the girl. I went through the routine of entering the room and found Hubert with his pants down—literally. The girl was shackled like all the others, her legs spread wide in order to receive *Meinheer's* attentions.

"Good evening, Hubert. How nice to find you here having fun."

The look on his face was priceless, somewhere between acute embarrassment and murderous rage, as his reactions and facial contortions moved up and down the register. He rushed over to a desk, pulling up his pants as he hopped, skipped, and jumped. I have to admit that my heart fluttered as he opened it. Knife or revolver? I hadn't enjoyed being shot while rescuing that kidnapped girl in Great Falls. Sure enough, he pulled out a weapon. I wasn't sure what it was—bigger than a pistol, but not quite a full-blown assault weapon. Whatever it was, it threatened serious business.

"Now what will you do, little princess? Do not think I have missed some of your funny looks when you think my attention is elsewhere. I think you should offer my fish a nice tasty breakfast." Hubert tried to hold the gun still with one hand while zipping up his pants with the other. He didn't quite master either task, risking a glance down at his flies, which gave me a chance to veer sideways so the barrel was no longer pointing at my chest and grab it. He managed to resist for a few seconds. Our grip squeezed the trigger, and it went off, shooting off the left breast of a voluptuous nude statue standing by his desk. The shock of how fast it happened, so fast his brain couldn't catch up, rendered him speechless for, oh, maybe a minute.

"Everything all right, Lin?" a voice behind me asked.

"Yes, thank you, Hunter. If you would be good enough to remove this young lady from the restraints, we can put Hubert in her place."

"You meddling little witch!" Hubert shouted, his face almost purple, and voice vicious.

"Thank you," I said. "I have a question for you. Did you clear your ancestor out of this room, or was that an earlier Herr Grunewald?"

"We hand the custom down from father to son." It sounded as if he was boasting about family honor. Maybe it was in his warped mind. "I did hear that one of my ancestors was found dead on the table in here by his son. His coachman was dead on the floor, too. Fortunately, he had started to train his son before he disappeared. It took the boy a year before he remembered a couple of initiation demonstrations with his father and thought of looking down here. A nice mess to deal with." He sighed and shook his head as if recounting some sort of *faux pas* at a tea party. I surmised that Hubert wasn't at all well.

His voice turned back to vicious. "Anyway, how do you know about that?"

"My little secret," I said.

"I have connections at the highest level. You won't get away with this." His manner had become calmy autocratic.

"Where are the keys?" Hunter asked me.

"On the mantlepiece." May the gods save us. It took Hunter that long to figure out he needed keys?

The girl stood next to me now, rubbing her wrists. She said something in German that caused Hubert's face to twist back into an evil mask. He practically spat his invective at her. I didn't understand the words, but I certainly caught the spirit of his denunciation.

"Time to get Hubert into position," I told Hunter.

"Oh, no, you don't," Hubert yelled as he made a dash for the door. I ran around him and pushed him into Hunter, who lifted the man over his head and dumped him on the table.

"I will knock you out if you try to resist," Hunter told him.

He did try to resist by clawing and kicking, most of which Hunter avoided. I was proud of him for not bonking the fellow over the head. I would have done that. We left the beast as I'd left his ancestor. We took the girl upstairs to sleep, which she did surprisingly fast. Most humans would have been too traumatized to drop off like that. Hunter and I had to square our stories for the police, but after that, we managed to drop off. Hunter went down for breakfast, while I stayed up here with the girl—Eva. When I heard the security people arrive, the three of us ran downstairs to await developments.

"It all went remarkably smoothly in the end. And we saved one girl from an end too nasty to contemplate. Funny thing, though, she didn't even say goodbye."

"She looked numb to me," I said. "Maybe it was delayed shock."

"Maybe." Lin shrugged. "Humans are so unpredictable sometimes. Other times, you know exactly what they'll say or do."

"Quite. Unpredictably predictable."

"Good one, Mary."

19

The flight back was smooth. Gerda and Gretchen wept at the airport while saying their goodbyes. After Gretchen left, with many a backward look and shy waves, we went through to passport control. Hunter had a letter from Gretchen's solicitor, also signed by her, permitting her daughter to travel with Herr und Frau Hunter Thoren.

Rose and Gerda held hands all the way through to the waiting area. Gerda looked as if she feared getting lost if she let go. Poor little girl, she'd suffered cruelty and shock. As we strolled down the concourse, we came to a bookshop. I wanted to look around, so Rose took Gerda over to the children's section.

"Look, Mama, can we buy this? It's got a story in English and German."

I skimmed through it. It had charming illustrations with the story in German on the left page and English on the right. And, believe it or not, it was about a baby fox. Hunter peered over my shoulder.

"Let us buy them one each," he said.

They sat close together, comparing stories, pointing out words and matching pictures, trying out pronunciation in the different languages. Auntie weighed in from time to time, helping them understand different phrases.

"I've mostly forgotten German," Lin said. "I spoke reasonably well when I was in Austria all those years ago, but never since. I understood a lot more than I let on, though. It's amazing what you hear when people think you don't understand."

We got held up in immigration in Dulles because of questions about Gerda, but it only took about half an hour to sort out, and we were soon on our way in two separate cabs. Gerda had become a little tense again, so we decided that Auntie and I would take her back to my house. She needed to have a quiet evening and feel secure during the night. Rose suggested that since she now had a queen-sized bed, Gerda would sleep with her until she got used to her new home. That made sense.

I ordered a pizza that night. Gerda had never had it before, but took an instant liking to it, to no one's surprise. I tried to keep the girls awake with a movie, but the time difference soon got to them, and they were in bed by nine, which wasn't bad. To my relief, Gerda was too tired for tears. I left cereal out so they could help themselves in the morning. I hoped jet lag wouldn't get me up too early.

But there I was, fully awake by six. When I got downstairs, I found the girls eating toast and jam in front of the TV. Fortunately, Rose had provided napkins. Auntie came down soon after, back to her youthful forty-ish appearance. Gerda's eyes widened, but she said nothing. Auntie spoke to her softly in German.

I knew the kids would want to spend most of the day at the beach. I let them go down on their own, with strict instructions not to go into the water until I joined them. I unpacked while Auntie kept an eye on them from the patio.

I put a load in the washer and changed into my swimsuit with its coverup. I liked the idea of a morning on the beach with a good book.

I found Rose sitting on her towel with her arms around Hyndla, who made little chirping noises of ecstasy as she petted and kissed him. Sam, whom Stan had dropped off at around nine, stayed up at the house beside Auntie, enraptured by the endless tummy rubs a guilt-ridden owner feels obliged to provide. Gerda was busy digging and building. They already had a good-sized sandcastle built with many turrets adorned with seaweed and shells.

"Have you been to the seaside before?" I asked.

She looked up. "Bitte?"

Rose said something to her in German. Gerda held up two fingers. "She's been to the seaside twice, Mama."

"How come you understood her after such a short time?"

"I just said words instead of putting them together properly. I said, 'How many? Sea.' That's all. It's going to be fun talking in another language. Can I have lessons?"

"I'm going to work with Gerda on her English. She's going to your school in just six weeks, you know. I think Auntie could work with you on German. She speaks it very well."

"That will be fun. Mama, when will Sam come home?"

"Stan brought him over after you came down here. Auntie feels so guilty for leaving him that she's spoiling him rotten."

"He deserves it. He's the best dog ever. I hope he'll be friends with Tor."

"I hope so, otherwise it will be very difficult."

Finally, Gerda was satisfied with her handiwork and stood up. She walked to the water's edge. She put one foot in, and then the other. Rose joined her. They stood together holding hands for a while, watching one of the ospreys bring a fish back to the nest on their platform nearby. The chicks were almost as big as their parents now. The platform must have been fixed by a neighbor years before, about six feet offshore at low tide. The ospreys came back every year; perhaps the platform was inherited by their offspring.

Soon, the girls were jumping up and down. It seemed that Gerda was not a confident swimmer. I guess she hadn't had much practice. But Rose encouraged her, and she started to do better. Auntie joined me and had the foresight to bring a beach ball, which she tossed out to them. They were soon playing catch and splashing each other, laughing and having great fun. It was a joy to see them, especially after Gerda's sad experience.

Curiosity was eating me, though.

"Okay, how do you go back and forth like that?"

"I just think it."

"Just like that?"

"Well, it takes a while. About an hour before we were about to leave for the airport to fly to Vienna, I sat, closed my eyes, and pictured myself as I used to be. Unfortunately, I dozed off, so it didn't work. I only had about twenty minutes, so I panicked. I screwed my eyes tight and pictured what used to be my morning routine when I got up in the morning, all stiff and achy. That worked. I hated it." She snorted and went back to knitting like a furious spider weaving its web.

"And when you came back?"

"That was easy. I think this is my default setting, as it were. I only had to think of myself running up the front steps of the Grunewald's mansion, and there I was. Back to thirty-nine."

"Thirty-nine, is it?" I tried not to laugh.

"It is, missy, and don't you forget it."

"Okay, you know best, Auntie. By the way, do you remember how I volunteered to work with Gerda on her English? I must get her speaking at least a little before school starts. And Rose said she wants German lessons. Would you be willing to tutor her?"

"Absolutely. She's smart. She'll pick it up quickly enough. They do at that age."

"It's Thursday now. Why don't we start on Monday? Every morning at nine for an hour or so."

"Tell you what, let's do an hour, then we'll have them together for another thirty minutes. Get them to communicate with each other in the two languages."

"That's a great idea."

"We're invited to the castle for dinner. I think I'll spend the night. Dora's getting a bit frazzled between looking after the baby and everything else." Auntie was always looking out for Dora.

"Should we speak to Lin? At least Dora doesn't have to do any cleaning now that Lin's hired a maid service."

Auntie thought for a moment. "I'll have to keep a close eye on all the other jobs she does. I know she takes care of the beds and the laundry, for example."

"That's a lot. Perhaps Lin needs to get the service to add a maid for that. If she only had to do the cooking, that wouldn't be so bad."

"You're right. I'll talk to her."

"All right, girls," I called. "Time for lunch."

There were the usual moans and groans, but I promised they'd be back on the beach soon.

After an afternoon on the beach, we all got cleaned up and drove to the castle, Hyndla draped over Rose and Gerda in the back seat. Sam sat on Auntie's lap in the front, sulking. I'd been worried about fights because Hyndla would be jealous of Sam, but Sam was the one whose snout was seriously out of joint.

Baby Penny was fussing in her playpen in the kitchen when we arrived. Rose immediately scooped her up and walked her around before laying her on a blanket in the living room. Gerda followed and seemed fascinated by her friend having a real baby to play with instead of a doll. Rose sat in front of Penny and sang to her. She was a very smiley baby, and loved the attention, especially when Rose told her a little story, using a miniature teddy bear as a prop. When Dora had laid the dinner out on the sideboard, she took Penny into the kitchen to be fed. Rose wanted to go with them, but I insisted she sit with the family. We had a good dinner, with a choice of steak or salmon. Most of us would prefer a change from beef, but it always had to be available for Hunter. Rose liked her share of her Papa's plate, too. She seemed to feel it tasted better than her own share, maybe because Hunter chose the rarest portions. Gerda chose beef because Rose did, and ate well. After dinner, Rose took Gerda to her room to show her the toys and books she kept there.

"Mama," she came to say while we sat having coffee on the terrace. "Can Gerda and me sleep here tonight? My bed is big enough. I want to play with Penny in the morning."

"But what about when you wake up and we're not there?" I asked.

"I think I'll stay, too," Auntie said. "I'll watch them."

I opened my mind to Hunter. "Yes," he said.

I liked the idea of having the house to myself.

"In that case," I said, "I think I'll be heading home. I'm still jet-lagged, I'm afraid."

I said goodnight, trying to ignore Lin's smirk, and left.

Hunter arrived a couple of hours later. "I had to read them a story sentence by sentence, while Auntie translated.

Chapter 19

I never did get beyond the basics in German. I hope Gerda learns English soon."

"She will. We start work on languages at nine o'clock on Monday morning."

We went upstairs, and when I awoke the next morning, Hunter had already left.

20

On Monday morning, I sat down with Gerda in Hunter's former study on the third floor, while Auntie worked with Rose at the dining room table on the ground floor. I had some of Rose's early reading books that worked well. They each had a story about a brother and sister, with a few sentences on the left page and a picture on the right. The first book was all about recognizing the shape of the words, rather than using phonics. The following book would introduce phonics. Although intended for teaching a child to read, I figured they'd work equally well for teaching a child English.

We got through the first book quite quickly, as Gerda had received a little instruction from her tutor in Austria. Once she got over her shyness and nervousness about making a mistake, she remembered her lessons quite well. I then moved over to the flash cards. I'd picked out ones that would be useful in our day-to-day lives: food, sea, weather, and numbers. I thought we'd revise those cards the next day, plus go on a tour of the house to cover the kitchen, bathroom, bedroom, and so on. We went downstairs.

Rose was having a stilted conversation with Auntie.

"She is doing very well," Auntie said.

"So is Gerda. I think they'll be chatting away very soon."

"Let's go into the kitchen to make sandwiches for lunch. That will be a good learning experience." Auntie summoned the girls in German and English to follow her.

We made ham and cheese sandwiches, which took care of some good words. Then we heated some tomato soup and poured glasses of milk. Everything was placed in the middle of the table and they had to ask for what they wanted in the language they were learning.

"We are good teachers, you know," I told Auntie.

"Well, they are good students," she said in both languages. Both girls grinned, pleased with themselves.

Sam employed his own language abilities to beg for scraps: little huffs and pleading eyes. The girls fed him tiny bits of their sandwiches under the table, under the illusion that Auntie and I didn't notice. After lunch, I demanded peace and quiet while I lay on my bed for an hour cuddling Sam.

It seemed to have clouded over outside. I hoped it would rain and got up to look out of the window. A strange man stood on the beach, hands on hips, staring at the house. I went downstairs to find Auntie watching him, too.

"I wonder what he wants?" I asked Auntie. "I don't like the look of him."

She joined me after picking up the binoculars from a side table. "I don't, either," she said. "Call Hunter."

I closed my eyes and sought him out. When we clicked, I thought, *Danger. Come.*

"Can we go to the beach now? Rose asked.

"Not just now. Why don't you both go up to your room and play? Mama has to take care of something."

Rose started, "But Mama..." but saw in my warning look that something was not quite right, so didn't make more of a fuss. She took Gerda's hand and led her upstairs.

The man started to walk toward the house. Sam started barking madly, as did Hyndla. He was tall and thickset with one of those buzz cuts that look sinister on such thuggish types. I locked the sliding glass door and put down its bar. The front door was already locked. We stood well back and watched him. He stood on the patio and peered in, beckoning us to come out. I shook my head. I noticed some dust on the grass by the road leading to the house fly up into some sort of eddy and knew help was at hand. I also noticed the neighbor who lived across the road toward the back of the property emerging from his front door with a rifle under his arm. *Damn.* We didn't need a witness to whatever would go down. When the stranger noticed our neighbor's approach, he got out a weapon of his own—some sort of pistol, I think. The neighbor beat a hasty retreat. I hoped he'd call the police. It had at least provided a distraction so that he failed to notice Hunter and Lin come to a halt behind him. We moved closer.

"What do you want?" Hunter growled.

The stranger whipped around in shock as Lin took the opportunity to disarm him while doing some serious damage to his wrist.

He clutched his wrist and said, "I'm here for the girl. Her father wants her back. He has a right to his child." He had a thick German accent.

"Herr Grunewald had no right to his daughter or anything else. He is in prison for serious crimes," Hunter said.

"Not for long."

"Why do you think so?" Lin asked.

"Because he is a powerful man. He will take his daughter and live in another country. He has money, so plenty will welcome and assist him."

Sirens blared not far away. The man tried to bolt past Hunter, but soon found himself pinned to the ground, face down and his arms behind his back.

A police car screeched to a halt and a couple of well-built cops sprinted over.

"What's going on?" one of them asked.

Auntie and I stepped out onto the patio.

"It's a long story, officer," Lin said. "Briefly, we have charge of a little Austrian girl with the permission of her mother. Her father has been convicted of murder, attempted murder, rape, and espionage in Vienna and is in prison. He is very wealthy, so he hired this man to kidnap his daughter. Apparently, he plans to escape and take his daughter somewhere that won't extradite him."

"Er," the cop said, clearly at a loss. "How do I know this is so?"

"It is not so," yelled the stranger. "It is all lies."

"This man threatened us with his pistol, which is over there." Hunter indicated the location with his chin.

Lin broke in at this point. "You need to lock him up and then call the police in Vienna to confirm the story."

"We were visiting them in Vienna because we had met them on another holiday and we all got on very well," Auntie said. "Due to my former career experience, I gradually realized that he was a spy during the Cold War who had given us the slip. And the Thorens here witnessed him attempting to rape and murder a young woman from his village in Austria, as he had done to several before. I will come with you and help you talk to the Vienna police."

The stranger tried to kick the cop while being handcuffed. Hunter kicked him on the kneecap, which kept him under control, if not quiet. Hunter helped get him into the car while Auntie climbed into the front seat.

"Better tie his feet," Hunter advised. "He's strong and determined to get away." The cop fished some rope out of his trunk and Hunter did the honors.

Lin and I watched them drive away. "I wonder what else Herr Grunewald has up his sleeve," Lin said. "Perhaps I should pay a visit."

"I promised to invite my sister and her children for a few days. I hope nothing strange happens while they're here. I really don't want her to find out our true circumstances. She is not the type to deal with it appropriately."

"Too bad Agna's not here. If she finds out anything she shouldn't, Agna could erase it from her memory."

"Can't you, now that your powers have strengthened?"

"I hadn't even thought about that. I must think about it. Maybe practice a little."

"On whom? Not me, I hope!"

"No, maybe a store clerk or someone like that. Anyway, I think I should go to Austria and see what's going on. Hunter's been talking about going to Copenhagen, too, to make sure that horrible gnome isn't planning his escape, either. He's a wily character, for sure."

"Why doesn't he just call the police there? He left on very good terms, after all."

"Yes, but I guess he wants to see for himself."

Auntie helped facilitate the phone calls to Vienna. The would-be kidnapper was sent home under escort, and Auntie heard later that Herr Grunewald was moved to a maximum security prison.

21

Events overtook Lin and Hunter's proposed visit as various groups, together with a few Quaker congregations, started to clamor for a visit from Odin, and various outlandish stories made the tabloids. Lin and Hunter hated the idea because it would almost certainly focus attention on them. There were—and still are—plenty of rabid religious zealots who could make life very unpleasant for the family, as well as attract the interest of government agencies.

Hunter communed with Odin, who said he would be delighted to speak to a crowd and assure them of his good intentions and encourage them to spread his message—that of embracing good and rejecting evil. Hunter said he seemed exhilarated by the opportunity.

The next decision had to be made: Who would organize the event and bring these disparate groups together? And then, the venue. The castle was out of the question. I'd heard that a local sculpture garden was going through hard times and wondered if they would welcome a paid event. Thanks to Hunter's generous offer, they did indeed welcome it, and we booked it for the Saturday after Labor Day. With that contribution to the proceedings, I was "volunteered" as the official organizer. I protested as I was afraid of repercussions. After all, I lived alone with a small child. I felt that the leader of the Maryland group I visited might be the best bet. He declined on the grounds that he lived too far away. I gave in but insisted on a cell phone dedicated to the event, a post office box, and a separate bank account for expenses that would be closed immediately after.

"Okay, okay. But I'm not starting before I've had my sister stay for a few days with her children. I promised. I can't claim to be busy all summer. And I can hardly tell her about this—rally, do we call it?"

"I see your point," Lin said. "Too many awkward questions."

"And family is family," Auntie added. "Blood is thicker than water."

"And we all share blood ties," Lin said. "But I know what you mean. By the way, that big dog is arriving on Sunday. He will be delivered here, so he can stay here until your sister has left."

I'd forgotten about Tor. Yet another thing to worry about. I called Lizzie that evening. She would arrive on Monday afternoon and leave on Friday morning. Today was Thursday, so I could make a few phone calls the next morning to firm up some details with the sculpture garden, or at least confirm how much of the site would be available. They were more than accommodating. I raced over to the post office to secure a P.O. box, then to the bank to open an account in the name of the festival. Since I already had a healthy account, there was no problem. Hunter had given me a check for a few thousand dollars, which I deposited right away, and they gave me a few blank checks. I drove over to the sculpture garden in the afternoon to put down a cash deposit—which took them by surprise. I explained that our event bank account had only just been set up. We went over some details, and they promised to draw up a contract at the beginning of the following week. I was exhausted by day's end. Thank goodness Auntie could take care of the girls.

Saturday was spent making up beds and shopping for the week. I knew they would be used to plain food, so wouldn't go much beyond a roast chicken, a meatloaf, and at least a couple of barbecues. Eggs, bacon, and cereals, sandwich stuff for lunch. And ice cream. Lots of ice cream.

I had to explain things to Rose, too.

"Rose, we will have guests staying here next week."

"Who?"

"My sister, your Aunt Lizzie, and her two children, your cousins."

"What're their names?"

"Jay and Jessie. Jay is ten and Jessie is eight."

"Older than us then. What happens if Gerda and I don't like them? Do we have to play with them?"

"You most certainly do. They will be our guests, and we must always make guests feel welcome. And they are your cousins. Part of our family. Auntie Peggy is their family, too, although they haven't ever met her."

"Maybe Auntie won't like them."

"Of course I will. Why wouldn't I?" asked Auntie.

"Because they're strangers, that's why."

"Well, you and Gerda were strangers until last Christmas," she said. "Now you are best friends."

Gerda broke in at this point, saying something to Auntie in German.

"Gerda says that there are rules about guests. They must feel welcome and given a nice time. And we must never be rude to guests."

"Stupid rules," said Rose. She went to the sofa and opened her German book. Gerda went to sit beside her with her English book.

"What on earth's got into her?" I whispered to Auntie.

"She doesn't want anyone to come between her and Gerda. Or me and her. Or you and her. Remember, you've never told her she has an aunt and cousins before."

This didn't bode well, but we'd just have to make the best of it. I knew just the thing to cheer her up.

"Tor is coming on Sunday. He'll be taken to the castle and stay there for a while."

"Why can't he come here, Mama?"

"It's too much with our guests coming. And I don't think Aunt Lizzie is used to dogs. Sam is probably enough for the time she's here."

Rose pulled a face and went back to her book.

The girls were excited to see Tor again, I, less so. I had Sam's reaction to worry about, not to mention Hyndla's. Tor could do them both serious damage if a dispute broke out. Added to that, very big dogs make very big poops. I didn't feel like dealing with that, either. Thank heavens he'd stay at the castle, at least for the time being.

We were all out on the terrace; the girls keeping watch for the van—I'd left Sam in our wing. Hunter had left the remote-controlled gate open for it. Eventually, it came rolling up the driveway. A scraggy young man jumped out, fingering his drooping mustache obsessively.

"Where d'you want 'im?"

Rose ran to the back of the van.

"Just let him out. He will stay by me."

Gretchen stood behind her. "Yes, he will be fine with us."

The driver looked at Hunter.

"Yes, you can do as they ask."

I noticed Hyndla get up and run to the edge of the woods. He must have smelled Tor.

The driver opened the van and pulled down a ramp. Tor growled. The driver hesitated.

"I suggest you wait in the van, and we will open the crate," Hunter said, trying not to show how funny he found the man's cowardly behavior.

"Okay, it's against regulations, but if you insist." He scrambled into the cab with comical haste.

Once the man was out of sight, Hunter unlocked the crate. Tor stepped down the ramp like a king, looking this way and that as if acknowledging his subjects. He nosed Rose first, gave a little yelp, and rested his head on her shoulder as if she belonged to him now. Gerda edged nearer, and he went to greet her, too. I thought I might as well ingratiate myself since I'd probably be his primary caregiver, so approached with one of Sam's treats. He sniffed the treat and snuffled it from my hand. I think I passed muster. Hunter slapped Tor's sides and told him what fun they'd have. Tor looked up at him and licked his hand. I selfishly wondered if—hoped that—Hunter might become attached to the dog and want to keep him at the castle.

We all went back to the terrace, where Tor spent a great deal of time sniffing where Hyndla had been sitting. He stared into the woods as if he knew that was where he'd find his quarry.

"Tor, you must be a good boy with Hyndla. He is my friend," Rose said. "And you have to like Sam, too. He's part of our family and we all have to love each other."

Tor stared at her. Suddenly, he raced toward the woods. I gasped, suddenly fearful for that lovely little fox. Rose went after him. But all he did was race around the lawn in huge circles, letting off steam after his long confinement. I noticed Hyndla sitting at the edge of the woods. Rose went over to him. I didn't think it was such a good idea to draw attention to what amounted to prey from Tor's point of view.

Tor noticed and stopped dead in his tracks. We all watched. What would it do to Rose to see her beloved fox torn apart? Rose sat with her arms around Hyndla. I could see her lips moving and soon found myself hearing what she was saying, even from that distance.

"Tor, I love Hyndla. He is very special. You are very special, too. You must be friends. I want you to protect Hyndla."

Tor leaned forward and sniffed Hyndla's snout. The fox sat staring straight ahead. Tor sat back and looked hard at Rose, then Hyndla, then back at us.

"It's okay, Tor," called Hunter.

I turned back in time to see Tor lay down next to Rose with his head resting on one of her legs. Hyndla's head rested on her other leg. The two dogs' snouts were not more than an inch apart. We all let out a sigh of relief. Now, we had to deal with Sam, whom I had left alone back at the house. One animal at a time.

"Mary, I know we agreed to keep Tor while your sister is visiting you, but why don't we keep Tor here at least a little longer?" Hunter said. "I think he needs more space to run."

"That would be best, I think. He's attached to Rose, but I'd rather leave introducing him to Sam's territory for a while longer. I think he'll become attached to you."

Hunter stood by Tor while Auntie and I fetched Sam. Auntie put him on a leash. I hadn't seen a leash for Tor, but he would have to have one—not that any of us except

Hunter or Lin could hold him back. I was gaining strength, but not yet to that extent.

Sam put the brakes on when he saw Tor and emitted a low continual growly rumble until Rose put her arms around him.

"It's okay, Sam," Auntie said several times. Hunter brought Tor closer. Tor stared down at Sam from his lofty stance without moving a muscle. Sam started to rumble again.

"It's all right, Sam. Tor is a friend." Rose pulled on Tor's collar. "Say hello, boys."

They sniffed in the usual intrusive way of dogs, and Sam quietened. After a few minutes, Tor led the way off the terrace and Sam followed. Hyndla watched them with a glint in his eye as the dogs chased each other around, having a high old time. Phew. All three of them seemed at ease with each other.

After dinner, we said goodbye. Rose and Gerda wanted to stay with Tor, but I reminded them that we had guests arriving the next day. Rose looked mutinous again.

22

It rained on Monday morning. I hoped the traffic wouldn't be too bad for Lizzie. It had mostly cleared by two, so the kids went to the beach to build yet another sandcastle. It seemed that Gerda had somehow calmed down Rose, who had chattered about making the hugest sandcastle with her cousins during lunch.

Finally, the car drew up. Auntie and I went outside as soon as we heard it. I had Sam on a leash. Lizzie stared up at the house. "This is yours?" she asked.

"Yes. My employers built it, then moved to a bigger place. Come on inside. You must be tired."

"Hello, Lizzie," Auntie said, gently.

"Oh, hello, Auntie Peggy. It's been a long time."

"Yes, too long. Your mother's funeral. I know you've been busy bringing up these lovely children."

That broke the ice a little.

"This is our dog, Sam."

"I want a puppy, but Mom won't let me," Jessie said, bending down to fondle his ears.

"I don't like dogs. Dirty things," Lizzie declared. Thank goodness I'd left Tor up at the castle. Jay and Jessie looked longingly at the beach, where Rose and Gerda still played.

"Mom, can't we go down to the beach now?" Jessie asked in a wheedling tone.

"When you've used the bathroom and changed."

"Let me show you to your rooms. Then the kids can change and get out there," I said.

I led the way upstairs. I put them on the second floor, where each had a room to themselves. They shared a bathroom. I showed them how to turn on the TV in the sitting room outside the bedrooms.

"Where do you sleep?" Lizzie asked.

"On the third floor. Auntie and Rose sleep on the first floor."

"Nice setup."

"Yes, I'm very grateful."

Lizzie and I walked Jay and Jessie down to the beach. I called Rose and Gerda to join us.

"This is your Aunty Lizzie and cousin Rose and her friend Gerda. Gerda is visiting us from Austria."

"From what?" Jessie asked.

"Austria. It's a country near Germany and Switzerland in Europe. They speak German there. Rose is learning German and Gerda is learning English so that they can talk to us and each other better."

"Oh," Jessie said. I'm not sure she'd been told about Europe.

"It is very nice to meet you," Gerda said, holding out her hand to shake Lizzie's. Lizzie obliged, but her children just stared and put their hands behind their backs.

"You are supposed to shake hands," Rose told them. "It's polite."

No response. This was going to be a tough week.

"Well, Aunt Lizzie and I are going to have some iced tea with Auntie Peggy, so we'll leave you children to play. No one is to go into the water unless one of us is on the beach with you. Is that clear?" I looked at each of them. All four nodded. Hot and humid as it was, I felt we should sit on the patio to keep an eye on them. At least the awning was out, shading the chairs.

Lizzie gradually relaxed as we sat enjoying our iced tea and cookies. Sam sat at a distance. He didn't like her.

"I haven't made a cake," I said. "I'm afraid I'm not very good at baking."

"I haven't made a cake for ages," Auntie said. "Perhaps I'll make one tomorrow. A chocolate one, I think."

"Ooh, yes, you made one for my birthday once," I said. "It was decadent. I've never had one as good."

"I don't remember you being around much when we were growing up," Lizzie told Auntie.

"No, I wasn't. My job involved a lot of travel. In fact, I lived in Europe for quite a few years on and off. State Department."

"Dad said you were a spy."

"Oh, nonsense," Auntie said, laughing. "Your dad always liked his little jokes. I was just doing secretarial work most of the time."

I laughed, too. The heck she was!

I was happy things seemed quiet on the beach. Just as that thought crossed my mind, I heard a yell and saw Jay come running up to the house with a nosebleed. I ran inside to grab a towel, which Lizzie held to his nose.

"Rose is a horrid girl. She punched me. I hate her!"

"Oh, dear, I am sorry. Why did she do that?" I asked.

"I jumped on their sandcastle. It was only a stupid sandcastle. I hate her."

"Well, that wasn't nice of you, but Rose shouldn't have punched you. That wasn't nice, either."

"I should think not," Lizzie said in a voice that was almost a hiss. "She'd better apologize.

"I will go and get Rose right away," I said.

She knew she was in trouble when I stood in front of her. "Why did you punch Jay? My sister is very angry now. You have to come and apologize."

Rose stamped her foot. "I told him lots of times that he had to use wet sand to make turrets for the castle, but he kept forgetting. So he got mad and kicked over most of our castle. We worked hard on it. Look at it!"

It was a sorry mess.

"He was not nice," added Gerda.

"He gets easily frustrated," Jessie said, briefly looking up as she worked to repair the damage.

"I know it's upsetting when you've worked so hard, but you know the sea will wash it away tonight."

"That's not the point." Rose stamped her foot again.

"Don't take that tone with me, young lady. Remember what I told you about guests? Punching them in the nose is against the rules. Come up with me and apologize right now. What do you think Papa would say?" *You sound just like your mother.*

"'Good for you,' that's what he'd say."

"Up to the house. Now."

My temper was not improved by Rose's sassy responses, as I looked forward to an evening of appeasing my sister. She realized she'd gone too far and meekly followed me. She planted herself in front of Jay, who cowered at his mother's side.

"You were very mean to destroy our sandcastle. But I shouldn't have punched you. I'm sorry."

Jay buried his head in his mother's shirt and sobbed.

"Jay, you have to say sorry, too," Rose told him.

"Sorry," he mumbled.

"Let's go back and make it better," Rose said.

"Okay."

She took Jay's hand and marched off with him back to the beach.

"Do you think he'll be safe with her?" asked Lizzie. "She seems a bit violent."

Auntie intervened when she saw my face. "No, Lizzie dear, she saw a boy bigger than her doing something she thought was unkind. I guess she felt words wouldn't work. I think they've both learned a lesson today. Let's leave them to sort out their differences."

I went inside to start dinner. I planned a barbecue but needed to marinate the meat and make potatoes and salad. I needed to cool down, too. Violent! After half an hour or so, I had to acknowledge that her behavior had been violent. Probably because a bigger boy posed a threat, she felt she had to deal with it firmly. I would talk to her again at bedtime. Lin and Hunter were coming over for dinner tomorrow evening. I wanted everything smoothed out by then.

The next day was uneventful. I noticed that Hyndla hadn't put in an appearance. Sam sulked in his daybed after Lizzie yelled at him to keep away from her. I wouldn't be doing this again anytime soon. Thank heavens Tor was staying at the castle.

For dinner, I'd decided on a big pot roast—two regular ones, actually—with carrots and potatoes. Once it was in the oven, that was it. A salad, which I could prepare well ahead of time, and ice cream for dessert. I arranged extra chairs on the patio and set a nice table. Everything was ready by mid-afternoon, so I decided to sit on the beach. Lizzie and Auntie were already down there.

I was setting up my chair near the others, and at a safe distance from the kids, when I overheard Rose telling Gerda it would be her birthday soon, on August 7th. I couldn't believe that I'd forgotten. So much was going on I think my brain had become addled. Then Gerda said that it was her birthday soon, too. August 8th. I'd given her details to the school over the phone when I called from Austria but hadn't really registered her birthday. My mind was preoccupied with other events at the time.

"We are almost twins!" Rose called out to us all.

"Yes, real sisters!" Gerda squealed.

"We have our birthdays in the winter," Jessie said. "That's much better because your school friends can all come and Mom gives us cupcakes to take to school and everyone sings 'Happy Birthday' to us."

"Well, we can ask some school friends if they're not away, but our family is big, so it's always a real party. And we can be on the beach. I like that best, and this year Gerda will be here." Rose turned to get another bucket of wet sand, ignoring Jessie's sour look.

Well, how would we handle this? Two cakes, two parties? I'd ask Lin and Auntie what they thought later. I needn't have worried. Rose and Gerda informed me of the arrangements just before dinner. They would each open their gifts on their own birthdays. But Rose would wait for the party and cake until Gerda's birthday. I kissed her and told her how sensible that was. Rose wanted to be at the castle on her birthday, and Gerda wanted to be at our house on hers. I suggested we have most of Gerda's birthday at our house, then go to the castle for cake, presents, and dinner so that everyone could enjoy it. They agreed to that.

Lin and Hunter arrived at around six. I made the introductions. Lizzie gushed a little, clearly intimidated by their good looks, expensive car, and chic appearance. The kids muttered a sullen "hi," not knowing what to do with themselves when Hunter was drawn down to the beach by Gerda and Rose to admire their rambling castle.

"Mr. Thoren is going to see your sandcastle," Auntie said. "Why don't you help show him?" The kids shook their heads and went upstairs.

"I'm afraid they are quite shy," Lizzie said.

"That's quite all right," Lin said. "They go through those phases. They'll grow out of it."

We all sat outside and I rolled out my trolley and fixed drinks. Lizzie and Auntie each had gin and tonic, Lin and I had our usual white wine, and I poured a glass of claret for Hunter.

"I heard from Gretchen," Lin said. "She's sent a gift for Gerda's birthday. Did you know it was coming up, Mary?"

"I just found out today. The day after Rose's. I told her what the girls had decided.

"Well, that sounds like a good solution. We'll need a big cake! Agna's coming over, Eir will come, Margareta and Sven, of course, Joe and Helen. Lettie I'm not sure about. I must tell them it's a day later."

"I think the girls want to invite a couple of friends from school ... if that's all right."

"Of course it is. We'd better keep Tor away from the food, though!"

I laughed. "All he has to do is reach over the counter. He doesn't even have to get up on his hind legs."

"Who is this Tor?" Lizzie asked.

"He's a huge dog we brought back from Austria," I said. "He belonged to Gerda's mother. She is moving to Canada soon, so it was easier just to bring him over here for the time being. He's a sweet dog. The girls love him. Sam is jealous, of course, but they don't fight."

"Ugh, thank goodness he's not here," Lizzie said, shuddering. "All that dog. I couldn't stand it."

"He doesn't take to everyone, either," said Lin. She loved Tor. I'm not sure he was suited to life in a small house. It would be better for Tor to stay at the castle rather than be confined to a small backyard in Toronto.

Lizzie looked embarrassed by Lin's rebuff. Auntie didn't chip in to save the conversation, but Hunter arrived to claim his wine. He flashed his irresistible smile at Lizzie, and she blushed for different reasons. I knew just what she was feeling—a little breathless, slightly weak at the knees, a flutter in the nether region. Lin smirked, as expected.

"I think dinner is ready to be put on the table," I said. "Could someone get the kids back up to the house?"

"I'll go," Hunter said, taking his wine with him.

"Can I help?" Auntie asked.

"No, you keep Lizzie company. There's really nothing much to do."

I called upstairs to Jessie and Jay to wash their hands and come down for dinner. No answer. Lizzie could get them. I didn't have the patience to deal with their nonsense.

I got everyone seated except Lizzie and her brats. The food was on the table, the wines sat in their holders, and we waited for a few minutes. After a while, I started to serve everyone. I didn't go to all this trouble to let the food get cold.

Finally, Lizzie stomped downstairs, followed by two sulky children. Jessie's cheek showed a red handprint and her eyes looked puffy. They took their places in silence. I served them while Auntie carried on a conversation with Lin and Hunter about a play that was coming to the Kennedy Center.

"When I sold my house in Salton, I bought a little condo so that we could have somewhere to stay when we want to see a show or do better shopping than we have down here. It's only got one bedroom, but there's a pull-out sofa and a pull-out armchair. So Mary, Rose, and I can be there together if we want."

"That's nice," said Lizzie, resentment poking through again.

"We did that, too," Lin said. "We like to go up there some-times. We got a three-bedroom because of our kids."

"How many children do you have?" Lizzie asked.

"Two, both in university. Sven is in grad school and Margareta just graduated. She's going to study medicine."

"They must be very smart."

"They are intelligent, but they are hard workers. That's what counts in the end."

"Hear that, kids? It's not enough to be smart, you have to work hard, too."

Lizzie didn't get much of a response, except for an eye roll. The kids were behaving really badly. Were they not used to mixing with grownups? Probably not used to mixing with people outside their social setting. In any case, they were embarrassing me.

After I cleared the dishes and brought out several tubs of different flavored ice cream, Jessie and Jay seemed to relax. Hunter even managed to engage them in conversation about the sandcastle. We adjourned to the living room for coffee and more wine. Lin and Hunter left at around ten.

"It's okay, Mary," Lin whispered to me as I walked them out to the car. "She's not used to different kinds of people. And she's jealous."

"I'm sorry, too. It wasn't a very comfortable evening."

"It's always nice to see you, Rose and Auntie. And I'm looking forward to the birthdays."

"I'll think of something special," Hunter said.

I waved them off before going back inside.

"Thank you for dinner, Aunt Mary," Jessie said as soon as I got through the door. "Mom says we have to go to bed now."

"Good night, Jessie. You are welcome. Jay?"

Jessie kicked him. "Ouch! Thank you for dinner," he muttered.

They trudged upstairs. Those stairs were not carpeted, so I could hear every stompy step.

"Where's Lizzie?" I asked Auntie.

"She took her wine down to the beach."

"Do you think I should go to her?"

"Why not just leave her alone? I think she feels embarrassed by the kids' behavior. No need to make her feel she has to apologize."

"She made a few unfortunate comments, too. She just can't get over her jealousy. It's sad, I have nothing in common with her. Most of the time, I don't even know what to talk about."

"Do you blame her for being jealous? She doesn't know much about your life, but she can see your house, your trips, your clothes, your friends, your education."

"She chose to marry early."

"Yes, we all make mistakes when we are young. Hers was one she is stuck with for years."

"You're right. I think I'll put Rose and Gerda to bed and go up to read."

I heard Lizzie creep up the stairs—as much as one can creep up creaky wooden stairs—just after I'd got under the duvet and opened my book. Our relationship would always be strained. She was family, but the sort of family one only sees after healthily long intervals.

23

I'd looked at the forecast on my phone for August 7th and 8th. Rainy both days. Stormy, in fact. When I got up on Rose's birthday, I found her and Gerda despondently eating cereal in front of the TV, with Sam sitting between them. I didn't usually allow eating on the sofa, or morning TV, but it was her birthday and a pretty dismal day.

"Happy birthday, my sweet!" I said.

"Thank you, Mama. Will the weather be better tomorrow?"

"About the same, I think. But you can have fun indoors, too."

"But outdoors is better. And supposing Papa had planned the surprise for outdoors."

"Papa is very smart. He will make it wonderful. Doesn't he always?"

"Yes, he does." She brightened. "Gerda, maybe we should have your birthday at the castle, too, if we can't go to the beach."

"Yes. That is good."

I hoped Hunter had figured out something special.

"Is that all you two are having for breakfast?"

"Are we going to the castle for lunch?"

"Yes, that was the plan."

"Then I don't need anything else. You know how Dora makes so much lovely stuff."

Indeed, I did. I let the girls watch TV all morning, which went entirely against my principles, but sometimes you just have to let things slide. Auntie read the paper and did the crossword, and I finished my British mystery—I'd been reading nothing but British mysteries for weeks and had become enamored of the ancient settings, eccentric characters, and intricate plots.

Finally, we all donned raincoats that were meant for cooler weather and set off for the castle. Hyndla bounded out to the car. I parked as close to the overhang by the side door as I could. We got out and dashed into the hallway, where Sam, predictably, shook himself. Hyndla had run in ahead and I knew I'd find them both in the kitchen, focusing entreating eyes on Dora. She always weakened after a few minutes.

Rose had been quiet during the ride. I thought she was still upset about the weather.

"Mama. I think you and Auntie forgot something."

"What did we forget?"

"My presents." Ah, the penny dropped.

"No, we knew we'd be here, so I left them with Lin a few days ago."

She skipped off to find everyone, ebullient now. Gerda hurried after her.

Everyone was gathered in the living room, with Penny standing in a playpen in one corner, her chubby fist clinging onto Rose's shirt. Many kisses and hugs later, Hunter popped open a couple of bottles of champagne. He popped open another bottle, too.

"Champagne for a birthday celebration. And we have a special children's champagne, too." Sven and Margaret passed around the drinks, making a point of serving Gerda and Rose first. They were thrilled to be drinking their "champagne" out of crystal flutes like everyone else.

"A toast to our birthday girls," Hunter boomed.

"To Rose and Gerda!" everyone called before sipping. The girls were pink and excited by this very grownup salute. Penny started to whine after being unceremoniously abandoned for the lure of champagne. I went over and picked her up for a kiss and a cuddle. I hadn't done that much lately. After ten minutes or so, Dora called everyone into lunch before handing Penny a bottle to keep her busy in the playpen. She had produced her usual extravaganza of roast beef, salmon *en croute*, and vegetables in a variety of sauces.

We all ate our fill and could hardly summon up the will to get up from the table. Sam still waited, ever optimistic that someone would offer a final scrap. I knew for a fact that Margareta, Sven, Gerda, and Rose, had all smuggled him a little something, thinking themselves unobserved.

"Cake later," Lin decreed. Even Rose didn't complain. In fact, her eyes looked heavy.

We all went back to the living room, where Gerda and Rose sat in Hunter's oversized armchair, one squished on each side. Before long, they were both sound asleep. I couldn't resist taking a picture with my phone. Very cute. I started to feel sleepy, too, so excused myself to go to my room and take a nap. I heard Auntie come to her room not long after.

Rose came to shake me awake. It was four already.

"Cake and present time, Mama," she said.

I went to the back of my closet and got out a small package. "I think the cake is tomorrow."

"Good things often come in small packages," she said, looking at what I held, at once doubtful and hopeful.

Auntie came out of her room with a wrapped gift and we went down the corridor that connected our wing to the main house and through to the living room.

I hoped Rose didn't receive so many presents that Gerda would feel jealous on her day. But probably everyone would think of that and step up. Rose got an adjustable gold bracelet from Lin and Hunter, a set of Beatrix Potter books and a German storybook from Auntie, a digital watch with an old-fashioned clock face from Sven, and a puzzle from Margareta. From Dora and Stan, she got a big, cuddly plush fox. My gift was a gold chain with two pearls suspended on it.

"I will add two pearls on every birthday until you are 21," I said.

"Gee, that's a lot of pearls," she said. "It's very pretty, and it's going to be even more pretty when I get grown up."

To her delight, Joe and Helen Paglietti arrived just as soon as she'd opened the last gift. She rushed to hug them. She liked Helen very much but adored Uncle Joe.

"I thought you weren't coming," she said. "I'm so glad you're here."

"Oh, we wouldn't miss your birthday! I'm sorry we're late," Joe said. "Helen's mother arrived this morning."

I'd forgotten about her. She'd been at their wedding last year, together with her awful husband and his even more awful sister.

"She's made her move, then?" I asked.

"Finally," Helen said. "I picked her up while Dad and Aunt were out. She couldn't pack everything, but she managed to bring what she wanted most. She's resting now. We don't have a landline anymore, so we bought her a cell phone ahead of time."

"How is she feeling?" Lin asked.

"Shaky, but relieved." Helen sighed. "Of course, he can claim abandonment, so I guess she won't get any support. But you never know what a good lawyer can accomplish. Most divorce lawyers are bull dogs. They don't let go."

Hunter said, "She would have been welcome to come, Helen."

"I know, thanks, but she's not up to it. I think it's the first time she's ever stood up to him. It's shredded her nerves."

Joe said, "We're holding up the proceedings. One more to open!"

Their gift was a set of DVDs, all Disney movies.

"We'll share, Gerda. These are lovely, Uncle Joe and Aunt Helen. Thank you so much."

Dora came in with a cake that was just big enough for everyone to have a slice.

"The big cake for you both is tomorrow, but we can't have presents without cake," she said. "Just one candle for today."

Rose looked delighted. I think she'd had second thoughts about postponing everything until Gerda's birthday. But everyone had made it special.

We had an early dinner before heading home. Auntie stayed at the castle, probably to help Dora with tomorrow's celebration. I'd promised Gerda she could have some time on the beach. Maybe the rain would hold off for an hour or two.

24

The rain did let up for a little while the following morning. After a quick breakfast, the children tore down to the beach. It didn't last long, and they were back by eleven, dripping wet. I made them hold up their feet in the rain to wash off the sand. Then, into the bath. I'd bought them each a similar new dress, which they'd picked out the week before during a quick trip to Annapolis. Rose's was pale blue with white embroidery around the neck and hem. Gerda's was pale pink with darker pink embroidery. They looked enchanting. Their coloring was similarly Nordic and now that Gerda had toned up and slimmed down, they were much the same size.

We went through to the garage and got into the car. When we got to the castle, we sat on the terrace under the newly installed awning. The rain was only drizzling by this time, and it was hot and humid. The mosquitos would be out for blood tomorrow. Penny sat on the two-seater swing between Gerda and Rose.

Lin told them, "I'm going to tell you a story about another birthday party that took place in one of the worlds of long ago called Alfheim, the land of the elves. We are waiting for another guest, which is Hunter's birthday surprise."

I'm glad Lin gave me some notice so that I could set my phone on record.

"Lin's stories are really good, Gerda," Rose said. "I'll help if you don't understand something."

Penny gurgled.

Tape 11,
Volume 4

The queen of the elves had a beautiful daughter called Folla, who had the most star-filled hair you ever saw. Every time she moved, tiny silver lights would twinkle as her hair rippled in the breeze. The queen made sure there was always a breeze as she never tired of gazing at her lovely child. As little girls do, Folla grew up and met a handsome young elf called Pilk, who had the most perfectly pointed ears she had ever seen, and the longest fingers in Alfheim. In his turn, he was enchanted by her twinkling hair and ice-green eyes. They fell in love. Luckily, the queen approved of Pilk, who was always deferential and charming in her presence.

I accompanied my Lady Frigg to the wedding, which was lavish in every way. Lanterns hung from trees throughout the land, sweet morsels filled tubs on every street corner, wine fountains gushed in every square, and musicians played in the palace day and night. Frigg presented the couple with a golden bowl of honey that would never be empty. They kept dipping their fingers in the sweetness and licking them clean like naughty children. I expected the queen to give them a good telling off, but she just looked on with an indulgent smile.

The bride wore a gossamer gown of palest green, studded with tiny pearls that were a gift from Njord, god of the sea. The groom wore a dark green outfit of the finest silk, produced by silkworms who lived in a remote part of Midgard and woven by the queen's own weavers. The wedding ceremony, conducted by the queen, was short and sweet, with the couple adorning each other with flower necklaces and swearing to be faithful forever. It was held on the palace grounds because elves are very small, so many of the guests couldn't fit inside even the palace's greatest hall. A banquet was set out on many tables. The plates were elf size, so we didn't bother to eat anything except a slice of the fairy wedding cake to be polite.

The little couple gazed into each other's eyes in the most touching way. I was still an innocent handmaiden then, so had never considered marriage—handmaidens were not destined to marry. But seeing those two together made me a little wistful for a wider life.

There was no sight of the king. Gossip in some quarters asserted that the queen kept him locked up because he'd gone soft in the head. Others suggested far worse. Whatever the case, he was seen at their star-lighting ceremony one night, never to be seen again. Apparently, the real story was that after he'd lit all the stars in Alfheim's sky, he absent-mindedly held a taper to the moon. The moon shrieked in pain and swatted him with a moon rock, hard enough that he lay on the ground unconscious. The palace servants carried him away, and it was as if he'd never existed. There was no funeral, so he was probably still alive, but no one dared to ask. The queen could be remarkably touchy, as I was to find out later when I tried to warn her about Ragnarok. The moon refused to shine for a full week, and the sun also went dark in sympathy, so I suspect that wide rumblings of discontent among her

subjects during a dark, cold week led the queen to guard
against any further unfortunate accidents.

"Gerda, Ragnarok was the battle that ended the nine worlds.
Only Midgard (the planet Earth) came back. Sadly, Alfheim,
the land of the elves, has never returned."

Gerda nodded. She seemed to understand everything Lin said.

We enjoyed the happy union and went back to Asgard,
where I soon settled back into our usual routine of saving
people. And then came the invitation to the first birthday
party for Folla and Pilk's baby daughter. I had just finished
dealing with a cruel husband who was making his wife and
her daughters utterly miserable. It had been rather taxing,
so I really didn't feel like going, but my lady said we had
to, or it would cause offense. I didn't say so aloud, but she
had two other handmaidens, so I didn't see why it had to
be me. Anyway, if she said I must, I must.

Again, the party was held on the palace grounds. We had
brought a golden chain on which hung a moonstone that
had magical properties that soothed aches and pains. Frigg
handed it to Folla, who kissed her on both cheeks as she
thanked her. Elves were not as immune to suffering as we
gods were. The baby hadn't been brought out yet.

I was so glad I went. The queen had arranged the most
wondrous entertainments on a wide platform, with the
woods as a backdrop. First came a dance performed by
stars that flashed their lights in different colors as they
spun and darted around the stage before they swept back

to their place in the sky as the music came to a close. Then came the golden horses, who leaped over each other, through flaming hoops, and did backflips. At the end, they lay on their backs juggling apples with their hooves, popping them into their mouths, one by one, the last apple being chomped on the final chord of a horn.

There were ballets danced by elves and fairies, who flitted around the stage with wings that almost vibrated like those of hummingbirds. There was even one performed by mermaids, who glided around in a massive tank of water as they writhed and tangled, untangled and stretched, all to the music of what sounded like modern-day harps. I looked around, but couldn't see any musicians. Their performance was strangely hypnotic. Frigg dug her elbow into my side at the end because I wasn't clapping. I wasn't exactly asleep … but in some sort of trance. When I thought back to it later, I felt uneasy about it. There hadn't been much applause, so I wondered how many others had experienced that feeling.

An old gnome came out on the platform, as ugly a gnome as ever I saw, and I've seen plenty. He held up a stick, blew on it, and flames flared along its length. He let it go, standing behind it as he waved his arms about, as if conducting an orchestra. The stick spun in a vertical circle so that the flames seemed to sear my eyes. Just when I felt I couldn't look any longer, the gnome produced another stick from the back of the platform and set that alight, too. The sticks fought a duel, back and forth, up and down, sparks flying every time they clashed with a sound like clanging steel. Next, they both stood straight above the gnome's head and brightened, almost unbearably, until they collapsed in a heap of ash.

As expected, the party ended with fireworks that burst into showers of brilliant color, one depicting a baby girl in a green dress, another depicting the queen in her carriage, and others forming the shapes of animals and birds.

All this while, the baby girl had been clapping her hands and chortling in the front row, crying, "More, more," between chattering excitedly to her parents. Apparently, elf children mature fast. I guess they have to, being so small. She wasn't even a foot tall. She certainly put away several slices of her birthday cake in a hurry, having first blown out the candles in one mighty puff. After that, she wandered around the grounds, saying hello to this guest and that, without her parents or the queen taking any notice of her whatsoever. I was glad to see she was wearing Frigg's pendant, otherwise one of the larger guests might have stepped on her.

A sudden movement among the trees alerted me to the fact that someone or something was hiding back there. Something big and black. I whispered to Frigg that I needed to check out a possible problem.

"It's big and black, and it's hiding."

"I'll come with you."

We moved as inconspicuously as we could, given our relative size. I noticed the queen fix her disapproving gaze on Frigg. We entered the wood well to the right of where I'd seen the creature, moving deep so that we could circle around behind it and tiptoed forward, stopping at the sound of a snuffle. We crept up behind a large tree and peeked around. It was a young giant, not yet big enough to cause a problem for us, but certainly big enough to eat an elf. I walked out in front of him. He cowered, raising his hands as if to ward me off.

"What do you want? Don't hurt me."

"I want to know what you are doing here."

"I'm hungry. My parents said I eat too much, so they brought me here and left me all alone. I'm so, so hungry. I need a nice, fat little elf."

"You will have nothing of the sort. These are our friends and that would be very naughty and rude of you. Did your parents say when they'd be back?"

"No. They told me to eat until I can eat no more. When I fall asleep, they will come and get me."

"Wait here," I told him. "I'll find you some food. But not elves. Their queen will kill you if you do. You don't want that, do you?"

He started to cry. "I'm sorry. I can't help it. I'll try to be good."

I ran back to the party, which was breaking up. I gathered as much of the banquet as I could and ran back to the boy. He gobbled it up in a minute. Elf food wasn't going to be enough. I ran back.

"What do you think you are doing?"

Her Majesty stood behind me, her hands on her hips, and looking very cross. I didn't want to tell her about the giant child, otherwise she'd probably have him killed. But I had to explain this.

"I noticed a movement in the woods, and we went to see if it was something dangerous. It was a young dragon who lost his way. He is very hungry, so hungry, he can't fly. He can still breathe fire, though. If I can take him enough food, he will fly back to his parents. We know the way and will guide him." I looked her in the eye. "We don't want his parents to come looking for him, do we?"

The queen looked startled and called for her servants. "Take all the remaining food to the edge of the woods," she ordered. "Lady Lin will put it to good purpose."

I took what I could carry, and raced back to Frigg, who I found comforting the sobbing boy.

"Here," I said, thrusting the food at him. "The queen's servants are bringing more to the edge of the woods. They think there's a dragon in here, so they won't come any farther."

I went back and forth with the food, and finally, he declared himself satisfied.

"I'll just take a nap under this tree, and they'll come back to take me home," he said, happy once more.

"Remember, no elves," I said. "Otherwise I'll tell the queen about you."

"I'll be good."

We went back to the queen and reported that all was well. She thanked us for dealing with the dragon, and we thanked her for her hospitality before heading home. We checked on the boy first.

"Do you think we should wait?" I asked Frigg.

"No need. Do you hear those heavy steps?"

I did. They crashed through the undergrowth like overgrown elephants. "We'd better make sure they go straight home and don't pick up any elves along the way."

"You are right. Let us climb this tree."

We just reached the tree top when two huge hairy giants came lumbering toward their son. Their heads were only just below our feet. Thank the gods, trees in Alfheim weren't small like the inhabitants. The father had a face that looked as if another giant had held the top of his head with one hand, his chin in the other, and squished them together. The mother was sort of the opposite, with a face like a big fat doughnut, her nose and chin barely in evidence. Without a word, the sour-smelling father scooped up the boy, and they both strode back to the portal between their world and Alfheim, soon disappearing into the misty ice that led to the frozen land of the giants. Our portal led us into a kinder, warmer world.

"Oh, that was a lovely story," exclaimed Gerda, clapping her hands.

"Oh, yes," Rose agreed. "I hope there won't be any giants at our party!"

"No giants. Just me," a gentle voice behind us said.

We all turned to find a slender, boyish figure dressed in blue. He carried a stick and wore a mischievous grin.

"Are you our surprise?" Rose asked, getting to her feet.

"I believe I am. Happy birthday, little girls."

"Thank you," they chorused.

"Come down to the lawn. I want to show you something."

"But it's raining," Rose protested.

"Not anymore," he said.

We looked out of the window. The rain had stopped, and the sun shone. Auntie picked up Penny, whom I'd put back in her playpen when she fell asleep.

"Ooh," the girls said, running toward the terrace steps, followed by their canine retinue.

"You boys stay here," commanded the stranger, pointing to Tor, Sam, and Hyndla, who all sat down with a disgruntled thump.

We all stood at the terrace rail to see what was going to happen.

"Who is that?" I asked Lin. "And where's Hunter?"

"That is Tok, a magic man recently awoken in Asgard. He loves showing off. Tok will put on quite a show for them because he is grateful to Hunter for killing Freya and setting him free. He used to be under her command. His powers were never very strong, but enough to entertain."

Hunter appeared at my shoulder. "I had to recover from getting Tok down here. He is rather flighty. I hope he pays attention and does not do something silly. Lin, you should ask Frigg to take him on."

I asked, "Lin, was that birthday party story true?" To say it sounded farfetched seemed odd under the circumstances, but it did.

"Mostly," she replied with a quick smile.

I turned my attention to the lawn, where the girls squealed as Tok spun so fast, he looked like a blur of cloudy sky. As he began to slow down, at the same time moving toward a rose bed, he stopped in the middle of the plants, singing a strange lilting tune that sounded almost like a lullaby. The roses pulled themselves out of the soil and he led them to the girls, waving his stick—a wand, I guess—as if conducting an orchestra. The flowers danced around the girls, their scent filling the air even up to where we stood.

"He's better put those back in good order," Lin hissed. She was proud of her roses.

"He will," Hunter assured her. He looked at me with a grimace that indicated he hoped so but wasn't so sure.

Tok stopped singing and, waving his wand once more, pointed it at the rose bed. The roses danced over there and wiggled their way back into the soil like pole dancers shimmying for the crowd. Lin peered anxiously as if expecting them to flop over.

Tok began to spin again, his wand held in both hands and pointing at the sun. The air turned dark, and it began to snow, although the temperature remained warm. The girls caught flakes on their tongues, dancing around the edge of the lawn to the music of what sounded like a symphony orchestra as the snow fell softly around them. I stood mesmerized, watching this crazy spectacle. The girls seemed bewitched as they pirouetted and leaped, their arms moving like wings. Tok watched, too, motionless now, his smile verging on a grimace. I began to panic. Would it stop? Would he make them dance until they dropped?

He looked straight at me and laughed. He raised his wand, conducting the music more and more slowly, until it died away. The girls curtseyed as we applauded. They didn't seem at all the worse for wear.

"I was becoming a little concerned," I whispered to Hunter.

"He wouldn't dare hurt them," he said.

"Would he have liked to?"

"He has his days. He can be mischievous."

"Oh, that's reassuring."

Don't worry, Mary. I'm watching closely. I kept forgetting about our ability to read each other's minds. I hoped the children didn't catch on to it anytime soon.

A loud chorus started up, with what sounded like heavenly choir singing "Happy birthday to you," and so on. All at once, hundreds of brightly colored balloons came floating down to the girls. They caught all that they could, running around the lawn with them streaming behind. Those that they couldn't catch floated up and down, and around in circles.

"Look," Tok called out.

All the loose balloons turned into brightly colored butterflies that flew into and above the trees and beyond until they were out of sight. The music stopped after repeating the song again and again. Tok turned to us and bowed. He blew a kiss to the girls, waved his wand, and flew after the butterflies. Rose and Gerda stood waving goodbye until they could see him no more.

More excitement was to come when Gerda was given her presents, which were a great success, and very similar to Rose's. Joe and Helen couldn't attend, but Rose had already promised to share the movies, so that was all right. To my surprise, Gerda burst into tears after she'd opened the last gift.

"Whatever's the matter?" I asked her.

She was sobbing too hard to answer. Auntie held her and talked softly to her in German. Soon, the tears were mopped up, and a smile reappeared.

"I have never had a birthday party. I have never had lovely presents. I am so happy." She almost started to cry again.

Rose hugged her tightly. "We all love you and want you to be happy," she told her.

"Time for cake!" Hunter called, relieved that the tears were over. He didn't know how to handle tears.

We hadn't seen the cake yet. I know Lin had ordered it from the gourmet grocery store in Salton, so it was bound to be special. It was quite a confection. Two tiers of tiered chocolate cake with raspberry jam between each layer and chocolate icing dotted with fondant roses. There were fourteen pink candles, seven in two circles, so they could each blow out their own. It was a work of art.

"That is the most loveliest cake ever," Rose said.

"Wonderful," Gerda whispered.

"Wait a minute," Lin said. "I'm going to call Gerda's mother." Gretchen had called Gerda earlier to wish her a happy birthday, but I guess Lin thought she'd enjoy seeing this.

Gretchen answered, and Lin held up the phone while they blew out the candles. Lin passed the phone to Auntie, who chatted with her while Dora and Lin argued about how best to cut the cake. The girls became fidgety. Hunter took the knife from Dora, cut two large slices from the bottom tier, and handed them to the girls, who bore them off to the terrace to enjoy without grownup interference.

"Don't give any to the dogs," I called out to them. "Chocolate is poisonous for dogs."

I hurried after them because I wasn't sure they'd believe me. I'd heard that coping with dogs after they've eaten chocolate could be an unpleasant experience.

Dinner was served a couple of hours later. The girls were exhausted from all the excitement and didn't eat much. They were more than ready for bed by eight, and took themselves back to our wing, saying they could get themselves ready.

"I'll go and check in a few minutes," Auntie said.

We both stayed the night and slept in the next morning.

25

The resumption of discussions about Odin's visit led to a very busy few weeks. So many details: rain date, dais, security, and publicity, to name a few. The garden's concession stand would be open. First aid? Probably not. I didn't bother with microphones as I figured that if anyone could make themselves heard, it would be Odin. I had no idea how many to expect, but arranged for two college kids to guide parking. I wondered how event planners could stand doing this for a living.

And while all this was going on, I had to get the girls ready for school. Gerda had made quite good progress with English, but she would still struggle with it. I knew Rose would help her. Auntie and I still worked on their languages every morning, and I noticed the girls would speak together in a sort of mixture of English and German words. I'd made sure that they'd be in the same first-grade class.

School opened on the Tuesday after Labor Day. Hunter drove us. Gerda was quiet, clearly apprehensive. I got out and walked them in, holding each by the hand. When we reached their new classroom, I introduced them to the teacher, Miss Bellmont.

"Pleased to meet you, Madame," Gerda said.

"Likewise," Rose added.

Miss Bellmont was a motherly-looking type, who drew the girls to her bosom, which startled them both.

"How lovely to meet you," she said when she released them. "I know you will be very happy here, Gerda."

"Thank you, Miss Bellmont."

"Such lovely manners," she said, casting a glance at Rose.

"Yes, thank you," my daughter said. Better late than never.

I wished them goodbye and left. When I picked them up later, they looked disheveled, tired, and happy.

"Good day?" I asked.

"Oh, yes," Rose said. "Everyone liked Gerda, and they all helped her with words. We had a lovely time on the playground, too."

I was so relieved. I'd been afraid that Gerda would be teased. Children can be so cruel. My sister was horribly teased for her stutter. It only made it worse. My mother homeschooled her for two years and managed to afford therapy. Once she could more or less control it, she was sent to a Catholic school with a different set of kids. She was never that academically strong but graduated, then married her first boyfriend. She ended up just like my mother, a put-upon wife and mother, always worried about money and losing interest in her appearance. At least Lizzie had smartened herself up.

That recollection raised another pang of guilt. When she visited me, we had little to say to each other. We were so very different. And my current circumstances were hardly shareable in their entirety.

Anyway, all went well for Gerda, and her English seemed to improve by the day. Since I was so busy, Auntie took over after school. She supervised homework and then went over language training with both, having them both read and translate.

Lin and Gretchen kept in touch. Gretchen called my phone every Sunday to talk with Gerda, but we only exchanged cursory greetings. The calls usually ended in tears, but Gerda's soon dried as time went on. Gretchen was now in Switzerland. The Grunewald estate had been sold to a hotel chain, and she had applied for a visa to emigrate to Canada. Coming to the U.S. had proved too complicated, as we thought it might. Meanwhile, she was taking English lessons and hoping for the best. The trial was long over, and her husband was in a secure prison, so finally she felt free.

"Even criminals don't like rapists," Lin said. "With any luck, one of them will solve the problem."

"One can only hope," I replied.

Later, I thought about how easily I fell in with that sentiment, that concept of rough justice. Well, look at the misery the men in that family had caused. I hoped he didn't have any sons we didn't know about.

One of the girls in Rose's class took ballet lessons. She brought her ballet shoes into school one day and demonstrated some steps. That did it. It reminded Rose of her wish to learn ballet, which I had forgotten about. Now Gerda wanted to take ballet, too.

"Please, Papa," was all it took. He'd already agreed to Rose taking classes, anyway.

I found a school that had good reviews. They taught an English method called "Royal Academy" and seemed to get good exam results. They could go straight from school once a week. I would wait in the lobby. This meant going to the store to buy the necessary gear, which meant a trip across the bridge to St. Mary's County one Saturday morning. Both girls were thrilled to bits with their pale blue leotards, pink tights, and pink leather ballet shoes.

They loved the class. I didn't know anything about ballet, so had no idea if the instruction was any good. I knew that the required repetition of exercises could be tedious, so wondered if it would last. Gerda had been a little tubby when she came over, but with all the outdoor playing and now ballet, she looked good.

26

inally, the day arrived, comfortably warm, but not too hot, and no rain in the forecast. Odin materialized while we were eating breakfast. To my surprise, he wore khakis, a white shirt, red tie, and brown loafers. The only oddity was an eye patch. He looked like an oversized Mormon. He laughed when he spotted my incredulity.

"I observe from afar, my dear. This is how those who spread the word usually dress, is it not?"

"Indeed, they do," I said. "You look the part."

He looked pleased. He followed Hunter into the study. Hunter would drive him to the gardens as if he were a normal person. I needed to leave earlier to make sure everything was on track for the 2 p.m. kickoff. Sven and Margareta had come home for this extraordinary phenomenon. Auntie would drive with them. Gerda and Rose would stay with Dora.

At noon, the Norse groups started to arrive. I welcomed the Maryland group, appreciating their numbers. It was nice to see those warm people again. Various other groups came in, too many to welcome personally. Around 1:30, many people arrived either in pairs or alone. A flock of devout Quakers filed in. No doubt others less obvious would be present. One group worried me a little, as they looked rough and angry. Several with unruly beards, all with dirty t-shirts with various nasty depictions emblazoned front and back, such as skull and crossbones, Love Jesus or Die, and so on. I went in search of the security guards to ask them to keep an eye on them. I found all three gorging themselves on hamburgers by the concession stand.

"Time to get to work," I said. "There's a group that looks as if they could be trouble." All three were moonlighting cops, and all three clearly regarded the job as a boondoggle. I felt as if I should be keeping an eye on them.

I was getting worried at five minutes before the start when neither Hunter nor Odin were on site. "Don't worry, they're here." I just about jumped out of my skin. It was Lin, of course, who had crept up behind me.

"I am worried. There's a group that looks like trouble."

"I saw them. I'll stay close. See, I told you."

I turned to the dais, and there they were. Two gods that looked alike—Odin larger than Hunter, neither of them betraying their age—incalculable in human comprehension—blond hair, and a sort of white glow surrounding each. The crowd suddenly quietened to an abnormal degree. There must have been around a thousand present.

Odin raised his arms. "My dear brothers and sisters. I am so happy to see you in front of me, with me. As you can probably guess, I am Odin. I have recently awakened from a very long sleep resulting from the terrible events of Ragnarok, the final battle. But now our heavenly Asgard is coming back to life, as are the gods.

"I do not come here to convert you, to pull you away from your own religious beliefs. I do not look to be adored or worshipped. I have seen many terrible crimes committed through the ages in the name of religion. I wish only for that to cease. It is unnecessary. Those of you who are Christians, read the gospels once more and follow their message of peace, love, and tolerance. Moslems, participate in the fourth jihad, that is, remove all wrongdoing from your heart. Jews, reflect upon the central message of your Torah, to love your neighbor as yourself. There is nothing in those holy books that asks you to hate those who are different or to turn away the needy. Embrace the good, throw away the bad ideas and thoughts that may have been invited into your spiritual life, usually by others with something to gain. The same is true for other religions, too. Read your holy books and look for the good in them. Then look for cruelty and hatred. I am sure you will not find these evil things."

"Heathen! Antichrist!" The man stood close to me—no one you'd give a second glance to. He raised a pistol and shot at Odin, who extended his hand and caught the bullet. He held it up to show the audience. Lin knocked the shooter to the ground and twisted both arms behind him until he cried out. Two security guards came running amid screams and people running in all directions.

"Stop!" Odin roared. And they did.

"Not you lot," Lin snapped at the guards.

The crowd turned to face Odin again.

"You see, this man is afraid. He has lived with his beliefs all his life, both good and bad. His friends no doubt think like him. They are a tribe. It is frightening to have these beliefs challenged, these ideas that are part of you, glued to your soul. It feels as if something is being torn out of your body if those beliefs have to be reformed and, in some cases, discarded. Fear of what we do not understand. That is what we must fight. As I said at the beginning, embrace the good, shun the bad."

The white aura thickened and they disappeared.

Some in the crowd left, quiet and frightened. Others talked excitedly among themselves.

I expected that at least one reporter would have been present. He or she would have rushed out to file their report. I walked some distance to a white statue of something I had yet to figure out—probably the sculptor hadn't either—and sat with my back against it. All that hard work had paid off. The shooting, while very scary, had not ruined Odin's speech. I hoped it would make a difference, that his word would spread.

"People don't give up their hatred that easily." Lin again. She sat beside me. "Despising others makes insecure people feel superior. And those who are angry because their lives are difficult need someone to blame. And politicians are only too ready to offer them a scapegoat."

"I know. I just hope some people will spread the word. Maybe the press will help."

"We'll see. People have short attention spans these days, and they're intrinsically selfish."

"Boy, you have a low opinion of the population."

"This population and others. Remember just how long I've been observing human nature."

I paid the guards and parking attendants in cash. The venue contract had included clean-up, fortunately, although I noticed there wasn't much litter. I felt exhausted as I trailed Lin to our cars. Had it been worth it? And what would happen to the would-be assassin? It's not as if they could find Odin. And they wouldn't know Hunter, either. At least, I hoped not. I'd used my mother's maiden name and had not given my address to anyone. I didn't want trouble or attention.

At home, I found Rose and Gerda in Hunter's lap—one on each leg, where he was applying an adhesive bandage to their wrists. They didn't look upset—quite the contrary. Odin stood next to them.

"What happened?"

"It's your turn next," Sven said.

Everyone had bandages on their wrists, even Dora, Stan, and Penny.

"What's going on?"

"I blessed you all with some godly qualities the first time we met," Odin said. "Now you are to be blessed with immortality. My gift to the family of Hoenir and Lin for their contributions to our heavenly rebirth."

I looked at my immortal daughter and her friend. They looked the same. So did Auntie. Odin took my wrist and made a small cut quickly and almost painlessly with a tiny silver knife. A few drops of blood welled up. His wrist was already cut open to a larger degree. He squeezed some white liquid—god's blood, I guess—from his own cut and mixed it with mine. A tremor shook me as I closed my eyes, feeling something like an electric current run down every limb, then into my head. My heart seemed to skip and dance dangerously but soon quietened. I opened my eyes as Margareta bandaged my wrist.

"You'd better sit down," she said.

Sam nosed my hand before sitting down and licking his foreleg.

"Him, too?" I asked her.

"Yup."

I looked for Odin, but he had left.

"We'll be together forever, Mama," my little Rose said, taking my hand and leading me to an armchair. "Forever and ever."

Gerda looked sad. "I will not have my Mama forever, though."

"No, that's true," said Rose. "But we will have each other."

27

The rest of October passed uneventfully, apart from media stories popping up of surprise appearances at Quaker meetings, Norse blots, and even churches and temples of people claiming they were representatives of Odin and preaching "Odin's Word." Sometimes these were welcomed, and sometimes not. Some of the preachers were clearly fakes. Lin said that Odin had begun to send some of those gods and goddesses that had woken up to spread the word. They were able to get away with it because they could suddenly materialize in the pulpit, or wherever the faith leader usually proclaimed from. Lesser mortals just barged in, which didn't go down so well. Materialization always tends to grab people's attention. A TV talk show managed to catch one appearance when a Quaker reporter happened to be present and could catch it on her phone.

Social media fairly buzzed with it all for a while. But it wasn't long before the appearances took on the normality of mass shootings. Notable, but not shocking. But various news sources reported how attendance at religious gatherings had increased and sermons had taken on a message of love and peace rather than one of sin and punishment.

Politicians were concerned, and one of the more right-wing factions had begun to clamor for congressional hearings. Just whom they expected to interrogate in their grandstanding procedures, they didn't mention.

We spent Saturdays, and often Sunday, too, at the castle. Both girls were devoted to Penny, and she responded to their attentions with delightful coos and gurgles. She was crawling now, so Dora was glad of their watchfulness. Sam and Tor kept watch, too. I remembered how Sam was with Rose—always on duty when she was a baby.

One rainy Saturday, I said, "Lin, we've hardly got any tapes for this year. I think we'll have to combine with next year."

"You said the same thing last year! But it's all right," she said. "Think about it. We are here for good. All of us. Time will keep passing and we will keep living. We don't want to draw attention to ourselves. Maybe these memoirs will never be published. But at least I get to reminisce and have a record of everything. Maybe we'll have to rise to heaven one day. Who knows what lies ahead?"

Strange as it may seem, I hadn't given a lot of thought to my immortality. But now, I realize that things will change enormously over the years to come and I will be here to see it all. Look at the twentieth century and how things changed in science and transportation, just to name two things. Who knows what would happen politically, apart from anything else? So much of the world was unsettled. The American political scene was a three-ring circus, and millions lived in misery. Even our planet might not survive. What then? This led to a sleepless night. I wondered if Auntie had these thoughts. It turns out she did. But she tended to be more philosophical.

"There was this popular song when I was young," she said. '*Que sera, sera*'. Whatever will be will be. Nothing we can do about it."

"Unless Odin manages."

"Evil is not so easily vanquished," she said. "And leadership attracts evil men. It's lust—for power and wealth. Of course, the exploitation of women comes along with that."

"What about women leaders?"

"Of course, they are sometimes evil. Just not so often. And if you look at a lot of them, they tend to have male characteristics."

"I've never thought of female leaders that way," I said.

I tried to put aside my worries and carry on as usual. When Auntie visited Dora, Hunter would visit me. I was trying to get used to thinking of him as Hoenir but kept forgetting. We never tired of each other. I felt completely bonded to him, and, to a lesser extent, to Lin.

Things were still going well for the girls. Gerda was thrilled to hear that her mother would visit the castle at Thanksgiving, and might even be able to stay until Christmas.

The ballet school would hold a little recital close to Christmas in their private school's auditorium. A few dances featuring some of the students in each piece. Gerda and Rose would perform a duet. I could hardly wait. I had to buy costumes, but thankfully had nothing to do with their acquisition or construction. I had a friend at school who took ballet, and remembered how her mother slaved away to sew her costumes for the recitals.

Parents were allowed to watch class once a month. The first time I went, it looked pretty basic, and the girls coped quite well. By the second visit a month later, they had been promoted to the next grade. That was after their immortality was granted, so no doubt godly qualities had something to do with it.

One Saturday morning in November, I'd dropped the girls off at the castle early, because I wanted to do some shopping across the bridge in St. Mary's County. There was a greater variety of shops over there. I left the shopping in the trunk and went through to the living room. Hunter and Lin weren't around, so I assumed the girls would be in the kitchen with Dora.

"Where are the girls?" I asked Dora.

"Tok took them out for a treat. He said Hunter knew all about it."

"I'm afraid I was outside at the time," Auntie said, wringing her hands. "I'm sorry."

"It's not your fault."

Tok took the girls. Did you tell him he could?

No, I'm coming.

What was Tok up to? Was he as kindly as he seemed? Fear gripped me. Where was Hunter?

I went out to the terrace and scanned the field to see if there was any sign of them. Fear gripped me. Only the animals were there, the dogs circling and sniffing. Hyndla, in particular, looked agitated, pacing back and forth. I remembered the funny look on Tok's face as he watched them dance. What did he want?

Where the hell are you?

No answer.

After a while, I heard Hunter talking to Dora.

I rushed into the kitchen.

"He just appeared. The girls were in here having some cookies and hot cocoa. The dogs were outside. He told me you said he could take the little girls for a treat. They were excited. He put his arms around them, spun in a sort of blue swirl, and was gone."

Hunter took my arm and led me back to the living room.

"I was trying to communicate with Odin. I could not penetrate his mind for some reason. I will try again. He will cast his eye over his world and this one to find them."

He leaned forward, holding his head in his hands. The veins in his neck stood out and his hands clenched. He sat up again.

"We are being blocked. I do not understand who or what has the power to do this."

"Do you think he is seeking vengeance for Freya, despite saying he was glad to be free?"

"That is possible. I hope not. If I cannot find Odin, I will have to go to Asgard to see if he is there. My little Rose. Little Gerda."

He looked close to tears. I know I was.

Lin came in. "I will go with Hunter. We will find them. Don't worry."

Of course, I worried. And Gerda's mother would be here next week. What on earth would we tell her if her daughter wasn't back? *Sorry, a magician spirited your daughter away.* She'd have us in straight-jackets, and possibly in jail.

"We will get them back," Lin said. "For sure. Tok isn't that clever."

I was sure he was clever enough to harm them if he wanted to avenge Freya.

Don't think that way. Hunter kissed my forehead before they both disappeared.

It was the next day before they returned, neither of the girls seemingly aware of their absence. In the meantime, I spent the time wandering, crying, and obsessively cleaning their bedrooms and ironing their clothes. Auntie tried to comfort me, to no avail.

"Hi, Mama!" Rose called as she appeared on the terrace. "We've had a lovely walk with Papa and Lin. Here, we picked some flowers for you."

I don't know how I didn't burst into tears, but I managed to accept the flowers graciously and kiss them both. Auntie didn't say a word. Dora appeared, holding Penny.

"Girls, why don't you come and have some milk and cookies? I made some fresh this morning."

Rose took Penny before they followed Dora into the kitchen, along with Auntie. I needed a good bawl, so excused myself and went to my room.

"We'll talk later," Lin whispered as I passed her chair.

I put the flowers in a vase without looking at them too closely, setting them on my dresser. Curled up in bed, I let it all out, just about emptying a box of tissues. I made myself stop and wash my face in cold water. I didn't want Rose and Gerda to see my swollen eyes. They clearly had no idea anything was wrong. I pushed down all the "what ifs" I'd been torturing myself with and resolved to pull myself together. The girls were back home, none the worse for their experience—whatever that was.

Hunter came down after a while and folded me into his arms. He said nothing—he didn't need to. His embrace calmed me. After half an hour or so, he kissed me and left.

I got up and looked closely at the vase. I cupped what looked like a rose in my hand. It wasn't quite like any other rose I'd seen. It was almost green and had curly leaves. But it smelled like a rose. Rose said they'd picked wildflowers. I guess she meant flowers that weren't in a regular flower bed. And there was a bright blue daisy that had no scent.

Otherworldly, indeed. I decided to press them before they died. A sort of souvenir, but one I wouldn't be showing off.

I went back to the main wing in time for dinner. I remembered it was Sunday. We'd have to go back to my house right afterward as it was a school day tomorrow. I thought they'd done most of their homework on Friday after school and Saturday morning. I'd taken to insisting on that when I knew we were going to the castle for the weekend because they didn't want to waste a moment doing boring schoolwork when they could be doing more important things. I'd check their bags when I got home to make sure it was all done.

There were the usual protests after dinner about leaving.

"But we just got here," Rose said, frowning.

"Time passes quickly when you're having fun," I said, wincing as soon as the cliché left my mouth. "It's Sunday today."

Both girls looked at each other, puzzled. I looked at Hunter. *Say something.*

"Your mother is right. Today is Sunday. I think that you lost track of time. It happens sometimes."

Lin saw us to the car. "I'll come over for coffee in the morning," she whispered after the girls were strapped in.

Lin arrived at eleven the next morning, armed with a cheesecake. I poured coffee, plated generous slices of cake, and we sat down.

"I'm going to stay sitting, so you can use your phone," she said, before forking a good chunk of cake into her mouth. "As you can see, the girls are confused about their lost weekend, but they remember nothing of the events in Asgard. They were unharmed. Tok wanted to punish Hunter, not the girls.

Let me finish my cake. I've changed my mind, I think I'll recline after that."

I finished my cake and coffee, trying not to appear impatient. I'd set the tape recorder just in case. Finally, she was ready.

Tape 12,
Volume 4

Arriving in Asgard was a shock. We saw nothing and no one. No palaces, no trees, no flowers. Not even any clouds. It was a void. Then we heard the children laughing, somewhere toward the horizon. We couldn't understand it, because there was nothing to be seen in any direction. Flat nothingness. We started to run toward the voices, but it felt like running underwater. We knew then that Tok had erected barriers, both physical and visual. He had become more powerful than we realized.

I don't know how long we ran, but we finally collapsed to the ground, spent. And you know how strong we are. We hung our heads, concentrating on replenishing our power. When we felt restored, we rose again, only to find a field in front of us. Both children were there, playing catch with a flying ball that threw itself around them and up in the air so they could grab it. Tok stood watching, calling out encouragement.

"Very good, Rose. You're better at catching the ball than your father ever was."

Rose threw the ball at him, which he caught on the tip of a finger. "My papa is good at everything."

We both surged forward, only to be smacked in the face. We extended our arms to feel where this barrier might begin and end. I even jumped many feet in the air. I felt it curve slightly high up, so it was a kind of transparent globe. We banged on the wall. It rebounded a little, but we couldn't break it. Tok ran over to us and blew us a kiss.

"You took Freya from me, so I have taken something precious from you," he yelled, dancing up and down. "You can't break this spell, and Odin can't help you."

"What have you done to Odin?" Hunter roared.

"Let's say he's frozen in time, together with all his gods."

I looked to see the girls' reaction to this exchange, but they were playing on swings now and had no idea we were here, or that Tok was shouting these taunts.

Hunter told me to do what I could there, and he would try to find Odin. I sat down and tried to think of some way to break the barrier. If only I'd thought of calling Agna. I tried communing with her, but couldn't get through, which didn't surprise me.

"What do you want?" I called.

"I want Asgard for myself. I will lead the gods to glory and force their worship on Midgard."

"Do you really think they will follow you?"

"They will have no choice. I am more powerful than any of them."

"Yes, I can see you have become very powerful. I don't remember seeing you practice your art with Freya."

"It was our little secret. Me and Agna. Only Agna betrayed her, and she will pay for it."

Good thing I hadn't brought Agna into it.

"I know Freya planned to rule the Aesir. But she wasn't strong enough in the end. Hoenir will not endanger his precious Rose. Will he choose Rose or Odin? I think we both know the answer to that."

"Of course. He will be heartbroken, but he will choose Odin. His duty demands it, you see."

"You know that isn't true."

"Why aren't you satisfied with living under Odin's rule? He is a just god."

"He killed my beloved. I cannot forgive that."

"Supposing I deal with Odin? Hoenir cannot, but I can. And I am just as strong. You know Hoenir is not interested in ruling. He is not a leader. He lacks wisdom, you see. And he knows it."

"What can you do to Odin?"

"During the many thousands of years on earth, I have learned many things. There are no witches on Earth now, but there used to be. And there are ways. Do you know how I can completely destroy Odin? I can look him in the eye so hard and bright it will blind him. I don't think you yet have the strength to do that. If he is blind, he can no longer cast his eye over the worlds and dispense wisdom and justice."

"Show me. Blind Odin and you can have the little girls. I'm not sure about Hoenir yet."

Something like a small tornado came swirling toward me from the right. A mighty thump revealed Odin completely encased in a block of ice, with Hunter hugging the ice.

"Trying to melt it," he gasped.

Tok laughed. "Not so easy, my friend."

Hunter tried to step away but found himself stuck. He pulled and tugged, swore and kicked, but it did no good.

"All right, do your worst. Blind the god, Lin." Tok stood, arms akimbo, grinning insanely.

"I can't do it through ice. There can be nothing between our eyes. No barrier."

"It's a trick!"

"How was I to know you'd iced him up? I thought you'd put him in chains or something."

"What are you talking about?" Hunter yelled.

"I promised to blind Odin in return for getting the girls back."

"You can't do that!"

"I think I can. Just as soon as he serves him up neat."

"Lin, no, Tok will ruin Earth after he ruins Asgard."

"Earth is ruining itself. Do you want your daughter back?"

Hunter started to cry. Suddenly, his arms were released from the ice and he lay curled up on the ground crying. In spite of the dire circumstances, I felt like writhing with embarrassment.

"Get up," I hissed. "Stop that at once."

He took no notice.

"All right, let's get this done."

Tok waved his wand, and the ice melted in a gush of water that soaked Hunter. He took no notice but continued his unseemly display. Odin straightened and stared at Tok, then at me.

"She is going to blind you, false god," Tok shrieked. "You are finished."

I moved to face Odin with my back to Tok. And winked. "I am sorry, my lord Odin. I have no choice. Tok will only give us back the little girls if I blind you. I learned many things on earth over the ages, and this is one of them. He has set a magic barrier, you see, so that we cannot reach the girls.

"Stop talking and get on with it." Tok's tone had turned from mocking to menacing.

"Look at me, Odin. Look me in the eye. Do you feel your eye clouding, pulling back into your head?"

Odin clasped the sides of his head in his hands.

"Do you feel the darkness, the desolation, the end of your vision and wisdom?"

Odin moaned, pleaded. "No, do not do this terrible thing. Please."

"Do you understand that it is all over now? That Tok commands Asgard and the Aesir?"

Odin fell to his knees, his hands covering his face. When he removed his hands, his eye looked empty. Hunter wept louder.

I turned to Tok. "Keep your end of the bargain. Take down the barrier."

He waved his wand, and I rushed over to the girls, picked up one in each arm, and ran back to Hunter. "Let's go," I said. Hunter embraced the girls, burying their heads in his chest.

Tok stood in front of Odin and Hunter. "I didn't say Hoenir could go."

Odin looked up, threw his arms around Tok, and roared. I snatched the wand out of Tok's flailing hand and broke it over my knee. It stung and burned me, but I barely noticed. Tok's screams became fainter and fainter as Odin crushed him. To say that Tok became a shadow of his former self is an understatement. Odin dropped his remains and stabbed a finger at them. They burst into flames.

I looked around to see gods and goddesses strolling in fields lined with trees and flowers. A magnificent palace shone in the distance.

"Go now," said Odin. "If you do not linger, the girls will remember nothing."

"Do you think he would have hurt them?" I asked Lin.

"I don't think so. They would have been in his service forever."

I shivered. "Thank heavens you tricked him."

"He wasn't as clever as he thought. Like his beloved Freya."

"But why didn't Tok blind him? He had powerful magic."

"Because he dared not look Odin in the eye. He could not overcome that power."

28

Hunter and Lin took the girls to Heathrow to meet Gretchen two days before Thanksgiving. Lin told me later that she was overcome by Gerda's growth and English language ability and also Rose's ability to converse in German. I wondered what Gretchen would make of a pet fox frolicking with a spaniel and a Great Dane.

Gerda and her mother went straight upstairs so that Gretchen could freshen up. We all waited for them in the living room. Margareta and Sven had arrived home for the holiday just as Gretchen and Gerda reappeared. Rose rushed to them for a welcome hug. Gerda hung back.

"Oh, come here, silly," Sven said, opening his arms. Margareta hugged Gerda, too. Introductions were made, and everyone sat while Hunter and Sven made drinks. Gretchen's English had also come a long way.

"I have been taking English instruction for three months every day," she explained.

"You have done very well," Lin replied.

"Exceedingly," Auntie added. "And Gerda has worked hard at her lessons."

"Ah, I have you to thank for that, Peggy," Gretchen replied.

"No, my niece Mary taught Gerda. I taught Rose German."

"Well, everything is good, then."

We sipped our drinks and chatted until called in to dinner.

"What are your plans, Gretchen?" Lin asked.

"My visa for Canada has come. I have a friend in Toronto and will move there. Quite soon, I think. Maybe February. My friend is keeping her eyes open for a good house."

"Excellent," Lin said. "Congratulations."

I noticed Gerda and Rose staring into each other's eyes.

"Mama, does that mean I have to leave my school and my ballet class, and Rose?"

"Of course. You are my daughter. We should be together." Gretchen looked hurt.

"Of course I want to be with you, Mama. But I would like to finish my year at school instead of starting a new one in the middle."

"Oh. Well. We shall see."

As every parent says so very often.

Gerda looked downcast.

"Gretchen, perhaps that is not such a bad idea," Lin said. "Gerda will finish first grade, her English will be even better than it is now, and you will be able to move into your house and get used to the neighborhood. You can visit anytime. Toronto is only an hour's flight away. You can look for a good school for Gerda, too. You will not be so rushed."

"But is it not too much for all of you? She has been here a very long time."

"No, we love her. And she is Rose's best friend. She is welcome anytime."

"Can Rose come to Toronto with me so we can explore together?" Gerda asked.

"Of course, *Liebchen*. For the whole summer if she likes."

The girls laughed and clapped their hands. I didn't feel that great about Rose being gone for a summer. But it wasn't Timbuktu. And I had never been to Toronto. I could see that Hunter wasn't that keen, either, but he kept quiet.

"I have been to Toronto," Auntie said. "It is a lovely city. Lots of green, good restaurants, good theater, and other cultural events. And nice people. Much nicer than New York." She continued in German, perhaps repeating what she said in English.

"I am happy to hear that," Gretchen said, looking happier. "Perhaps you should come soon and help me to settle."

"I would love to," Aunty said, looking excited.

After dinner, we went back to the living room for coffee. The girls were taking care of Penny, who seemed to be teething and was fretful. At nine, I thought it high time to get Rose home and into bed.

"Rose, it's time to go." Both girls got up. "Gerda, you will stay here tonight with your mother."

She looked embarrassed. "Yes, of course. I am so used to going everywhere with Rose."

"I'll take care of Penny," Margareta said, picking up the baby from the rug on the floor. She took her to the far end of the room and started to talk to her, just like I remembered her talking to Rose at her first Christmas all those years ago.

"Papa," Rose said in a wheedling tone she kept for him, "do I really have to go now?"

"What did your mother say?"

"She said we have to go."

"Then that is what you shall do."

She pouted, kissed everyone, and we left.

I said, "The day after tomorrow is Thanksgiving, so it will be a lovely day. And Gerda and Frau Grunewald's first Thanksgiving. So, very special."

Rose said in a flat tone, "We learned about Thanksgiving at school, so at least she knows the story."

I wondered which particular story they'd been fed.

29

The table looked even better than usual. Margareta had found slender branches with crimson leaves and created a spectacular centerpiece with dried orange slices and nuts wound among them.

I briefly explained to Gretchen the meaning of Thanksgiving in the U.S.A., and she told me how farmers and other agricultural organizations come to Vienna every September to give thanks for the harvest, showcase their products, and offer educational programs for city folks on agricultural matters.

Joe and Helen came, which delighted Rose, as we hadn't seen them since her birthday. Eir, of course (she'd told me to drop the "doctor"), Lettie and a new beau named Charlie, and all of us. The loud chatter and happy greetings lifted my spirits—not that they'd been low—and everyone looked relaxed, even Gretchen. The kids would sit at a separate table with Margareta and Sven presiding, with Penny in her high-chair between Rose and Margareta. Even the Thorens' large table wouldn't comfortably accommodate so many people if the kids sat with us. Lin felt that Dora and Stan should not be left out in the kitchen, but must join us as members of the family. Dora, of course, would be up and down, but Auntie and I could help carry things in and out.

Rose frowned when she found out she wouldn't be sitting next to her beloved Papa and Uncle Joe, but when I explained Penny needed someone to look after her, she readily acquiesced. She loved the straw turkey that adorned her table, too.

The meal was magnificent, as always. The turkey was golden and succulent, and the sides, which I always enjoyed the most, were many and varied. I was just waiting to see what Gretchen made of the pumpkin pie. It wasn't to everyone's taste anyway, but to a foreigner who had never heard of it? She loved it, loved everything. She was dressed more elegantly than when we met, first in Denmark, then in Austria. The sweet lady smiled a lot and chatted away without worrying about making mistakes like she had in the past. Finally, Gretchen was amongst people who liked her and appreciated her. I hoped she'd meet a nice man soon. But perhaps she wouldn't trust her judgment. She couldn't have been more than in her mid-thirties and was a very attractive woman.

One thing Gretchen did not know about was her daughter's immortality. I wondered if Gerda would tell her. Would she be happy about it? Or angry with us for letting it happen? And she had no idea about the gods. The whole situation would come as a shock, as I well knew. Well, I didn't see how she could be angry about her daughter's guaranteed forever life.

Rose and Gerda were telling Margareta and Sven about their ballet school recital the week before Christmas. They both promised to attend, as exams would be over by then.

"What are they saying?" Gretchen asked.

"The girls have been taking ballet lessons," I told her. "We are allowed to watch the class once a month. Next week is the one. I'll take you. They love it."

"I did ballet dancing when I was a girl," she said wistfully. "My father made me stop because my marks in mathematics were not very good one summer. I cried a lot."

"They are very good at it," I said. "I'm sure there are very good ballet schools in Toronto."

"I am sure," she said. She looked uneasy.

"What's the matter?"

"She is so happy here with her school, with you and Rose, and her activities. I do not think she will be happy to leave all of you."

"No, she won't. But children adapt quickly. And if Rose comes with her for a while, that will make it easier."

"Yes, you are right. How strange it is. When the girls met, they were friends at once, and they could not even talk to each other. It is quite special, is it not?"

"Very special," I said. "They will miss each other. Perhaps you will bring Gerda sometimes. You will both be very welcome. Why don't you bring them back for their birthdays next summer?"

"They'd like that, as will I. Thank you. I think you are all wonderful. And in the summer, why not come with us to Toronto?"

"I'd love to." I patted her hand, and we smiled at each other. I didn't have friends anymore—outside the family, that is—and I felt I might have found one.

30

Gretchen and I went to the girls' ballet class the next week. We sat in the row of chairs in the usual studio as the girls started to file in. Where were they? Their teacher spotted me and came over.

"They are in a different class. They both progressed so quickly that we moved them up to Grade One. It's the studio next door."

We got seated a few minutes before class started. The girls were already at the barre, chatting in a small group. Soon, class started. The teacher roamed along the line of students, correcting positions here and there while rapping out counts and orders.

"I can't believe how good they are," I whispered to Gretchen.

"Me, too," she replied.

The teacher shot us a venomous look. We sat up straighter.

Not only had the girls mastered the new material, they were better than all the others. I didn't know much about ballet, but they looked and moved like dancers. I was entranced for the full hour. At the end, the teacher came to talk to me. I introduced her to Gretchen.

"Your girls are doing beautifully," she said. "I would like them to take their Grade One examination in June. The examiner will be visiting from England and touring the East Coast to conduct examinations for a couple of weeks at that time. Unfortunately, it means going to Baltimore. There are not so many schools in Maryland that teach the Royal Academy of Dance method, so they have to consolidate. The end-of-year show is only a week later."

"I appreciate it," I said. "I will get them there."

"Thank you," Gretchen said.

We went outside to where the girls were getting ready to leave.

"Did Miss Bartlett ask you about the exam?" Rose asked. "Can we?"

"Of course," I said. "You have both done so well. Of course I'll take you."

"And I will make sure to be here for you," Gretchen said. "I would not miss this show for anything."

Both girls squealed and hugged us.

"I think the whole class is taking the exam," Rose said.

"I know you will all do very well," Gretchen said, smiling at them all. They mostly smiled back. I had picked up a touch of hostility from some of the girls. Jealousy, I supposed.

When we got back to the castle, the girls went outside to see if Hyndla had come over. He hadn't, so they went to find Penny instead. She crawled around like a frenzied beetle and was already trying to pull herself up on her feet by hanging on the furniture. She could say a few words, too, such as, "Wose, Eda, Sen, Ita." Quite advanced, which wasn't surprising. I had wondered how she'd turn out, seeing as how her mother was an erstwhile wood nymph and her grandparents, leprechauns. She was a very pretty baby, to my relief. Dora was quite pretty, Stan was Stan, and her leprechaun grandmother, a fright.

"How was it?" Lin asked.

"Wonderful, just wonderful!" Gretchen gushed. "I could not believe how beautifully they dance."

"They certainly seem to be talented," I told Lin. "They have been put in a higher class and will take an exam in Baltimore in June. They look so good."

"I should take it up again," Lin said. "I think I told you, Mary, that I progressed too fast for the beginner class, but not fast enough for more advanced work. Maybe I should try again with private lessons."

"It's good exercise, for sure," I said.

"If it was only exercise I wanted, I'd go to the gym. I want the music and the feeling of dancing to it with graceful movements. One day."

31

The few weeks leading up to Christmas went by fast. Rose and Gerda were excited about their school's upcoming concert and, more especially, the ballet school's Christmas show in which they would dance a duet.

Margareta and Sven would return by the middle of December, and Lin was preoccupied with shopping for gifts. Anyone would think we were normal. I took Gretchen to a big mall near Salton to do some shopping and decided to try Annapolis, where there was supposed to be a particularly good mall, according to the mother of one of the girls' classmates. The good mall turned out to be in the suburbs, but after a late lunch, we managed to find parking and look around the old town. I find shopping tiring and hard on the feet. Gretchen seemed to enjoy it—perhaps because it was a form of sightseeing for her. I liked shopping in foreign places, too, after all.

We all went to the school concert where the children's sweet voices nearly moved me to tears. One girl in sixth grade was dressed like an angel for her solo, "Silent Night," and she sang like one, too.

CHAPTER 31

We all went home to hot chocolate and home-made cookies.

"I can see why Gerda does not wish to leave her school," Gretchen said, her voice sad and wistful. "How I wish I could settle here. But it was not to be."

"You will not be so very far away," Auntie said. "We will visit back and forth."

Then came the dance recital. It was a simple affair in the auditorium of the girls' school, without costumes or scenery. The girls performing solos wore little pull-up tutus over their leotards, which made them feel like real ballerinas.

We sat through several dances before our girls appeared onstage. They danced to the bluebird music from Tchaikovsky's "Sleeping Beauty" score. I am not exaggerating when I say that they enchanted the audience. They moved like bluebirds, flitting with darting little steps, with each other and apart, sometimes giving the impression they really were flying. Their steps were precise, their arms soft and undulating, and they were one with each other and with the music. I reminded myself that we were in the presence of gods. I glanced at Lin as she watched them intently, tense and excited. Gretchen's mouth hung open as she marveled. I felt the same way. When the music drew to a close, and the girls held their final pose, the applause was deafening. The little dancers held hands and curtsied before exiting to the wings with regal ballet walks. These girls could turn professional one day.

We all sat around the living room when we got home. Everyone rhapsodized about the girls' performance. They looked about ready to drop, so I suggested they go to bed, which they did with only a symbolic protest or two. Hunter promised to kiss them goodnight if they hurried. He, Gretchen, and I went through to our wing about twenty minutes later, only to return almost immediately. They were fast asleep—in my bed. Sam and Hyndla had made themselves comfortable on the duvet, while Tor lay beside the bed, only opening one eye when we came in.

"I guess I may as well go home," I said.

"It's getting late. I will drive you," Hunter told me.

The evening thus ended very satisfactorily.

Lin called me the next morning. Hunter had left early.

"Can I come over for lunch?" she asked. "I have a story I'd forgotten all about."

"That would be great," I said. "We are a bit short of stories for this year."

"Well, like I said, it really doesn't matter so much anymore. But this is a ballet story, sort of."

"Omelet okay?"

"Sure."

We enjoyed our mushroom omelets with a glass of sparkling water and a slice of cheesecake before getting down to business. It was Saturday, and the girls were at the castle, so we had the place to ourselves.

Lin assumed her usual effigy pose on the sofa, near which I had already set up the tape recorder.

Tape 13,
Volume 4

Mary, you might remember that I moved to London from San Francisco just before the 1906 earthquake. One of the benefits of living in London was, and still is, the rich theater offerings. I managed to get tickets for a performance by Anna Pavlova at the Palace Theatre. I think it was 1910 or so. She performed The Dying Swan so delicately, so movingly, that tears spilled down my cheeks as I watched that careworn fluttering creature breathe its last. There was complete silence for at least thirty seconds before the applause pealed out through numerous curtain calls. I have never forgotten the exhausting sorrow and jubilation I experienced that evening.

As it happened, my companion at the performance knew her husband, Victor Dandré. We were invited to a garden party at her house in Hampstead that June. It was an airy, spacious house with a huge center room she used as a studio, and a balcony on the second floor that ran all around it.

Anna appeared about a half hour after we arrived, dressed as a shepherdess, which I thought rather affected. As it turned out, though, she and her latest partner, Laurent Novikoff, planned a performance on the lawn to entertain the guests. With flowers in her hair and golden sandals, she looked more like a nymph than a shepherdess. Again, I was transfixed. I vowed to learn to dance ballet, to transfix others that way. I made a few tame attempts, but never quite followed through. Something always intruded. But Rose will do it. I know she will. I feel it.

Lin sat up and I turned off the recorder.

"I think both of them will pursue ballet," I said. "It is clear that they are both very talented. But, it's early days. They might get tired of it. It's a hard slog, from what I understand."

"Rose will not give up. She feels dance in her soul. As long as I can watch ballet, I don't need to do it."

"Don't you realize how you transfix people with your beauty and strength?" I asked.

Her eyes sparkled. "I guess I do. All my world's a stage."

She took out a package from her tote. "This is for Rose when she is a little older. Don't give it to her now, it might make Gerda jealous. I'll give her a book about Anna Pavlova for Christmas."

"What is it?" I set my phone on record. Lin had both feet on the ground.

It's a pair of Anna Pavlova's ballet shoes. I ran into the studio dressing room and took them as a souvenir. There's a little glass ballerina in the toe of one of the shoes. I think it's from Sweden. She made quite an impression on King Gustaf, you know. It has little pearls all over the tutu and diamond dust in its hair. I took that, too. Her shoes were in a cupboard with her name on it. The ballerina stood on a table next to a dozen other trinkets. It didn't take me long. The bathroom was next to the studio, and that's where I darted into once the coast was clear. When I heard voices, I flushed and emerged with my spoils concealed in special pockets in my capacious and fashionable boa. I love mementos.

"Lin! Wasn't there an enormous fuss?"

"I didn't hear anything. She may not have noticed for some time. Celebrities like her are showered with gifts. I doubt they even remember half of what they've got."

"Lin, you are incorrigible."

"Oh, well. I am what I am."

"Can you believe it's been nearly a year since Hunter climbed Yggdrasil? Has there been any talk of more appearances?"

"I know, although a year doesn't mean much to me. Such changes for all of us. I think Odin wants to awaken more gods to take his word to the masses. I'm not sure it's going to do any good. Too many people are so entrenched in their hatred. Next year we should see some movement. And we've got to get you and Rose up there, too."

"Is it safe for us? We are not of their blood, not truly."

"You are now of Odin's blood. They will respect that."

"Does Gretchen know about Gerda?"

"No. I suppose I should tell her."

"Maybe talk to Gerda. She might want to keep it to herself. And she might not know what it all meant."

"That's a good point. I'll ask her what she remembers. We might want to talk to her more when she's older. Well, I must be off. A little more shopping to do. Christmas is coming!"

"And you always make it spectacular."

"I try."

Soon, I heard her car back out of the driveway and peel away.

This gift was historically important, and I wasn't sure how to explain it being in my possession. I thought I would hide it on the top shelf of my closet, wrapped in the same sheet as my beloved, ancient teddy bear, whose skin was too fragile to mend anymore. I lifted him down and laid him on the bed, opening the cloth. I tucked the package under his arm. He still wore the same kind expression that had comforted me as a child. I had never shown him to Rose because she would have demanded him for herself, and he couldn't have survived her loving attention.

One day, my mother gave me my usual snack of milk and cookies when I got home from school. My sister was still at soccer practice. I suddenly noticed how puffy her eyes looked. She had been crying.

"What's the matter, Mom?"

She sat down and tears started to roll down her face. "It's Grandpa. He had a heart attack. He's gone."

"I'm very sorry." I gave her a big hug. Disconcertingly, this seemed to make her cry even harder.

I didn't like Grandpa much and didn't mind never having to see him again. He was bad-tempered and didn't seem to like children. He never sent us a birthday card, let alone a gift. According to him, me and my sister would never amount to anything and would end up just like our mother. Not that my mother was bad in any way, but often short of money and overwhelmed. He was so mean. I didn't understand why she was so upset. I was too young to understand these things.

After doing our homework and eating dinner in uncomfortable silence, we went to bed. I cuddled Teddy and imagined how I would feel if my father died. That made me cry for a long, long time. Just thinking about that made my tears flow again, because my father died not long after, and my mother six months before I came to the Thorens. I was grateful for still having blood ties—Auntie, Lizzie, and Rose. And the Thoren household was family, even before Odin mingled our blood.

Once again, Teddy absorbed my tears. When my sight became less blurry, I stared at him, gawping like a dolt. His fur was renewing itself, a soft golden pelt that gradually spread over his body, and the awful tear in his cheek had closed up. His black thread eyes, sewn by Mom after one of the glass ones with its dangerous spike popped out, became black and shiny once more. He was becoming whole, thanks to my—godly?—tears. Teddy would not be shut in a closet ever again. The ballet shoes and figurine could nestle in this sheet up there on their own.

New strength arises from knowing and remembering, lovingly holding and touching. With my self-discovery, I resolved to become more mindful of the difference between substantial matters and trivial ones.

I carried Teddy down to the beach to introduce him to the sea, cradling him like a baby. I rocked him like I used to rock Rose. The chill breeze didn't bother me so much these days. I felt the bite but without the discomfort. Teddy seemed to push back against me a little. I held him under his arms so that he could look to the horizon. The sky and the sea were almost the same washed-out blue. I could hardly discern the horizon. Teddy began to shake a little, then a lot.

A huge black shape undulated over and under the water. I'd heard that dolphins occasionally showed themselves in the Bay, but I'd never seen any. After a while, I realized that this thing was not several creatures, but one. A very large, scaly one. It reared up and turned its massive black dragon eyes toward us, its long black tongue flickering. It swayed for a few minutes and let out a deafening screech before crashing down into the water and disappearing. I could see where the water eddied around its underwater undulations. It was moving in the direction of the castle beach.

It took me a few minutes to regain movement in my limbs, paralyzed as I was by fear. I held Teddy close to my chest. He buried his head into my shoulder. How could I let the children swim here anymore? What could I tell them? I'd have to talk to Lin and Hunter. Given the stories I heard, maybe Agna should be consulted. I looked down at Teddy. Had I imagined everything? No, he was still golden, sleek, and gorgeous.

Just when I thought things were calming down, this had to happen. I trudged back to the house. Hunter sensed my distress.

What's the matter?

I've just seen a monster swimming in the bay. Huge, terrifying. Snaky. No, more like a dragon. Didn't you hear it scream? It's moving your way.

Yes, we have seen it, too. We will ask Agna to deal with it before next spring. She is good with water things.

Why didn't you tell me?

We did not want to upset you.

I'm upset now.

Sorry.

Can it come out of the sea onto land?

We do not think so.

Think so or know so.

Do not worry.

For god's sake, whatever next? Whichever god heard that, please don't answer.

Hunter's laugh was so deep and loud that I couldn't tell if the sound was still in my head or coming directly from the castle.

What's so funny?
Nothing. Why?
You were laughing.
I was not.

Book Club Questions

1. What are the main concerns of various characters about Hunter climbing Yggdrasil, and what do those concerns say about them?

2. Do you think Hunter/Hoenir is becoming a more pro-active character in the series?

3. Auntie Peggy has proved to be a dark horse. Would you like her to become more powerful in different ways than she already is?

4. Mary's horizons are often widened by travel. How do the foreign settings widen your horizons with respect to the story?

5. Some of these Norse god-worshipping groups exist in the United States and other countries. Does that surprise you?

6. Do you think Odin's Word will be heard and accepted among the general population? If not, why?

7. Did you expect Mary to be granted immortality? If you were Mary, would you be ambivalent about it? If so, why?

8. What are the pros and cons of Gerda hiding her immortality from her mother?

9. Why do you think animals play an important part in the story?

10. There are many legends about monsters that live in large bodies of water. Can you think of any?

Author Bio

D. A. Spruzen grew up near London, U.K., graduated from the London College of Dance and Drama Education, and earned an MFA in Creative Writing from Queens University of Charlotte; she teaches creative writing in Northern Virginia when not seeking her own muse. Her publications include the first four books in the "Sleuthing with Mortals" series: *The Turkish Connection*, *The Witch of Tut*, *The Knight, the Gnome and the Fox*, and *Odin's Word*; a historical novel *The Blitz Business*; and a poetry collection, *Long in the Tooth*. Her poems and short stories have appeared in many online and print publications. She resides in Northern Virginia and Southern Maryland.

Discover more at
4HorsemenPublications.com

10% off using HORSEMEN10